MADE FOR SIN

MADE FOR SIN

CELIA MAY HART

APHRODISIA

KENSINGTON PUBLISHING CORP.

http://www.kensingtonbooks.com

KENSINGTON BOOKS are published by

Kensington Publishing Corp.
850 Third Avenue
New York, NY 10022

All Kensington Titles, Imprints, and Distributed Lines are available at special quantity discounts for bulk purchases for sales promotions, premiums, fund-raising, and educational or institutional use.

Special book excerpts or customized printings can also be created to fit specific needs. For details, write or phone the office of the Kensington special sales manager: Kensington Publishing Corp., 850 Third Avenue, New York, NY 10022, attn: Special Sales Department, Phone: 1-800-221-2647.

ISBN-13: 978-0-7582-1465-2
ISBN-10: 0-7582-1465-0

First Trade Paperback Printing: February 2007

10 9 8 7 6 5 4 3 2 1

Printed in the United States of America

Prologue

Lucy Waverton writhed against the stuffed leather seat. Behind her closed eyelids, flashes of light alerted her to sunlight flickering through the drawn blinds of the carriage. But his hands on her body wrought a heat deeper than the sun's.

Her entire universe existed within this rolling carriage and the man who plied his sensual skill upon her willing body. His hands and mouth touched her everywhere, his mouth trailing wet paths across her breasts and down.

Her breasts ached, her nipples rising in hard confusion. Wave after wave of heat washed through her, sparking all of her senses into wakeful eagerness.

His mouth covered hers, kissing her with ruthlessness, making her head spin. The sweet scent of brandy tickled her nose and she tasted it upon his lips. Even in a state of intoxication, his sure caresses elicited wild emotions Lucy had never felt before.

His mouth slid down her neck, nipping and suckling the tender flesh. Her head fell back against the bolsters, inhaling the dusty air in a desperate fight against the breathlessness his touch invoked in her.

He returned to her mouth, raining kisses upon her lips. His own lips changed from soft and sensuous to hard and demanding. He coaxed a luscious bloom within her that devoured her fears from the uncertain start of this journey. Combing her fingers through his hair, desire and need consumed her.

His thumbs stroked her bared breasts, heating her to her very marrow. His broad thumbs swirled around her nipples, so hot and alive. He pinched them lightly, making her gasp, and then harder, making her cry out.

He hauled her onto his lap, making her grab the seat behind his head. Underneath her, he found her mouth with his once more, drowning her in impassioned kisses.

Lucy didn't care that the hem of her skirts lay across her thighs, or that her bare knees pressed into the leather seat. She gave as good as she got, telling him with ardent kisses of her overwhelmed senses, telling him by tangling tongues that she wanted more, a lot more.

Still kissing her, he pulled at the tapes of her high-waisted walking gown and tugged the material down over her arms and to her waist. She leaned into him, letting him explore the bared contours of her back. With a single touch, she arched her back for him, breaking their kiss and presenting her breasts to his eager, skilled mouth. He pushed aside her little heart locket to nuzzle the warm hollow between her breasts. Her hair tumbled down her back, her mane of hair caressing his moving hands.

In the next instant, the stricture of her stays about her waist vanished. He pulled them out of the way, the cotton grazing her skin.

Her pushed-down sleeves trapped her arms at her sides, her hands coming to rest on his lap. Panting for breath, she pressed down. Something hard and long seemed trapped within his pantaloons. Her fingers curled about it, unable to get a good grip.

He groaned, burying his face between her breasts. His whole body tensed, poised on the brink of action. His fingers dug into her flanks. He laid kisses upon her skin, nipping and sucking at her collarbone, the sides of her breasts, below them.

He slid his palm along her bared thigh and down between her parted legs, searching for the cleft there. Lost in the maelstrom of sensation, Lucy didn't notice this liberty until he touched her there.

A burst of energy shot through her from the top of her cleft straight out of her head. She cried out, in both shock and joy. He rubbed her wet flesh and delved further down her cleft to where the wetness grew.

She never knew her body had the ability to respond like this. Every sense reached out to him, wanting more. She didn't want this to end. Beyond heavenly, his fingers slid over her slick cleft, arousing her to even greater heights. Lucy sobbed for breath, rocking her groin against his working hand, her own hands shifting in the same rhythm against his crotch.

Another groan burst from his lips and his hand slid away from her cleft, burning for more from him. She mewled in disappointment. Would he not assuage her itch?

He lifted her hands, unbuttoning his pantaloons one-handed before grasping her waist and lifting her. He urged her to slide even closer.

Closer. Precisely what she wanted. How did he know?

He nuzzled her breasts a moment more. He lowered her. Something hard, yet fleshy probed her wet slit. It fitted against her, like he belonged.

Her slight weight bore her down and her flesh was parted by his, wider than his thumb and much longer. She cried out, unused to this stretching of herself, but still and still he burrowed further inside her.

She rested at last, crotch to crotch, his wiry hair mingling with hers. His hips thrust up, making contact with the little bud of wet flesh and sending fresh fire through her.

A quick student, she rubbed herself against him, her hips shifting up and down, bringing her excited flesh into contact with his crotch and away again.

His own thick flesh slid in and out of her, evoking new sensations that made her sob.

"Yes, yes," he grunted. "My cock aches to spend itself."

So that's what it was called. He'd named that part after a rooster? A smile twitched across her lips and vanished, dispelled by a moan as shudders washed through her body. Every muscle tensed, waiting for something to happen, some crescendo to the incredible sensations he'd shown her.

"Make me come," he groaned, grabbing her hair and tilting her head way back. He nipped at her swollen nipples. "Faster, faster."

She rode him like a horse, although she'd never ridden any way but sidesaddle before. Her cries burst out of her with each staccato thrust.

Again and again, he filled her. Again and again, her little nub of raw need flamed until she couldn't breathe, consumed by fire.

His grip tightened on her hair, his fingers dug into her hip. He bellowed a roar, holding her in place while he pumped his hips wildly against hers.

"Yes, Danielle! Yes!"

Her muscles tensed again, the relief she sought abandoned in a cold wash. Who the devil was Danielle?

1

Alex Radbourne, the Earl of Radbourne, woke in a mild state of panic. *Where the devil am I? Why does my bed rock in such an alarming manner?* He forced open his gummy eyelids.

He blinked, a bright shaft of light piercing the gloom. *In my carriage? What the devil am I doing in my carriage?*

His memories came rushing back. He bit back a groan, not wanting to upset the girl. He'd been an idiot, but he'd decided to do the right thing by her.

He blinked again, his eyes adjusting to the light. The girl. Where was she?

He roared, pounding on the carriage roof, bellowing for the coachman.

At once, the carriage drew to a halt, and his coachman opened the door. "Yes, my lord?"

"Where the devil is the girl?" he demanded.

The coachman started, staring beyond his master into the carriage's interior. "She—she is not in there?"

"I know that," Alex snapped. "What I want to know is where she is *now*."

His coachman took an inadvertent step backward. "We just went through the town of Durham, my lord. Had to slow the carriage. Perhaps she chose that moment to leave?"

Alex cursed. "She could have killed herself. What made her act that way? She—" He broke off, remembering their wild, abandoned lovemaking in the carriage. It would not do to speak of that before the help, although surely the man had heard them copulate.

"Women!" he cursed. "I'll never understand them."

"What do you wish to do, my lord?" the coachman prompted after a short, angry silence.

"We'll have to go back to Durham, of course, and see what has gotten into that girl. Can't have her wandering about the countryside on her own. It's not safe and she's under my protection, whether she likes it or not."

Lucy slammed through the undergrowth. Thin, flexible branches whipped her outstretched palms and tore at her high-waisted skirt.

She sobbed aloud between gasping breaths. She had to get away. She had to.

She ducked under a spreading tree branch, twilight making it difficult to discern shapes. Leaves batted at her face, sticking to her wet cheeks. Some of them fell away again, but Lucy had no time to care about her appearance.

She had to get away.

Lucy stumbled into a clearing and at once put on an extra burst of speed, ignoring the stabbing pains in her booted feet.

Her eyes clouded with tears, she slammed headlong into someone. Someone whose arms caught her involuntarily. Her impetus knocked them both to the ground.

It knocked the breath out of her. Eyes closed, she fought him, panicked cries escaping her lips.

He'd found her.

"Hush, shhh," the man murmured, expertly fielding her flailing fists. "I won't hurt you."

The soothing tones of his voice penetrated her panic, her fear. It was not him. She stilled, gathering her breath and her wits.

He patted her back awkwardly. "Are you all right, miss?" His common north country burr, combined with the odor of sweat, leather, and—Lucy struggled to identify the other smell—gunpowder brought Lucy fully back to her senses.

She must be squashing the man.

Lucy pushed off him and sat in the dirt beside him.

Night had almost eclipsed the last of the twilight. She made out the pale oval of his face—not as pale as her own lily-white hands, which she held up in the air for comparison. A giant white *X* glowed across his chest.

She'd run into a soldier.

"Help me," she whispered, her voice hoarse from all her tears. "Someone is after me."

At once, he scrambled to his feet, a long dark shadow of a rifle gripped expertly in his hands. She gazed up at him, struck by his commanding, alert air. He reminded her of a predator, sniffing out prey in the night.

A brief frission of fear washed through her. Would she become his prey?

Lucy tried to calm her breathing while the soldier stood over her, his posture stiff and still. She whimpered, half out of fear and half from the incredible raw maleness of the man. She gripped the leg of his trouserlike overalls.

"Hush," he growled under his breath. "I'm listenin'."

She covered her mouth.

"There's no sound of pursuit," he said at last, holding out a hand to her.

She gripped it and he hauled her to her feet. Unbalanced, she fell against his chest. Her fingers hugged the edge of the thick white leather crossbelt crossing his torso. Clay crumbled against her hand. He hugged her, keeping them both balanced.

Embarrassed, she ducked her head, rubbing her cheek against his woolen coat. In an odd way, it comforted her. She'd never been comforted by a stranger before, but this man took it all in stride, rubbing her back in a soothing circular motion, making her feel like a helpless child.

The scent of him—male sweat from heavy exertion and something undefinably herbal—took her from her comfort zone into the self-awareness that she clung to a *man* and she was a grown woman, not a child.

She didn't let him go, breathing him in.

"I have a camp nearby," he said, keeping his voice soft and even. "I can take you there and we'll get you where you need to be in the morn."

Where would that be? Lucy's choices of refuge had shrunk dramatically over the last few days. A hiccuped sob escaped.

"D'you understand, miss?"

She nodded, abrading her cheek against his coat, catching the chill of a button on her skin. "Yes. It is just . . ." Tears overwhelmed her once more. She'd made a catastrophic decision that changed her life forever. This stranger didn't know the half of what had happened to her. Couldn't know.

More kindness existed in his simple courtesies than in a hundred of the, well, Upper Hundred or *beau monde*.

"Hanky," she snuffled.

"Sorry, miss. Sergeants don't carry handkerchiefs."

Unable to make out the sergeant's stripes in the dark as proof of his words, she wiped her eyes with the back of her hand, sniffed hard, and gestured to him to lead the way.

He must have caught her movement, for he turned, leaving her only the glowing *X*-mark of his uniform as a guide. Lucy hastened after him, lifting her shredded skirt hem from the ground.

At length, firelight flickered ahead, gradually forming shape as a cheery fire with the dark outlines of people seated around it. She identified another uniform and hung back as her rescuer strode into the group.

He must have realized she didn't follow him, for he turned and gestured to her to approach. "Come, we won't bite ya."

Lucy took a frightened breath. She gazed down at herself, aware of the disorder of her clothing, the tears in her skirts and sleeves. How could she appear before others like this?

He beckoned her again, a little more sharply. "Come on, miss." He faced toward the fire. "Joe, you have a spare blanket, right?"

A soldier on the far side of the fire shifted and rummaged in something at his side. He rose and circled the fire to join the sergeant.

By now, all the denizens seated around the fire stared at her with frank curiosity. Somewhere in the dark, a donkey brayed.

Lifting her chin, Lucy stepped toward the warmth of the fire, even if the others around the fire did not seem inclined to show a friendly face. She drew closer, accepting the settling of the blanket about her shoulders from the sergeant, and meekly followed him to a place about the fire.

The sergeant made a sharp motion to another of the men, who disappeared into the darkness. In the firelight, Lucy got a better look at her rescuer. He wore a soldier's uniform, his dark, mussed hair remained unpowdered, tied into a simple queue at the nape of his neck. A dried leaf clung unnoticed to his hair.

The flickering ruddy light made his features look harsh, in stark contrast to the gentleness he had shown her. Would daylight smooth the dark ridges that lined his cheeks and the corners of his eyes and mouth?

It was a handsome face, she decided. One that matched his wiry strength, for he was no taller than she and not of stocky build.

More than that, he seemed more masculine than anyone she had met in London, more masculine than starched fronts and refined airs. This sergeant was all man, raw and real.

Lucy settled onto the cold ground, draping the blanket about her. She gathered the folds close under her chin and stared at him. He mesmerized her and she couldn't say why. His every move drew the eye, totally at ease with the latent power he emanated.

"Maggie, got any of that stew left?" the sergeant asked.

One of the women rose, her red hair straggling unwashed about her face, and spooned a bowl from the black pot warming by the fire. She thrust the bowl under Lucy's nose.

"Where did you find 'er, sarge?" Maggie asked, shooting wary glances Lucy's way.

Lucy ignored her, shoveling the stew into her mouth, burning her tongue. *When did I last have a proper meal?*

"Where d'ya think?" the sergeant returned, not unkindly.

"Bit of a mystery, ain't she?" Maggie observed. "Fancy get-up all torn. Could be a whore but she don't seem to have any brass."

Lucy swallowed and smiled sweetly up at the woman. "Please do not speak of me as if I am deaf."

Maggie shrieked an amused cry that ended in a chuckle. "Talks fancy, she does," Maggie said to the crowd before returning her attention to Lucy. "Wot's yer name?"

The sergeant stepped in front of Lucy. "Leave her be, Mags. The girl's had a shock. Time enough for her tale tomorrow."

Maggie harrumphed and resumed her place by the fire.

"Thank you," Lucy murmured under her breath.

The sergeant sat next to her, shrugging. "M'name's Michael."

"Lucy." She didn't know these people. Would she be safe in giving her whole name?

"Try 'n' rest. We'll 'ave to get an early start to get you home."

Lucy nodded, too tired to argue with him. Tears welled again. *Home*, she thought. Can I ever return there? *Will I ever see it again?* She pushed the bowl toward Maggie and lay down, still wrapped in her blanket.

What was she going to do?

For a long time, Sergeant Michael Hall stared up at the night sky. Tiny stars sparkled overhead, unconcerned by his disturbed thoughts.

Where had this girl—this woman, for he'd been made all too aware of her shapely curves during both collisions—come from? He and his troop traveled off the main byways, the presence of soldiers not always welcomed on the roads south to Dover.

He'd learned that lesson on his first trip south. The memory almost made him nostalgic for those carefree days when he didn't know the darkness of his future.

His thoughts turned back to this woman, to Lucy. Maggie had already pointed out the quality of her gown and he knew that from touching it when he'd held her. Even though she'd been upset and hungry, every word and gesture indicated her cultured upbringing.

Part of him hoped he hadn't picked up trouble for their little group. The other part stirred into an aching awareness and reminded him of the fun that could be had with an adventuress.

Lucy stirred beside him and rolled over to face him, still wrapped in her blanket. He watched her, her face shadowed by the dying firelight.

After a moment, she shivered, part of the blanket trapped beneath her, baring a single lower limb. She edged closer, sighing when her knee came into contact with his leg.

Michael stiffened. *The lass had to be used to roaring fires and heavy down comforters. She must be freezing in the night air*, he thought. He bent over and tugged the blanket free and covered her with it.

It didn't seem enough. She wriggled closer until her head nestled on his shoulder, and her legs lay along his. Her hand rested on the ground between them for a moment before creeping across his coat.

He didn't move. He didn't breathe. *What the devil was the girl about?*

He'd made a mistake. Having not been rebuffed, the girl snuggled in against him and almost against his will, his arm drew her closer.

She sighed, gripping one of the buttons on his coat.

Michael made himself relax. Her blond hair, white in the moonlight, smelled faintly of roses. For one poetical moment, it spoke to him of lush innocence and wealth beyond his dreams.

Lucy let out a soft snore. Michael's lips twitched in response. She was too exhausted to complain about her place of sleeping but surely he'd get an earful in the morning.

He started to drift off to sleep, the warm bundle nestled next to him more of a comfort than he'd suspected. He had never made the habit of sharing his blanket. Ever. His eyelids fluttered shut.

The girl squirmed again, but he was used to it now and paid it no heed, sleep claiming him. Her arm drifted lower, resting across his stomach. His abdominal muscles tightened and sleep escaped him again. Would that dratted girl wriggle all night?

Her hand slid lower and beneath the flat band of his overalls. Michael squeezed his eyes shut. Heavens above! Her fingers curled around his limp cock, cradling him like a baby chick.

He didn't know which was worse: that a woman had touched

him while his cock remained asleep, or that she'd done this in her sleep. The girl would be mortified to discover them in such a position when she woke. Or would she? A gentlewoman didn't behave in this manner.

He had to do something about it. His cock had already started to respond. End it, or allow it to continue? Mischief tweaked his lips upward.

But no . . . Gingerly, he clasped her forearm and inched it toward the safer ground of his chest.

Her hand gripped his cock harder.

Michael let out a string of almost-silent curses and let her arm go. His cock stiffened, trapping them both within his overalls.

Lucy murmured something.

He tensed, expecting her to wake and cry out an alarm.

But no. Her head turned and she pressed soft kisses against his coat. So soft that at first he hadn't realized what she did. Was she awake?

"Lucy," he whispered. She hooked her leg over his, but gave no other indication that she'd heard him.

And then her hand moved forward and back.

Good God. The woman stroked his cock!

At once, Michael knew Lucy's true identity. A high-class whore, possibly one of those courtesans who only plied their favors with the filthy rich. Not the filthy. Not him.

But tonight, tonight she wanted him.

Tonight, he didn't need to be responsible. Especially as he appeared to be getting it for free. More than happy to oblige her desires, he unbuttoned his overalls, his cock springing free, Lucy still gripping it. She gently squeezed him, not moving her hand at all. The head of his cock swelled.

He gnawed his lower lip in frustration. Her rhythmic squeezing of his cock accompanied her crotch pulsing lazily against his hip.

Lucy snored again. Michael bit back a groan, his cock pulsing in the sleeping girl's grip. She still slept? Or was this a game she played at? Michael couldn't pretend to know the mind of a courtesan.

"Hot," Lucy muttered. She shrugged the blanket off, exposing a creamy white shoulder.

Michael slipped a hand into her bodice, which had somehow come loose while she slept. Her breast nestled cool in his palm, her flat nipple soon budding into tautness at his touch.

His eyes widened in the dark. No stays? A gentlewoman wouldn't be caught dead without them.

"More," she whispered, in such a sexy sigh that Michael's hips gave an involuntary jerk.

He rolled onto his side and captured Lucy's sleeping mouth with his. She moaned against his lips and he eased off, gazing down into her upturned face.

Her eyelashes fluttered, but her eyes remained closed. Her lips puckered. He accepted the unspoken invitation and kissed her again. He longed to lay claim to her mouth, really kiss her, hard and deep, until they fought for breath, but that would dispel the charade Lucy insisted on playing.

He explored her soft contours, the swell of her breasts, skimming over the material of her gown. Sliding his hand down the slight incline of her belly and out to her hips.

She made a small noise, a wanting noise, urging him on. He kissed her again: her mouth, her pert nose, her chin. He pressed his mouth against the upper swell of her bosom, inching up her skirts.

His palm skated across her thigh and she opened immediately to him, giving him easy access. He held his breath, brushing her cunt with a fingertip. She shivered, her groin jerking up.

Finding moisture, he delved a little deeper, parting her cunt's lips. She sighed against his ear, more a breathy moan. He probed deeper, finding her wetness rising to meet him.

A whore was always ready.

Swirling his finger against her tight hole, he pushed one finger in, then two. She rewarded him with more wetness. His cock throbbed with the urge to be the part of him to plunge inside her.

He shifted then, rising above her, pushing her legs apart further. He guided his cock along her slit, stroking her with it.

She moaned and her hands rose to grip his coat. Startled, he looked into her face. Her eyes were still closed, her mouth parted in soft, panting breaths.

Biting down on his lip, he pushed inside her. Her breath caught. "Yes, yes," she breathed. She welcomed him in, her cunt muscles clutching at him.

He longed to pound into her, to rid himself of his tense need, like he would with any other whore, but that would destroy Lucy's game of pretended sleep, and a high-class courtesan needed a little more care.

Michael sank into her by increments, his entire back strung tight with his enforced self-control.

In for a second time.

Then a third.

It didn't matter that he thought she was a whore, even the lowest of the low didn't deserve to be taken without her assent. Unable to bear the guilt any longer, Michael withdrew and covered her with her blanket. He cast himself away from her. With his back to her, he frantically jerked at his cock until his jism flew from its throbbing head.

At last, he allowed himself to relax, his breath rasping hard in the night air.

He started at a light touch on his side. "Thank you," Lucy whispered.

Thank you for what? he wanted to ask. He tensed all over again, wondering what he had done that had been right—or wrong.

Damn courtesans and their games.

When Lucy woke in the morning, her private parts still throbbed. Her explicit dream haunted her. It had been nothing like what she had experienced with Radbourne. The sex had been soft and gentle. The dream ended before she'd had a chance to experience that release.

She sighed, sitting up and wrapping her blanket more tightly about herself. Her unseen lover in the dream had not been Radbourne.

Lucy glanced aside at Sergeant Hall's blanket. The ground was bare, the blanket folded up and attached to a brown leather pack.

Without moving from her place, she searched for him. She didn't find him near the campfire with the others. The woman called Maggie glared at her, stirring what smelled like porridge over the fire. The other women in the group either ignored her or smirked knowingly at her, especially those closest to her sleeping place.

One of them, seated right by her, spoke. "He's gone ahead to scout, love. He'll be back before we leave."

Lucy gnawed her lower lip. Did that mean he'd gone and re-traced her path to see where she had come from? She knew he would find nothing, unless he encountered Radbourne on the road. Would Radbourne come back for her, or be relieved to be free of his burden?

If only she hadn't—

"So you are awake," snapped the sergeant.

Lucy gazed at his polished black boots. The sergeant must not be a morning person, she decided. "Yes," she said meekly.

"Good. Get something to eat. We're moving out soon." He strode away.

Gulping, Lucy approached the formidable Maggie, holding out the bowl she'd eaten from the night before. Without a word, Maggie lumped a large spoonful of porridge into the bowl.

The moment Lucy finished eating, the sergeant gave the command to break camp. Around her, his little troop burst into action. Possessions disappeared into bags and into a small cart, the fire extinguished.

The men fell into line, followed by the small cart pulled by a donkey. Its rough wheels somehow made it over each bump and hollow. The women gathered behind, a fair distance behind the cart. Lucy lingered in the rear. Should she join them? No invitation had been extended.

Sergeant Hall marched down the line's length and fixed her with a cold glare. "You. Walk with me." He turned and stepped into place behind the last of the men and the first of the women. Lucy joined him as he barked the order to march.

The day's journey began in silence for her and the sergeant. Behind them, the women chattered, although Lucy was too far ahead to discern precisely what they said.

Instead, she focused on putting one foot before the other. She'd not taken off her boots from the night before and her feet already ached with that headlong rush. Her big toe throbbed, reminding her of the rocks she had stubbed it on. Her tender heels warned her of getting rubbed raw. How did he expect her to walk all day?

"What are we to do with you?" Sergeant Hall demanded.

"I'm not going back!" Lucy declared, hearing her voice sound shrill with fear.

"You were tired last night," Sergeant Hall began, his words so clipped Lucy almost missed them. "I would like to hear your story now."

Lucy raised her chin, realizing with his curt words she had become a burden to yet another man. Was this always a woman's lot? Was that why her elder sister chose to stay home rather than endure another year of the marriage mart?

Yet even though his brow furrowed and his sensual lips thinned, his dark eyes glinted with amusement or anticipation. Who wouldn't want to be a burden to a handsome man like that? In full daylight, this sergeant was a feast for the eyes. His glossy black hair shone in the sunlight, edging a sensual face that promised much sexual satisfaction.

"Your story?" the sergeant prompted.

Why did he make it sound like she'd spout a work of fiction before she even started?

"My full name is Miss Lucy Waverton. This year is my first season in London. I . . . I learned to gamble and to enjoy doing so, but finally one of my fellow gamblers decided to teach me a lesson, I think, and demanded what I owed him." Lucy thought it best not to name names at present.

She continued. "I agreed to meet him in a not-so-public location on the outskirts of London."

Beside her, the sergeant sucked in his breath.

A little irritated, Lucy replied to his unspoken accusation. "Yes, I know *now* that it was a mistake, but I hadn't wanted to tell my chaperone about it. She would have sent me home in disgrace."

And where am I now? Lucy became aware that the women behind them had crowded closer and heard much of what she had to say.

"His carriage arrived soon after . . ." Lucy's voice trailed off, each moment a blazing memory. It pained her to speak of it.

In her mind's eye, she saw Radbourne's carriage door open, saw her hand extend up with the small leather bag of coins clutched in her grip.

Saw his hand coming out of the darkness, grabbing her gloved wrist and hauling her inside.

Then . . . then darkness. Struggling to free herself from his clutches, to escape his boozy breath. He'd roared for the coachman to go and she'd been thrown against him in the sudden jolt forward.

"'Miss' Lucy?" the sergeant inquired.

Lucy returned to herself, aware of her intent audience, aware of the sergeant's angry and sarcastic use of her title, meager though it was. Did he not believe her?

She swallowed and took a steadying breath. "Instead of accepting my payment, he abducted me. He—he forced himself upon me."

Would he and the others pierce that lie? Her shame ran too deep to speak the truth. Radbourne had been too drunk at first to do more than grope at her, terrifying enough. But later, when he sobered, he gave the order to ride north. He'd apologized profusely, promising to make it right for her.

Sweetly, ever so sweetly—for she *had* liked him until that frightening abduction—he'd seduced her, speaking of making her the happiest of women. He awakened all her senses, freeing her to experience them at the fullest.

Or so she had thought in that breathless seduction. But all his protestations of love had been lies. He spoke another woman's name. Not hers.

"He raped you?" The sergeant's anger swept from hot to icy cold. "Is that how you lost your stays?"

Before Lucy responded, one of the women behind him snorted in laughter. "And is it no different to you bedding the poor girl last night?"

Lucy stumbled, unable to breathe. "What?"

"Should've got your facts straight first," the crowing woman continued.

"You wanted it," the sergeant told Lucy, his dark gaze shifting away, his shoulders hunched. At last he fixed her with a dark-eyed gaze that made her burn.

She concealed her anticipatory shiver. "I . . . I wanted it?" she echoed. He'd bedded her? She tried to remember the details of her dream. She remembered seeking warmth, finding it. What had she done?

"I know you are lying to me, but we will speak of this later," he growled. "Without an audience."

Lying? But she had only a little, and not about last night.

"You better do right by her," crowed another of the women. "These posh types do like their roll in the muck, but you better return her in pristine condition, or her papa will have you strung up."

"Enough!" he barked. He stabbed a finger at Lucy. "And you, miss. You decide where we shall take you, even if it's no farther than the nearest inn." He strode off to the front of the line.

Leaving her to be swarmed by the women. They continued to move forward. Sergeant Hall left her to be picked to pieces by these common vultures.

Decide where to go? How could she even . . . She had nowhere and no one to turn to. Her fall was complete.

One of them batted the rest of them off, a petite, dark-haired woman. "Leave her be."

In a quieter voice, the woman said, "The sarge doesn't like liars. You should tell him the truth 'cause you made him look bad just now."

Lucy gave a short, worried nod. She would if she knew what the truth was about last night. Had he slept with her unknown to her? But to be honest about her little lie? "It's just . . . just so embarrassing." She took another ragged breath. "You know, to speak of . . . of, well, such things to a man."

Maggie volunteered, "You tell us an' we'll tell 'im for ya."

Lucy shook her head, startled and afraid. "No, no, I—"

Maggie cut off her protestations with a burst of harsh laughter.

"Leave her be," the kind woman repeated. "Let the sarge decide what he wants to do with 'er."

Maggie barked another laugh. "I reckon 'e already has." But she backed off, leaving Lucy and the other woman at the head of the female column.

"Thank you, ahh . . ." murmured Lucy to her defender.

"M'name's Jane, plain and simple. My man's Private Jones." She gestured ahead. "Stick with me and I'll show you the ropes." Jane glanced sidelong at Lucy. "'Course, that depends on how long the sarge'll let you stay."

2

Alex Radbourne cast himself out of the carriage and onto the cobbled streets of Durham. On the hill above stood the cathedral, a long squat building that would no doubt collapse if he looked more than once at it.

He cursed. It was Market Day and Durham's main street and market area was filled with bustling people from the city and the surrounding areas. How was he ever supposed to find her in all this?

Dratted girl.

He turned to his coachman. "You know who we're looking for?"

The coachman's long pause in replying gave him all the answer he needed.

"Stay by the carriage. If she happens to return, keep her here."

He strode off into the crowd, alert for a well-dressed blond woman. Did she wear her bonnet? He squinted, cursing the bright sunlight and his boozy, aching head. In the market, women abounded, most of them wearing caps or bonnets, their hair concealed.

Scents assaulted him, from the stench of blood from the butcher's stall, to the echo of rich loam in the vegetable stalls, to the sharp sting of the ironworkers.

Alex knew he'd recognize Miss Lucy the moment he spotted her. He shoved past a gaggle of farm women bartering with the local butcher, ignoring their annoyed shouts.

If he didn't find her, he'd head for the Continent. No longer would he be able to hold his head up in Society, having shamed, then lost, the girl. Where was she?

His height should have made this easy. He towered by a foot over almost all the shoppers. If he couldn't find her on the streets, he'd search each hostelry to see if she had passed by.

He combed the streets, an efficient quartering of the city until he had to admit defeat. Miss Lucy Waverton was not to be found out-of-doors in Durham.

He headed for the nearest post-house, a building he had passed on the way into the city. It might be she'd left the town straight away. He passed by his carriage, and his coachman dolefully shook his head.

The courtyard of the hotel that also served as the highway's post-house bustled with activity. A coach from the north had just pulled up and its passengers were taking the opportunity to stretch their legs and grab a bite to eat.

The golden smell of straw and the rich stink of horse dung suited Alex's nostrils better than the rank smells of the market-place.

Better was the sight of a diminutive female, blond hair peeking from under a sturdy bonnet, arguing vociferously with the innkeeper.

He dashed forward, grabbing her by the shoulder and hauling her around to face him. "Lucy! What the devil do you think—"

A beautiful woman confronted him. Her features echoed that of Lucy Waverton's and yet were uniquely hers. Her mouth hanging in a pretty pink O, her wide hazel eyes stared up at him.

Releasing her, he delivered a short bow. "My apologies, madam."

The woman didn't seem inclined to forgive him. "How dare you, sir?" She took a breath, no doubt to heap further invective upon him and she paused. The pitiful change in her voice made him shiver. "Lucy? You said Lucy?"

Alex sucked in his breath. This woman looked like an older version of Lucy, and if it were possible, more beautiful, although her skin reddened with anger. He decided to proceed with caution. "Yes, madam. I mistook you for another."

"For Miss Lucy Waverton?"

He nodded, eyeing her laden reticule with caution born of years of experience.

"Are you some London beau come in pursuit of her? I am searching for transport north myself . . ."

It would have been easy for him to lie to her, tell her what she wanted to hear. "That will not be necessary, madam. I have lost the girl."

She stared at him, her gorgeous lush lips open in a little O. "You—you lost her?" she whispered, her voice sounding remarkably even.

He bowed again, offering his head to be whacked. "I am afraid so. I look for her even now."

"You!" The woman poked him in the chest with her finger. "You stay away from my sister! I should have you arrested."

Alex cast a startled glance over her head, relieved to find the innkeeper had left this virago to him. At least it meant nobody would call the local constable. "I can explain everything, madam." He paused. "Wait, Lucy is your sister?"

"Explain! Explain? What is there to explain?" Lucy's sister exploded, pummeling him now with her weighty reticule. "You were seen, sir! Clear as day in Regent's Park! Your actions are inexcusable!"

"Woman, calm yourself." Alex captured her angry fists. "Your rage is, I fear, justifiable, but you are making a scene."

He didn't expect that to have so swift an effect. She stilled at once, staring up at him, her green hazel eyes filled with hatred.

"Let me go." Her low, calm voice filled with the same disgust reflected in her otherwise beautiful features.

"If you promise not to make a scene." When she nodded, he released her hands.

She rubbed at them as if he had caused her pain. He hadn't meant to grab her that hard. He hadn't meant a lot of things.

Lucy's sister spent the time reviewing their altercation. "Sir, or excuse me, I should say 'my lord' to give you the proper respect you do not deserve, but you say you lost my sister?"

Alex smirked at her impertinence and winced at her reminder of his folly. "Yes."

The beauty's lower lip trembled. "She is . . . she is dead?"

"No." He was swift to reassure her, gathering one of her hands in his, more gently this time. "No. At least, I hope not. She gave me the slip during the night."

"Here in Durham?"

"It was my hope," he affirmed, drinking her in. *Gorgeous.* He spoke with Heaven herself.

"I wish you would not stare at me so, my lord. It is unseemly."

"I had never reckoned on Lucy possessing such a divine sister. How have I not heard of you?"

She pulled her hand out of his grip, as if she had just remembered he had it in his possession. "This is not the time to speak of me, my lord. If my sister left you in Durham, she might be making her way home even now."

She moved to step around him. "If you will excuse me . . ."

"Not so fast, my girl." He caught her by the elbow, swiftly relaxing his grip. "I'm coming with you."

Her wide-eyed horror made him laugh. "If you think I am going to . . . going to associate myself with you, you are much mistaken. Go home to London, my lord. I shall take care of my sister. I am sure the last person she wishes to see is you."

He released her, but fell into step beside her. "You don't understand," he said, the shadow of the courtyard's stone gate falling over them for a moment. "I am honor-bound to rectify my mistake. I intend to marry her."

"It is clear to me that my sister has no desire to wed you." Her fists curled up tight. She walked with her head held high, her back stiff.

Alex realized Lucy's beautiful sister had a shrewish quality, which might explain her single state, and, if he guessed right, she was a prude as well.

"There was a misunderstanding," he said, following her down the main street, toward the market stalls.

She looked at him over her shoulder, her pretty face filled with arch disbelief. "Misunderstanding? Is that what you rakes call it these days?"

"If you'd let me explain."

She covered her ears. "Not interested in your foul excuses, my lord. And please stop following me."

Alex noticed his coachman come to full attention. "I have no intention of doing so, madam. However, I have a carriage available if you would allow me to drive you to your home?"

She turned at this, folding her arms. "Do you receive some sort of prize for attempting to abduct both sisters in a family?"

He barked a laugh. By God, he could bed this perverse wench. "I am doing my duty as a gentleman, madam."

Her eyebrows shot higher. "Gentleman? You lost your claim to that title three days ago."

He glowered. "Very well. Good day to you, madam, and

good luck in finding your sister. I wash my hands of her." He strode angrily to his carriage and boarded it, slamming the door shut behind him.

His coachman appeared at the window. "Your instructions, m'lord?"

"Wait a moment and then let's skirt the city." Alex gazed after Lucy's sister's retreating form. "I'll wager she's heading straight for home again. We'll follow her. Hopefully, Miss Lucy will be there also."

The coachman tugged his forelock and disappeared. The carriage turned and made its way back out of the city.

Alex reclined against the leather bolsters, considering his next move. If Miss Lucy had arrived safely home, he needed only to secure her father's permission and be on his way with her to Gretna again.

If only that stiff sister of hers didn't also pique his curiosity. Already he regretted losing his temper with her. No matter. Making it up to her provided a brief diversion while Lucy remained unattainable.

His lips curled upward with excitement at the thought.

When the travelers stopped for luncheon, Lucy took her bowl and sat apart from the others. She flexed her feet, constricted by the boots, but too afraid to take them off for fear of what she'd find. Her heels burned and the soles of her feet echoed the prick of every rock she'd trod upon.

Sergeant Hall had avoided her all this time. If he wanted to speak with her privately, here was his chance. She wanted to know exactly what he'd meant about her lying and about what the others had meant by his bedding her.

Lucy watched him skirt the perimeter and then crouch beside her. "Sergeant." She nodded.

"Have you made a decision?" he snapped.

She gazed up at him, knowing despair filled her expression.

Despite his cruelty this morning, she wanted to stay with him. There had been that gentle, sexy dream after all. "There is nowhere to go."

"Miss Lucy, I would a word in private with you." He glanced across at the others. "They have big ears."

Maggie visibly sniffed and Lucy stifled a giggle.

It elicited a brief smile from the sergeant. He rose and offered her his hand. She accepted it, rising and following him farther apart from the rest, trying not to limp.

He began without any preamble. "I don't like liars, Miss Lucy, and am not inclined to help them. I want the truth. I know you are not what you say you are, some wronged little miss. I know you for a whore."

Her hand whipped around and slapped him hard on the face, her face burning with guilt. "How dare you!" The tears sprung into her eyes. It wasn't fair. She couldn't help it if she'd enjoyed Radbourne's attentions. Did it really make her a whore?

"A very pretty display." The sergeant's face remained grim and unforgiving. "Now the truth."

Lucy drew herself up to her full height, meeting his gaze squarely. "I am exactly who I said I am." She didn't allow her gaze to flicker. "I want to know what those women meant by you bedding me."

"Don't change the subject." Michael Hall's gaze shifted away to the gathered women and then back to her. He couldn't explain why he wanted confirmation of her low state when his eyes and body already knew. Why did he wish her as other than a whore? Whores were far less complicated to deal with when bedding for sport.

"If I'm the whore you say I am, I do not believe that is what I'm doing," she retorted, fists clenched at her side.

"Must I spell it out?" He folded his arms and glared at her, hoping to scare her into a confession, one way or the other. "I played your little game last night. Why do you protest your innocence? I *know* you."

Lucy took a step back, her eyes wide. "I think you must be quite mad. What game?"

A smirk tweaked the corner of his lips, breaking his fearsome stance. By God, even arguing with her, he wanted her. "You deny that you stuck your hand down my overalls while you pretended to sleep?"

"I—I what?" She choked. "I—I did?"

Hall cocked his head to one side, surveying her. Her skilled dissemblance almost convinced him of her innocence. Not a whore, but an actress? "You truly don't remember."

She shook her head, her hands covering her mouth. "Then . . . then the dream I had . . . That was you?"

He gave a stiff nod. "It doesn't explain how a woman recently raped—" Lucy winced at the word "—would seduce a stranger in her sleep."

She gazed at him, her eyes round. "Do you think . . . do you think that now I've lost my virginity, I am wholly a fallen woman? Is that why I—?"

Michael watched her expression flit through a series of emotions. Her eyes remained wide, but realization replaced horror and her lips pursed into wantonness.

"You have been very kind," she whispered. "I do not blame you for thinking as you did, but it was your kindness and warmth that I reached out for."

She expected him to believe that? He examined her face, looking for some clue of her lies. He saw the truth in her eyes: she truly didn't remember. He'd never had much time for manners, but it didn't matter if she were a whore or some man's mistress, he'd taken her without her conscious permission.

He squirmed, squirreling away his anger. "My apologies," he murmured, reaching out to touch her cheek with the rough pad of his palm. "When you acted so, I had assumed . . ."

Lucy closed her eyes. He watched her swoon, and wondered anew at her innocence. Would a whore be overturned by such an innocent touch?

"Had I known you were—you were truly asleep . . ." He swallowed. "I did not mean rape."

Opening her eyes, she stepped closer until their noses almost touched. "I do not remember force," she whispered. "I remember gentleness. And even though I know it is wrong, I remember feeling disappointed when my dream ended too soon."

She dropped her gaze and Michael wondered at what secrets she hid.

With the crook of his forefinger, he tilted her head back, made her look at him. "It was unforgivable of me." Unbidden, his gaze dropped to her lips. He still wanted her. Even though she'd lied to his face, he still wanted her. "I should have made sure first."

"Now that we both know what happened, there is no harm done," Lucy murmured, her own gaze falling to his mouth, the tip of her tongue unconsciously peeking out and brushing her upper lip. "You have shown me that I need not fear a man's touch."

"Have I?" He thumbed her cheek. "I have abused you much today."

She managed a small smile, trembling and crooked. "I will admit my feet are much tired by all this walking."

Did she remind him that her station was much too good for him? His lips twisted, growing thin and hard. "I am afraid my resources do not extend to providing carriages for her ladyship."

"Sergeant," she reproved, her eyes shining with unshed tears. "I merely tried to make light of—of what happened. What we did . . . It scares me."

"That I—" He stared at her. He'd never bedded a woman

who ended up frightened of him, no matter how much he scowled afterward.

"No," she hastened to reassure him. "No, that I still want . . . it. I crave your touch, sergeant."

His body stirred at her soft, sexy words. If an innocent, did she realize what she said? Lust swept over him and he struggled to contain it. She wasn't for him.

"In my dream last night I felt safer than I have in a long time."

He blinked at her, disconcerted. She still wanted him? "There are consequences to this," he warned. He toyed with the tiny gold locket about her neck.

"I have already suffered them," she whispered. They were consequences any young miss ought to be wary of. She laid her hands against his coat and he trembled. "There can only be healing."

He stepped back, shaking his head. "You bewitch me, but I am too common for—" *An innocent miss.*

She cut him off, not wanting him to finish. "But uncommonly kind. Please, Sergeant . . ."

He returned to her, his arms going around her. "I think perhaps you had better call me Michael."

She smiled, leaning her forehead against his. "Michael," she breathed.

He kissed her, canting his head so that their lips fit together. She returned the kiss, matching his light pressure on her mouth.

Lucy heard a faint roar of approbation and realized his crew cheered. Michael broke off the kiss to glare over her shoulder at the applause and cheers of his men.

"There will be no privacy," he warned.

"We'll find ways," she returned. "They do."

He nodded. "You are sure about this? We will need to discuss your future. Where is your home? Is it on our way? Do you want to go back to London?"

She covered his lips with the tips of her fingers. "I don't have all the answers yet. Let me think on them, and tonight . . . Tonight, we will talk." She glanced over her shoulder at his assembled responsibility. "They will need to know, as well. It will affect them." She glanced back at him. "And I will not be a burden."

"You are not."

Lucy nestled her head against the strong column of his neck, holding him tight. He froze for a moment, before bringing his arms around her. The depth of her trust astonished him. It might all be an illusion, but Michael decided then and there that he'd enjoy it while it lasted.

She drew back. "What if he comes after me?"

He regarded her, wondering what new complication she cooked up for him. Was it possible the girl was not right in the head, for all her intelligent speech? "There's been no sign of pursuit."

"I left him unconscious. I hope that gives us a sufficient delay." Her teeth grazed her lower lip. "He does have a carriage and horses . . ."

Michael drew her into another tight hug. "And we are armed. Never fear, we will protect you for as long as you are with us."

She felt emboldened enough to kiss him. She drew breath to thank him, but his lips covered hers and drew her into a deep, searching kiss.

Michael pulled back, cradling her face in his hands and gazing into her eyes. "As long as we are honest with each other, we shall do all right by each other while we are together."

She smiled at him, relieved. "Yes."

"If you betray me . . ."

She covered his mouth with her hand. "I will not."

He nodded, satisfied. "Let us return to the others. We have a long way to go before we make camp for the night."

* * *

Caroline heard the rattle of carriage wheels behind her. She stepped to the side of the wheel-rutted track, walking on the green grass.

Instead of passing, the carriage drew to a halt. That evil man, handsome as sin, stuck his head out. "Madam, would you care for a ride? The sooner you get home, the sooner you will find your sister safe."

"She'll not be safe if you are there," she retorted. Caroline didn't need to wonder why this man made her behave so rudely to him. He had as much admitted to being a common villain. No matter what, she'd protect Lucy from him.

"With a household full of servants to stand between me and Miss Lucy? I assure you, madam, I intend to do the honorable thing by her."

"Having already done the dishonorable thing?" Caroline retorted. "How kind of you." With a dismissive toss of her head, she resumed her trek home.

He followed her.

The wretched man followed her all the way home, plodding along in his stately carriage. Along the tree-shaded country path, through the gates of their country home, and up to the front door. She tried to conceal her fear and discomfort, walking at a steady pace, but she feared perspiration appeared under her arms.

She tossed her head again, almost dislodging her bonnet with the force of it. She didn't sweat from fear, but exertion. The sun had risen much higher since her early morning sojourn to Durham.

Caroline heard the crunch of gravel under his feet. She hurried up the few stone steps in the front door, and slammed the door in his face, much to her satisfaction.

She tugged at the wide ribbon bow beneath her chin and pulled off her bonnet, casting it onto the side table.

The butler hurried into the hall. "Miss Caroline! You're back?"

"Yes. Is Lucy here?" Caroline started for the grand staircase.

"No."

Caroline turned in time to catch the butler's frown of puzzlement. Someone pounded on the door. "Do not answer that."

"But—"

"Trust me on this one, Gibson." Pulling off her gloves, she continued, "I have received information that Lucy has escaped her captor."

She ignored the continued thumping on the front door. "She may be on her way here this very moment. I'll need the men to go out and search south of here. She may have tired or hurt herself and that's why she's not here yet. Tell Mrs. Gibson to have someone prepare her room."

Gibson bowed. "Yes, miss. But the door?"

"Ah yes, the door. I will take care of that." With the butler gone to do her bidding, Caroline hurried down the hall to her father's study.

Over the fireplace hung his flintlock, now retired from hunting. She stood on a chair and reached for it.

"Madam, I assure you it is not necessary to blow a hole in me."

Caroline, stretching up, froze and gazed toward the door. "You! Who let you in?"

"You neglected to lock the door, madam." Radbourne stepped into the room, extending a hand to her. "Allow me to help you."

Instead, Caroline unhooked the gun from the wall and pointed at him. "You will leave. Now. At once."

Raising his hands in a conciliatory gesture, Radbourne approached. "That gun isn't loaded and I doubt you could hit me in any case, even at this range."

"How little you know, my lord." Caroline sighted him

down the flintlock's barrel, raised her head, and pulled the trigger.

A deafening roar filled the study, accompanied by the acrid stink of gunpowder. The gun's kick knocked Caroline off the chair and onto the carpeted floor.

She struggled to sit up, shaking her head to free herself from the ringing in her ears.

The figure of Radbourne lay prone, his legs poking out from the far side of her father's large mahogany desk.

Caroline got to her feet and staggered over to him. Had she killed him? What a way to end the Waverton family tree. One daughter disgraced and the other a murderer.

Radbourne groaned.

She folded her arms, annoyed at the rush of relief surging through her. Not that he didn't deserve to die.

He sat up, his hand going to his head. He pulled his hand away and looked at his bloody fingers. "Witch," he got out between groans. "Next time you try and kill somebody, I recommend going for the torso. At least you're guaranteed doing some damage." He looked up at her, his blue eyes dark.

"Next time I will aim lower." She directed her gaze at his lap.

He barked a hoarse laugh. "Now, help me up, wench."

"Get yourself up and get out. You are not welcome here." Caroline wanted to breathe normally again. She either had not enough breath or too much.

Radbourne grabbed the edge of the desk and hauled himself up. Swaying, hand held to his head, he gazed down at her. She hadn't noticed before that he stood taller than she. "Lucy's not here, is she."

His saying that as a statement rather than a question annoyed Caroline to no end. "I would not tell you."

He grunted. "She isn't. Do you think you could stop hating

me long enough to see to my head? It's bleeding rather an awful lot."

"Baby."

He slumped against the desk. "Fine, I shall simply bleed to death all over your nice rug."

Blood seeped through his fingers, matting his fine blond hair. Caroline gnawed at her lower lip for a moment before giving an explosive sigh. "Oh very well." She righted the chair she'd knocked over and gestured he sit. "Don't move. I will return."

All the way to the still room and back, Caroline chastised herself. Why should she take the slightest bit of pity on this man who had destroyed her sister?

She returned and set about cleaning and bandaging the bloody gouge she'd made along the left side of his head. Radbourne remained silent until she'd finished cleaning the wound.

"I wish you would hear me out," he said, his voice low and even. "I admit I made a mistake—"

She sniffed, too busy concentrating on applying a bandage to speak. She'd already given him a piece of her mind and then some.

"I never meant to abduct your sister."

In response, she pressed down on his wound, all tenderness absent.

The breath hissed out of him. "She came to pay me a debt—"

Caroline froze. "A debt? What debt?"

"She'd taken to gambling, Miss—ah . . ."

"Caroline. Miss Caroline."

"Not married?"

"No." She swathed his head once more. "I find it hard to believe my sister gambled."

"I cannot say what drove her to it. I heard she never lacked for partners to dance."

She had her own theories as to why Lucy had avoided the marriage mart and it didn't make her happy. She tugged the bandage's knot tight.

He hissed again. "How much damage?"

Caroline busied herself with putting away her medical supplies. "It's not bad. I used to be a better shot."

He chuckled, annoying her more. "I should be glad of that, I suppose."

Caroline leaned back against the desk, arms folded. "So tell me the rest of your Banbury tale."

Radbourne bowed his head and ended up clutching it. "Thank you for agreeing to listen, Miss Caroline. When the time came to meet Miss Lucy, I already regretted insisting on the debt being paid. It wasn't the gentlemanly thing to do, but anyone could see she was getting in too deep. Where her father was, I don't know—"

"He is upstairs, unwell," Caroline lied. Her father was miles away, hunting with his cronies and his brand-new rifle.

"Ah."

"My aunt is Lucy's chaperone."

"I suggest you fire her immediately." Radbourne delivered this pronouncement with a straight face.

Caroline had to concede the point. She had yet to hear from her aunt regarding Lucy's disappearance, having gotten the news via a fast rider from one of her London friends. "You regretted forcing the debt," she prompted, vowing not to interrupt him again. The sooner he told his story, the sooner he'd be gone.

"I did. Alas, when I regret something, I drink. I drank far too much and quite forgot who I was supposed to meet. Thought it was my mistress." He winced, preparing for her verbal onslaught.

Instead, she presented him with her raised eyebrow and serene expression. "Go on."

"So I hauled her into the carriage. Lucky for her, I was too inebriated to be of any—ahh—use, but the damage had been done. I resolved to do the right thing by her and marry the girl. Thus our trip to Gretna Green."

"No special license from the bishop?"

"Your sister needed to be convinced that this was the right course. And a bishop is hardly likely to give me, a notorious rake, a special license, even for money."

Caroline noted the sarcasm in his voice and sniffed. He had no right to complain about being labeled a rake. It was justly earned. "Dare I ask how you convinced her?"

"With words, mostly."

She wanted to wipe the smirk from his face. "So you seduced her before your wedding night. You couldn't wait?"

"She didn't think the married life would be pleasurable."

Caroline didn't blame Lucy for thinking that.

His blond brows rose. "Oh-ho! You share your sister's sympathies." A grin flashed across his face. "In any case, last night your sister decided to take her leave—from a moving carriage, I might add—and I only noticed this morning."

Caroline frowned, her arms curling more tightly about herself. "I only wish I knew where she was."

"So she isn't here?"

She shook her head.

"Would you object to my staying the night in case she returns? I am obligated to marry her, after all, and it will remove all this scandal."

Caroline stared at him for a long moment. He seemed sincere: was that one of a rake's tricks? In any case, a marriage solved the taint of scandal. "Very well. I'll have a room made up for you."

3

Nightfall descended. Talk around the travelers' campfire grew raucous. Uninvolved in the raillery, Michael, Lucy, and Jane sat slightly apart.

"What will you do now?" Jane had heard her story and now glanced worriedly between Lucy and Michael.

Michael's arm tightened about her shoulders. Lucy tried not to think of the white clay piping from his crossbelt messing her gown.

Lucy wondered what answer he wanted her to give. "I—I think it best if I return to London as if nothing has happened. Explain it away, somehow. Such as I got word that my sister had fallen sick and I went back home to take care of her."

"What about going home?" Jane asked. "Where is it?"

"Outside of Durham."

"But we—" Jane fell silent at Michael's stern glance.

Lucy didn't miss the silent exchange. "Is it not far from here? I'm afraid I have no idea how far we have traveled."

"It's two days' journey behind us," Michael said, poking a stick in the dirt before them.

Lucy regarded him, watching the harsh planes of his face in the flickering firelight. "I cannot ask you to retrace your steps. Where do you go?"

"Dover." Michael bit off the word. "And then on to the Peninsula to fight the French."

Lucy swallowed her gasp. She didn't expect the sudden stab of fear at his traveling overseas. A soldier, so easily killed in battle. "Then I will travel with you until London. That is, if there is no objection."

"I have none." Michael's gruff voice grated.

"Me either," put in Jane. "The others will expect you to pull your weight." Michael nodded in confirmation.

"With your help, Jane, I'll do what I can," Lucy said, twisting her heart-shaped pendant between her fingers.

Jane smiled. "I will leave you two be. My man will be wondering what I am about." She rose and walked to the far side of the fire.

"Oh good," Lucy sighed, at once tugging at her bootlaces. "My feet are killing me." She slid off one leather boot and sighed in relief.

Michael picked up the discarded boot. "Not made for long distances, is it?"

Lucy shook her head, tucking her wounded feet under her skirt. "I didn't want to complain in front of Jane."

"She has salves that would help," Michael murmured. "I will speak to her in the morning. You shouldn't be shy in asking for help."

"But . . ."

"I know, lass." He gave her shoulders a squeeze. "But you shouldn't worry about it so." His breath puffed at her cheek. "Lucy, you said earlier that you wanted to continue what happened last night . . ."

"Yes, I did, and I meant it." Disbelieving her luck, Lucy

practically held her breath, waiting for his kiss. This is what she had longed for all afternoon.

The kiss didn't come. He gripped her hands, almost tugging her gaze to his face. "Lucy, you must understand. You and I have no future. I am off to war, and you will return to your people and dazzle Society."

She choked out a laugh. "Hardly."

"You will. You are truly a golden angel." His lips brushed her cheek. "I won't hurt one hair on your head."

"You won't," she whispered.

"Don't fall in love with me, lass," he warned, his voice rough.

Lucy turned to him, stroking his cheek. "I would not dare." She leaned forward and kissed him. She pressed her lips against his until he softened.

His lips parted and his tongue feathered across her mouth. With this encouragement, she let him in, his gentle kiss an exquisite delight, firing all her senses without overwhelming her. Radbourne had overwhelmed her.

Lucy closed her eyes and forbade herself to think of him any more. Michael's fingers tangled in her hair, catching in the knots from the windblown afternoon. She winced and kissed him all the harder, leaning into him.

He broke off the kiss and his gaze swooped over her features. "That was not an innocent kiss." His head canted to one side. "Nor was it very experienced."

"Michael, are you going to analyze my every action?"

"Sorry." His fingertips brushed her cheek. "You still remain a mystery to me."

"I want to feel like myself again," she whispered, mimicking his move and caressing his cheek. She heard a little intake of breath from him. "I feel like I have these ragged holes in my soul."

"I promised to heal you." He kissed the tip of her nose.

"Here? In front of everybody?" Lucy gazed at the people around the fire.

"You will see that they will be too busy with their own love-making to pay us any heed."

His mouth found hers and gently coaxed her lips and teeth apart, exploring more of her. Lucy longed to take him hungrily, as Radbourne had taken her, wanted to show him how much he attracted her, but she didn't dare. She held him to her and found herself lying on her blanket, with Michael's hip pressed against hers.

Michael broke away to nuzzle at her neck, his oral caresses inflaming her sensitive skin. She gasped, curling her fingers in his black hair.

"Michael," she whispered, trying to keep control of her rebellious senses. "What did I do to you last night? Exactly."

He paused in his kissing. "You . . . you slid your hand into my overalls."

Lucy sucked in her breath, wishing she remembered that part of her dream. "May I?"

Michael made a strangled noise Lucy took as permission. She slid her hand over his coat, sensing even through the layers he had sucked in his stomach. Her fingertips found the flat band of his overalls and slid under.

She found his male member, his "cock" she remembered Radbourne calling it, already swelling. Her fingers curled around its thick length and her groin melted into liquid. "You want me," she whispered.

"Heaven help me, yes," Michael replied, examining her face. "My eagerness to heal you—" He gave his head a shake. "It was wrong of me."

"It is not wrong if I want it too," Lucy coaxed. "Not just your healing, but you."

"Why?" His handsome face filled with puzzlement.

"Because you have been so kind to me, Michael. You didn't have to. I'm sure we've passed a village or two where you could have left me. But you didn't. And you are far more masculine than any man at Almack's. You are not repressed by the latest fashions. You are you: a soldier, raw and real."

She thumbed free the top button of his overalls, watching him blush. "Now show me, Michael Hall, just how much you want me."

"I won't rush you," he murmured and kissed her again. She had never experienced a kiss like this. Michael took sure possession of her, not just her mouth, but her entire form. He remained gentle, but for the first time, Lucy tasted his hunger. Oh, sweet Heaven!

She responded, pressing her body against his, her hand trapped in his overalls. She squirmed against him, wanting to show him how much she wanted him.

He retrieved her hand from his overalls and rolled on top of her, between her parted legs, although constricted by her skirt.

His kisses grew hungry, demanding. Lucy returned each one with equal fervor. His hands explored her body, finding the rents in her bodice and capturing a breast in one hand, his rough palm sliding over her soft skin, arousing her.

Still clothed, he thrust his hips against her, his hard cock pressing against her groin. She rubbed herself against him, until he groaned into her hungry mouth.

"I want you, Michael," she whispered in his ear, her tongue flicking out to catch his earlobe.

His breath hitched. "This is madness." His teeth grazed her bared collarbone.

"Insanity," Lucy agreed, clutching his back. Her hands slid lower to grab at his tight buttocks. "A joyful insanity," she amended, sighing in pleasure.

Michael worked his way down to the edges of her bodice and peeled it back, revealing her milky white skin to the rising moon. "Beautiful," he breathed. "You are so beautiful."

"So are you," she whispered, untying the leather ribbon that held his hair back and letting it tumble forward.

He chuckled, his eyes dark, unreadable. "Hardly." He cupped her breast. "This, though, is perfection." He bent over her, covering her nipple with his mouth and kissing it.

Her fingers tangled in his straight black hair. "Oh, that feels so good."

He switched to the other breast, making sure it received the same attention. He teased her with hand and mouth until her entire body strung tight with delicious tension.

Four days ago, she'd never have guessed she'd end up here, on a rough blanket on the ground, being ravished by a common soldier. He worshipped her body with an awe-inspiring, sweet, hungry reverence. Nobody had ever loved her like this. Not Radbourne, who despite his freeing wildness, used her like a commodity, easily forgotten, easily discarded. Well, she'd left him before he had the chance to abandon her.

Her back arched, thrusting her bosom into his face, demanding more and more. Her insides burned with a now-familiar fire, racing toward some unknown threshold.

Michael shifted above her, getting out of the way to hitch up her skirts and finish unfastening his overalls. His cock sprung free, grazing her thigh, leaving a light smear.

His hand sought out her private parts, finding her slick and ready for him. Lucy wriggled against his hand. Radbourne had explained the importance of all that wetness and this time it came to her naturally.

He fingered her, teasing her wet flesh, and she moaned, turning her head to bite his coat at the shoulder. The sweet tension built and built, breath escaping her and not coming back.

Trembling beneath him, she grabbed his coat, fumbled for

the buttons. She wanted him closer to her, closer than the thick wool cloth allowed.

He helped her with the buttons, groaned as her hands plunged past the wool to press against his chest. She reared up, pressing her lips against the open vee of his shirt, his upper chest coated with springy black hair.

Michael captured her mouth again, his tongue sliding in deep while his fingers went back to working her slit.

She sobbed into his mouth, kissing him back hard. Could this act be any more wonderful and exciting?

He covered her, his cock pressing against her wet slit. Oh yes, she remembered this in her dream. The slow, easy entry, filling her and filling her.

Michael slid in, burying his entire length inside her, and she moaned. Her hands slid under his coat, clutching at his back, her fingernails digging into the broad muscles of his shoulders.

He set up a steady rhythm, thrusting in and out of her. Her slit fluttered around his cock and he groaned. "I can't ... I can't ..."

He bent his head, burying it against her neck and pounded into her, fast and hard and deep.

Lucy thought she would stop breathing. Her need swelled and filled her, overflowed, bursting its banks like a storm-swollen river, flooding her. Flooding her and flooding her until she thought the gorgeous beauty of it would never end.

She hung on to him, riding out the storm of release. Sweet tension exploded into a wonderful, soul-shattering moment. A tear escaped her, running down the side of her face into her hair.

Incredible. He'd satisfied her, beyond her knowing. Radbourne's seduction never felt this good.

Above her, Michael tensed, his cock thrusting and thrusting into her sweetly aching quim until he gave a hoarse cry, gushing into her slit and collapsing upon her.

Lucy cradled him in her arms. She thought she'd fallen for him before, watching him that first night around the campfire. But this. This!

She kissed his brow. She would never let him go now.

Caroline felt the first pangs of hunger rumble. She glanced outside at the early afternoon sun slanting across the green lawn. She'd only nibbled at breakfast that morning, gathering in reports from her servants returning from the search for Lucy.

She'd pinned a map up in the study, marking how far south each of them had gone. She'd relied on Radbourne's information and now she had wasted almost two days looking for Lucy close to home.

Where could she be?

"Morning," a sleepy voice said behind her. Radbourne had finally shifted himself.

"Afternoon," Caroline corrected without rancor. She kept her attention on the map.

He joined her, looking at the map. "What's this?"

"We've been unable to find Lucy. If she was headed home, she'd either be here or we would have found her." She turned to him, forgetting for the moment that he was the cause of all her troubles. "What if she's lying dead in a ditch somewhere? How could you *lose* her?"

Her eyes filmed over with tears. Tears she had vowed never to shed in front of him. He stepped in and embraced her. Caroline froze in shock. How dare he touch her?

He patted her back, unconcerned. "There, there. We'll find her."

Caroline shoved him in the chest, stepping back out of his loose embrace. "We?" The white bandage on his head gave sufficient sign that there could never be a "we."

"She is to be my bride," he insisted.

"She is *my* sister," Caroline retorted, ignoring the pang of annoyance she had whenever he mentioned marrying Lucy. "I will find her."

She moved to step past him but he took her arm. "Take me with you," he said. "I have a carriage at your disposal and I can show you where she might have left me."

"Do you think I would blacken my reputation by being seen with you?"

"Which is more important?" Radbourne asked softly. "Your reputation or your sister's safety?"

Caroline covered her mouth, muffling a moan of despair.

Radbourne raised his right hand solemnly. "I swear I will not lay a finger on you . . . not unless you wish it."

"As if I ever would," she snapped. "Very well then. We have wasted half the day. I shall pack a few things and be ready within half an hour."

"So fast!" His sandy eyebrows rose. "I will endeavor to be ready by that time."

"We're searching for my sister, not going to Almack's." Caroline grumbled under her breath and quit the room before she heard his retort.

More than anything, she dreaded stepping into the carriage with him. Doing so sealed her fate. What precisely that fate was, she couldn't say, but the dull urge to flee back into the house to safety seemed an ill omen.

Radbourne had minimized the problem of his carriage being closed by rolling down the shades, making them as visible as possible.

He helped her into the carriage, his gloved hand holding hers almost dispassionately. Did she imagine his thumb brushing the underside of her palm when he released her? She cursed her weary mind for imagining such lunacy.

They set off through the rolling green countryside in silence. She glanced at him out of the corner of her eye. Part of the bandage peeked out from under the brim of his hat.

The long silence remained unbroken until the coachman flipped up the trapdoor above them. "We're back at the spot where you woke up, my lord."

Radbourne ordered the coachman to slow down. Both he and Caroline scanned the countryside for any sign of the missing girl.

They reached a village and stopped, the twilight making it difficult to see anything. Caroline sat in the carriage while Radbourne made sleeping arrangements at the local inn. She choked back a sob. Not a single sighting of Lucy. Caroline feared the worst: Lucy had been killed and she'd never be found.

Wordless, she let Radbourne lead her from the carriage and into a private dining room reserved for those who could pay for it. He guided her to a seat and sat her down. "I've ordered dinner for the two of us."

Caroline stared out of the window into the inner courtyard. "Thank you."

He knelt by her side, drawing her gaze. He frowned, his eyes searching her face. "Where is my fiery Caro?"

"I am not your Caro," she replied without emotion. She clasped her hands in her lap to stop them from shaking.

"We'll find her."

She didn't expect him to express gentleness. She closed her eyes in an effort to stop the tears from falling. "Will we?"

"We will. John the coachman is making inquiries in the general taproom now. Maybe someone found her and took her in."

Caroline took a deep steadying breath and opened her eyes, gazing down at him. "You think so?"

"Lucy's an adventuresome spirit. She's out there somewhere." He patted her knee. She sucked in her breath. "I wish I could reassure you of that."

Somehow, she managed a smile. Radbourne kept trying to do the right thing. "I think I might have wronged you, my lord."

"Finally!" He fell back, raising his hands to the sky in a mock hallelujah.

A laugh spurted from between her lips. "There's no need to make fun of me for making that admission."

"My pardon." He rose from his knees, sitting across from her. He shifted in his seat. "Damned uncomfortable chairs, here."

"Language," she murmured.

He made a quarter-bow of insincere apology. "I am glad you have changed your mind about me. I am not as evil as my reputation suggests."

Caroline wondered exactly when she had come to that conclusion. Was it because he hadn't laid a hand on her until just this moment and then in comfort? Because he had respected her space? Because he hadn't made a single lewd remark, except for the occasional case of swearing?

"That suggests some evil," she replied warily. A maid entered laden with a tray holding their evening meal.

He chuckled. "No man is perfect. Once we get to know each other—"

"Know each other?" Caroline blinked at him.

"If I am to be your brother-in-law, we shall be practically family," Radbourne reasoned. "But now, we can behave like civilized people, without resorting to the use of firearms, bed warmers, or pokers."

Her lips twitched with amusement. "I scarcely see how I shall ever come into possession of a bed warmer when I will not be in the same room as you."

Radbourne shifted again. "Ah, yes, well . . . There's only the one room . . ."

"And you will be sleeping here, then?"

"I did give the impression we were a married couple. Wouldn't do for you to be running about the countryside unchaperoned. Wouldn't look right if I stayed down here."

Caroline groaned, covering her eyes. "Then we must stage a fight—which won't be difficult, I assure you—and the innkeeper will think we've had a falling out."

"You think fast," he said in what sounded like admiration.

"Thank you." She turned her attention to the simple fare before her. "I think it is best that we argue violently."

"If you insist. That shouldn't be too difficult." Radbourne sampled the cheese from the platter before him.

She gaped at him for a long moment and then glared at her plate. Did he mean to start the fight now?

The coachman interrupted their eating. "Found her."

Caroline leapt from her seat with an excited exclamation. She bumped against the corner of the table and stumbled forward.

With surprising swiftness, Radbourne caught her. He didn't appear to be otherwise interested in her person, turning to the coachman. "Where?"

"Farmer in the bar saw some tinkers cross one of his fields. He thought there was a blond woman with them."

"Tinkers?" Caroline covered her lips in one-handed horror.

"Actually, ragtag soldiers, miss." The coachman winced an apology at his employer.

"Let's hope they are decent men and haven't harmed her." The rumble of Radbourne's voice soothed her. He patted her shoulder.

Caroline realized she hadn't moved since he'd caught her and extricated herself from his loose embrace with deliberate care. "Did he say where they were headed?"

"South."

Caroline looked at Radbourne. "Then south we must go."

"I couldn't agree more." He stopped her with a hand when she moved toward the door. "But not tonight. We have a carriage. They are on foot. We shall catch them up."

She nodded and sat back down at the table. Hunger claimed

her. The good news about Lucy dared her to relax. She devoured the food before her—meat stew, bread and cheese—and
drank the red wine that Radbourne poured for her.

"So tell me," he said, while she wiped her plate with a piece
of bread, "who is Miss Caroline Waverton?"

She frowned, confused. "She sits before you."

"Indeed, she does," replied Radbourne equably. "She is also
an incredible beauty who has chosen to hide herself away from
Society. Why is that?"

"Not that it is any of your business . . ."

"Had a beau die on you?"

She glared at him. "Are you purposefully trying to provoke
me?"

"I am merely curious why you still live in the family home
and are not married."

She wiped the corners of her mouth with her napkin. "It's
still not any of your business."

He waited her out, sipping from his glass of claret and examining her from over the rim. The liquid glinted like blood.

Caroline heaved a sigh. "Very well. My mother died when
Lucy was little and I old enough to mother her myself. It was
my first season in London and I received news that Lucy was
deathly ill. I came home and didn't go back."

"Why not?"

"By the time Lucy had recovered, the Season was over."

"But the next year?"

She didn't want to tell him. Radbourne no doubt thought he
was on to a good thing in snaring a beautiful young wife.

"Caroline?" he prompted.

She waved him away. "I didn't want to tell you for you will
count yourself doubly blessed in landing Lucy. All anybody
was interested in was money. My money, my inheritance. Nobody wanted me for *me*. I would have thought, at that point,
having given my childhood to my sister, I'd find someone to

share my future with. Not someone wanting to fritter away my fortune."

"You need not worry about me on that score. Although it is vulgar to say so, I am filthy rich. Monied women no longer attract me."

"Then why force Lucy to pay?"

"To teach her a lesson," he replied, his voice even. "Perhaps stop her from gambling her fortune away."

"You did indeed give her the scare of her life." Caroline hoped she kept her drollness to a minimum.

"It wasn't perfectly executed," he admitted. "But she did agree to marry me, Caroline. I don't understand why she ran out on me." He stared into his wineglass, his shoulders slumped.

Caroline rose and moved her chair to sit next to him. "Do—do you love her?" she whispered.

Radbourne looked up from his glass and met her gaze. "No," he admitted. "But I made this mess and I will do the honorable thing in fixing it."

Something in his expression made her dare to reach out and rest her hand on his back in comfort. Almost at once, she realized what she had done. She had touched him! She ignored the pleasurable sensation of stroking his strong shoulder and snatched her hand away. "I fear, I fear I may have had a little too much to drink."

"I think you are right, Miss Caroline," Radbourne replied in utter seriousness.

She frowned at him. Who else had been refilling her glass?

"It does explain your delightful frankness," he continued, "but you may trust that I shall keep your confidences."

That didn't make her feel any better. She folded her arms about herself, regarding him warily.

"Do you not wonder what it would be like to have a husband?"

"Aside from losing my rights?"

He raised an eyebrow at that. "Do you have any rights under your father?"

"When he's aw—ill, someone has to run the estate."

"Ah," he nodded. "But I was not speaking of administrative details, but those of the bedroom. Have you ever been kissed, Miss Caroline?"

She stared at him, wide-eyed. Had he heard something? She swallowed and baldly lied. "No, no I have not."

"Don't you ever wonder . . . ?"

Of course she had. A thousand times. In London, in Durham, even in the cathedral. The kisses, the touching, the almost-scandal. Those she had fled.

She feared she'd dry up, become old and bitter, but her other alternative didn't bear thinking about. "What use is it to wonder? Even if I experience it the once what does that leave me with?" Even tipsy, Caroline realized Radbourne aimed for seduction. "Knowing what I have lost, instead of guessing at it?"

"Caroline," he soothed, "it is not too late for you to find a spouse. You are a gorgeous, spirited woman that any man in his right mind would be proud to call wife."

"You flatter me because you wish to bed me," Caroline said and gasped at her rude, audacious words.

Radbourne did not take umbrage, but chuckled instead. "It is true. I want to bed you. Repeatedly, in fact. Most of all, right now I want to kiss you. Just one kiss."

Radbourne wanted to bed her, he had said as much, but she wanted to be kissed. It had been so long since any man had shown her such affection. The wine warmed her inside, arguing who better to receive a kiss from than a man practiced at it.

Before she talked herself out of it, she leaned into him, and pressed her lips against his. A sweet, maidenly kiss, rather dry.

For half a breath, their kiss lasted. Caroline wondered if she ought to pursue it, to show him she knew how to kiss, or to continue with the fiction she remained an innocent.

He let her kiss him. After a brief separation, he returned the favor, his lips soft and moist. His tongue teased over her closed mouth. Breathless, she parted them. Would his kiss be as good as the others she remembered?

His tongue flicked across her teeth and delved deeper. Caroline leaned into him, giving herself up to the sensation, every part of her reawakening. She pressed against his chest, the buttons from his coat sticking into her. She moaned, a breath of sound into his mouth, and he pulled back.

In a daze, she watched him study her, knowing that with one kiss, he melted some of her defenses. Not all, not all. She would never be *that* foolish again.

"I think," Radbourne said in a voice that shook, "we should adjourn upstairs where we are guaranteed our privacy."

Caroline licked her lips. Part of her screamed to deny him, to keep her darkest secret safe, but she yearned to taste more of him. "Privacy, yes. Your kisses are . . . are . . ." She reached out, her fingertips brushing his lips.

He smiled, capturing her hand. "Yes, I am sure they are." He rose, drawing her to her feet. "Come. Come with me, Caroline."

4

Radbourne choked back a laugh. At once, he'd seen through her pretense, thanks to her hesitation before she confessed that she'd never been kissed.

Given that Caroline had raised her sister, should he be the slightest bit surprised Caroline had also, apparently, passed on her wildness? He looked forward to finding just how far her experience lay.

He led her upstairs, in a one-armed embrace, which made the innkeeper's wife coo with delight. Caroline kept her head against his shoulder, turning away from the taproom crowd, her cheeks warming.

Such a change from the fiery shrew of just hours ago. He hoped her fire would translate into more carnal matters. He couldn't quite put his finger on it, some tale tickled in his memory, but he suspected she was a right hellion in bed.

It would be fun to prove it.

On reaching their room, Caroline parted from him, putting all possible distance between them. "This is a mistake. We should argue and you should leave." She gazed at her reflection in the window, almost not recognizing herself in the wavy glass.

"Caroline, you have never struck me as a coward." He closed the door behind them, but didn't move any closer. "But I will not force you to do anything you do not wish."

She turned from the small window. "You won't?" she asked in a tiny voice.

"I made a mistake with your sister, drunk out of my mind, and I didn't bed her then. I won't have you making a similar error." He forced a stern visage. She actually looked annoyed. Had she been planning to use that excuse the next morning?

"You are promised to my sister," she whispered. "I cannot take what is hers."

She had a point. Fortunately, he had an answer. "She ran away, remember. Lucy doesn't want me."

"She must be mad." Caroline said it under her breath, but he heard it.

"Perhaps. Her flight doesn't suggest any logic, especially after I thought I had explained everything to her." Lucy's flight did bother him. In that he had found a much prettier, more intriguing sister.

Caroline's hands twisted before her. Radbourne guessed she warred with herself. "One more kiss," she murmured. "One more and then we'll fight and you'll leave."

"Agreed." Radbourne doubted they'd get to the arguing stage. He devoured her with his eyes, her bosom captured in that tight pelisse bodice, the hint of curves beneath. He wanted to unbind that honey-colored hair and have it fall over her shoulders. He wanted to undress her. Hell, he wanted her and he didn't care if she saw the evidence.

The dip of her eyes and the sharp hitch of breath indicated she had seen his cock outlined against the soft linen pantaloons. His head pounded, lust reminding him of his wound.

They met in the center of the room. He drew her toward

him, feeling her soft curves against him. She tilted her head to meet his lips, and this time, he took her mouth without apology, possessing her in a long, tender kiss that made his knees tremble, for by God, Caroline kissed him back with such fervor.

She gripped him tight, clawing his back as if she wanted to gain a stronger purchase on him. Her leg hooked around his. She rubbed against him, utterly lost in his endless kiss.

They lurched toward the wall, missing the bed by a foot. He bore her back against the windowsill and in the next instant hoisted her onto the narrow ledge. She clung to him, her kisses peppering his mouth and face in between sweet, soft moans.

She didn't complain when he hitched her skirts past her knees, burrowing in between them until his trapped cock pressed against her quim. He longed to put his hand there. Was she wet for him already?

Caroline tugged at his coat, hauling it off his shoulders, and he let go of her long enough to shake it off. He returned the favor, unbuttoning her pelisse and revealing the fine lawn bodice of her gown beneath. The translucent fabric revealed the swell of her breasts and her lack of stays. Her nipples poked at the fabric, already hard and eager for his touch.

He obliged, tugging at them through the thin muslin, aware of her hands smoothing down his back and over his buttocks. She cried out, her fingernails digging into him.

Oh God, he'd stripped more than her coat away. He'd stripped away her façade, her pretense of being a demure and proper lady.

He tugged at a nipple with his teeth. Her head fell back against the glass and she writhed against him. Her hands, oh her hands, found his breech fastenings and dealt with them.

His cock sprung free. But not for long. Her hand wrapped around him, pulled at him with sure strokes, making him even harder, thicker. No maidenly fumbling, this.

Pushing her hand away, he lifted her. Her body slid down and onto his waiting cock. He entered her, smooth, sure, and deep. Her sweet cunt, so deliciously wet, squeezed his cock.

He groaned. He had no need for delicacy. He plowed into her, fucking her again and again, until her happy cries filled the room.

Her legs wrapped around his waist, he pushed off from the wall, heading for the bed. He had every intention of discovering tonight how abandoned Caroline could get.

Grunting with effort, he bent over the bed, letting the bed take her weight. She clung to him, whimpering when he pulled out.

"Roll over," he commanded.

Her hazel eyes wide, she obeyed. Her skirts had fallen down to her knees and he lifted the hem, revealing the pert, white rounds of her rear. He caressed them, his palms fitting around them as if she had been made for him. She wriggled beneath his touch, hiding her face against the faded coverlet.

Radbourne hauled her back to the edge of the bed. His cock nudged at the crack between her buttocks. Her hips reared up to meet him. He parted her butt cheeks and his cock slid down the crack, finding her cunt and sliding in.

She seemed wetter than before. He grabbed her hips, giving her cunt long, deep thrusts. His gaze traveled along the length of her back, the rumpled fabrics masking her lovely body.

He would love to do this again with her utterly naked before him, running his hands along the smooth planes of her back, with her utterly submissive to him.

Like now. She mewled beneath him, her body racked with shudders, her hands fisting in the coverlet.

All at once, her cunt clutched him, squeezing him so hard, Radbourne's balls threatened to fill his cock with semen. Caroline cried out, muffled by the coverlet, squeezing and squeezing his thrusting cock until he too came with a violence that made his throbbing head spin.

Radbourne grabbed the collar of her pelisse and pulled it off her before flipping her over. "Now, undress," he said. "I want to see you naked."

No! Her body defied her mind, and still lying across the bed, she loosened the ties of her gown, shimmying out of the dress.

He joined her, lying on his side, but Caroline had other ideas. He'd shake her off tomorrow, disgusted, and so she planned to make the most of this night.

She sat up and pushed him onto his back, swinging her leg over his torso. She hauled his white linen shirt up over his head, with his assistance.

Planting her hands on his shoulders so that he lay back upon the faded counterpane, she crouched on all fours over him. "We are not finished yet."

His sandy eyebrows twitched in amusement. "We are not?"

Flexing her fingers, Caroline lightly scratched his chest, drawing her hands down to his concave belly. "Not even close."

Her hands slid up, fanning out over his wiry blond chest hair. "Isn't this what you wanted, Radbourne? To be satiated by a willing bawd?"

"You have done that," he allowed. His blue eyes narrowed, watching her.

"But what about my needs?" She raked her fingers down his chest. "What about what I want?"

He licked his lips. "What do you want?"

She slid down further, sitting on his thighs. His spent cock lay curled between them. "I want to ride you like you rode me. I want your eager cock inside my juicy quim, so deep inside that it makes me scream." Caroline gave her head an abrupt shake, her warm, blond hair falling into perfect disarray. "Will you oblige me with an erection?"

"Willingly, ma'am, if you would but give me a moment to recover." A grin flew across his face. "You were splendid."

She blushed, but tried to recover the advantage. "And what will you have me do while I wait?"

He whispered hoarsely, "Touch yourself."

Caroline smiled, wide and lazy. Rising up off her haunches, she let her fingertips trail over the peak of a tightly budded breast and down her creamy belly until her fingers laced into the dark golden curls at the junction of her thighs.

Two fingers parted her folds, a third in the middle dipped into her slit. "Mmm," she moaned, gazing down at him through a curtain of hair. "I am all wet and creamy from you." She brushed over her clit. The breath hissed out between her teeth. "Oh, and so sensitive."

Radbourne grunted and his quiescent cock gave the first stirring of life. Tilting her head to one side, she remarked, "My, it doesn't take much with you, does it?"

"Not when faced with a vision like this." His hot gaze filled her with fresh longing. She examined him, a leonine, powerful man at idle rest, his cock standing to attention.

Her fingers gathered more of their combined juices, lathering the jellied stuff over her clit and her pubes. She rocked into her hand, making contact with her clit and gasping.

She closed her eyes, blocking him out, letting the pleasure swell through her. Every nerve ending tingled with anticipation and she felt a certain perverse pleasure in performing such an intimate act for him.

With her free hand, she teased her nipples into an even deeper, burning heat. Her breasts flushed red, dark as her blushing cheeks.

She swirled around her clit, brushing over the very sensitive tip by accident. The tension built, ready to break.

Opening her eyes, she gazed down at Radbourne's rock-hard cock. The devil stroked it. She pulled his hand away and moved forward until his cock brushed the innermost part of her thigh.

Grabbing him at the base of his cock, she sank down on him, stopping halfway and sliding out once more. God, he felt so good. His cock probed at her flesh again, filling her and stretching her, drilling a line to her swollen clit until she thought she would explode.

His hips lifted under her, bringing her back to herself. She buried him all the way inside. Grinding her pelvis against his in a circular motion, she planted her hands on his chest. The head of his cock inside her rubbed at her horny tunnel, bringing her closer, ever closer.

She flung her head back, gasping for air and moaning. She bounced on his cock, bringing him in hard and deep each time and then swirling her cunt around him and squeezing him.

He fitted and stretched her like a custom-made glove. No part of her was private to his cock. It probed every part of her cunt, thanks to her swiveling hips, returning again and again to a certain spot that made her almost stop breathing.

She'd reached the crest, the line of it sparked golden in her mind's eye. She moved harder, faster, ignoring the grunts of the man beneath her. She had to come first, she had to come first, or all was lost.

She breached the crest, the power of it washing over her. She bore down, squeezing his cock tighter and tighter in her cunt, milking his bucking balls for all she was worth. Once again, he filled her with his jism. She screamed her release, her climax washing over her again and again until she thought that it might never end.

At last, Caroline collapsed forward onto him, panting for every breath. His hands stroked her sweaty back until her breathing had calmed and she rolled off of him.

He rolled onto his side, propping his head up with a hand.

Their thighs touched, his spent cock dribbling the last of his jism onto her skin. "Suppose you tell me who you really are."

She frowned up at him. "I didn't give you a false name."

"I believe that," he replied, lazily stroking the side of her breast. "However, you are no maiden—"

"Certainly not now," she retorted.

He placed a finger on her lips. "You were not when we entered this room, Caroline. Do not dissemble toward me. I know a woman's body and have had my share of virgins. You are not one of the latter. What are you? Some kind of succubus who deceives men by pretending innocence and then sucking every last ounce of procreative juices from them?"

Caroline laughed at that. Perhaps Radbourne had had more to drink than she thought. "You are waxing poetic, Radbourne, and not making much sense at that."

He smiled at her, tracing a trail across her sensitive nipples.

She stifled a gasp.

"You are alive to my every touch. You revel in sexual pleasure. You are most definitely not the self-sacrificing miss I thought you. What's your story?"

His finger resumed its lazy trails over her bosom.

"What does it matter?" Caroline saw no hope of lying to Radbourne. She had let her desires run ahead of her, ahead of everything she held most dear. She tried very hard to regret it, but her body still throbbed with the joy of their coupling. "You have cleverly found me out. But I assure you, I have not been bedded by a man for a long time."

"Was there more than one?"

Her outraged intake of breath should have been sufficient answer, but you can never tell with rakes. "No." She shivered, realizing she lay naked with a practical stranger—and still wanted him with such a deep aching need it scared her.

Radbourne leaned over her and pulled the coverlet over her legs and hips, as the night grew chilly.

"Thank you," she whispered.

"We should rest. With luck, we shall catch up to your sister tomorrow."

She winced. Poor Lucy! She rolled into Radbourne's embrace, burying her face against his chest. The scent of him filled her nostrils, all aroused male and sandalwood and rich red wine. She wanted to regret her foolish act, but found she just couldn't.

Let her shame come with the morning sun.

It had rained during the night. Lucy woke to heavy gray skies. Still clasped in Michael's arms, parts of her remained dry, the rest utterly sodden and streaked with white clay that had dissolved off Michael's cross-belt. After a cold breakfast, the wood too wet to accept the flint's spark, they squelched their way southward.

By mid-afternoon, they rejoined the road, a muddy track that bogged the cart's wheels. The rain tapered off to a light mist, enough to keep them wet and uncomfortable. The soldiers' crossbelts had faded into a dull brown. Lucy's ruined gown chafed at her skin and she worried at being rubbed raw.

But there was no use in complaining, no matter how much she longed to give voice to it. There wasn't even a barn in sight where they could take shelter.

For the thousandth time, she wiped the moisture from her eyes. Ahead the road dipped, and already she heard the wild rush of rising water.

Michael trotted back down the line to the women. "We're crossing the ford ahead. The water's high, but we can still make it. We'll need everyone to help push the cart across." His lips parted in a cheerless grin. "Safest to hang on to something as we cross anyway."

He darted a concerned look at Lucy, making her feel so much more aware of her bedraggled state. She didn't even have a coat or scarf to keep out the weather. She shivered, wrapping her arms about herself and moving forward.

The donkey balked at entering the water. Lucy couldn't blame it. The dark and gray water swirled with fury, tossing branches upon the tiny wavelets as it made its downhill rush to the distant ocean.

Michael yelled. "It won't go pulling the cart. Jones, Smith! Unhitch her and lead her across!"

The soldiers unhitched the donkey, three of them tugging it across the narrow ford to the other side. Lucy stood and watched them, shivering. She wanted nothing more than a warm drink, a warm bed, and a hot fire. Her companions traveled rough. Would she ever get used to that?

She gazed at Michael, who yelled instructions to his men. At least her bed was somewhat warm with Michael in it.

The soldiers tied the donkey to a tree and waded back across the water. The water rose to mid-thigh on them and seemed to be getting higher. Lucy shuddered.

A slight decline led down to the ford, enabling the group to get a good start on pushing the cart well into the water.

Everyone took positions about the cart. Lucy stood at the rear, next to Jane. She gripped the wooden slats before her, the wood digging into her soft, unprotected hands.

"One, two, three!" bellowed Michael and everyone pushed against the cart. Down the slight hill it went, everyone continuing to push it.

With a splash, the cart entered the water. Icy cold water submerged Lucy's ankles, rising to her knees the further they went in.

Gritting her teeth to stop them chattering, Lucy clung to the cart, pushing it feebly. She thought it impossible to get colder, but the swollen river proved her wrong. Beneath her feet rolled smooth pebbles and under that, a harder packed surface. Man had added to this natural fording spot at some point.

The water rose, tugging at her skirts and her legs, threatening to take her under. Lucy gripped the wooden boards before her, despite the splinters entering her palms.

Jane shrieked beside her.

Surprised out of her misery, Lucy saw Jane swept away by the current.

Giving a yell, in case the others hadn't heard Jane over the roar of the water, Lucy jumped in after her, swimming to reach Jane sooner.

Jane's dark head disappeared under the water and resurfaced. In a few moments, Lucy reached her, holding the woman's head above water.

Jane fought her, dragging them both under.

Lucy surfaced, spluttering. "Jane, it's me!" Jane's dark, frightened gaze met hers. "I will hold on to you. Just relax! Lie back."

The weight of Jane's heavy wool jacket and woolen skirts kept them down.

Lucy held on, kicking her legs forward and under Jane, encouraging her to lift her legs. If their clothing didn't drag them under, and if they didn't freeze to death from the cold, she might be able to get them to shore.

Over the water's tumult, Lucy heard faint shouting. Glancing toward the far bank, she spotted Michael, running at breakneck speed, clutching his rifle in one hand. Close behind him panted Jane's husband.

He noticed her looking. "Hang on!"

Lucy had no intention of letting go.

Jane lay atop her, a sodden weight that dragged both of them down. Only their faces appeared above the surface, tilted back to breathe. The stiff and heavy wool prevented attempts to remove their pelisses in the water. Jane clung to Lucy's arm clasped around her bosom.

Lucy tried to kick them toward shore, but the wild currents

of the river, stronger than Lucy, had different ideas. It would have been difficult even if she swam in this alone. With Jane, it was impossible.

Lucy struggled to take breath. The cold water seemed to suck all the air out of her, numbing her fingers and toes.

"Lucy!" Michael called out her name. "Lucy!" She blinked the water out of her eyes and peeked across at him. He'd drawn ahead of them slightly, still sprinting, his head turning to check on her progress. He saw her looking and pointed ahead of them.

Ahead, a narrow wooden footbridge crossed the river. The base of it would brush their heads if they passed under it. Lucy saw at once what Michael had in mind. He'd outrun them and catch them before they went under.

If she grabbed one of the overhanging bushes by the bridge's base she had just as good a chance of getting badly injured in the attempt.

Lucy hoped they'd be able to hold on. In her arms, Jane coughed and gasped. The water kept tugging at them, dragging them under. Tangles of weed grabbed at their ankles.

Michael made it to the footbridge ahead of them. The sight of running redcoats had caught the attention of nearby villagers and they too clustered on the narrow bridge.

The little bridge seemed to groan under the strain of so much added weight, but Lucy reasoned the locals wouldn't all be on it unless it was safe.

Michael pushed his way to the center of the bridge. In turn, Lucy tried to swim back to the middle of the river. People on the bridge bent over, holding out hands to them.

Michael lay on the bridge, Jane's husband by his side. Another fellow, a stranger, offered himself as a counterweight.

I can do this, Lucy thought. *This will work.*

Lucy held her breath and at the last instant of reaching the bridge, she propelled her arm out of the water, hand blindly seeking rescue.

The effort plunged both her and Jane underwater, but someone grabbed her: first, her slippery wet wrist and then her forearm.

She torqued in the water, making them face the river's onslaught. Someone held her tight. The joints in her arm and shoulder screamed in agony.

They broke the surface of the water, Jane coughing up half the river. Blinking upward, Lucy saw Michael's face in an ugly grimace.

His fierce blue eyes communicated to her. *He held on to her. He wouldn't let her go.*

Lucy sobbed. "Jane! Jane!" she cried. "We are safe!"

Jane gazed up at their rescuers.

Michael's grip slipped. Jane screamed. Lucy's hand closed tight about his.

"Jane! Reach up!" Lucy encouraged. "They'll pull you out of the water."

Jane extended a shaking arm, and then another. Her husband and another man grabbed her arms and hauled her up. Everyone within reach strained to get a purchase on Jane.

It was the last thing Lucy saw before the water swept her under the bridge.

5

Michael held on, his heart almost bursting when Lucy, freed from Jane's dead weight, disappeared under the bridge.

He held on to her. He would not let her go, or let her die, and he meant to hold that promise. He glanced down at her white fingers in his grasp, the blood squeezed out of them.

Joshua, one of his men, knelt by his side. Michael didn't need to look to see Jane had been shepherded off the bridge. "I'll hold you, Sergeant, if you go over a little more."

Michael grimly shook his head, the wooden boards imprinted in his straining biceps. His entire body shook with tension, his booted toes hooked over the far side of the narrow bridge.

"Try and reach her," he shouted to Joshua. "See if we can pull her up."

He heard Lucy cry out, an angry, despairing cry. She still fought for life, her head at least above water.

Joshua grabbed her upper arm, his beefy fingers sinking deeply into her white flesh. It pained Michael to see her handled that way, his precious lady, but Lucy must be saved.

The two of them heaved on her arm and out of the murky water Lucy's other arm swung up and grabbed Michael's wrist. Her nails dug into his skin, but Michael didn't care. It meant she lived.

She thumped against the bridge and her grip loosened on his for a moment. It tightened again and they continued to haul her up. A burly man crouched by Michael's side, ready to lend assistance.

At last, they hauled her onto the narrow bridge, her thin clothing plastered to her body, her pale blond hair sticking darkly to her skull.

Without a word, Michael scooped her up in his arms and carried her off the bridge. A woman waited with a blanket. He lay her down upon it and wrapped her in it. Rubbing the warmth back into her limbs, he looked for a sign of life on her white face. A faint puff of air escaped her blue lips.

Her pale blue eyes fluttered open and she stared up at him. "Is she . . . is Jane all right?"

Michael swept her up into his arms and hugged her tight. "Thank God. Oh, thank God." He pulled back just far enough to push the wet hair from her face and kiss her.

Her icy lips warmed beneath his and she kissed him back with fervor, her arms twining around his neck. He willed his own heat into her body, kissing her and kissing her, until someone tapped him on the shoulder.

"Sergeant, bring her to the Green Burn Inn here. We have room aplenty for your women to dry and change."

With reluctance, Michael pried his lips from Lucy's. "Thank you," he said, picking Lucy up once more, quilt and all. "My Lucy has no other clothes than what she wears."

The woman who had held out the blanket nodded sagely. "I have some of my daughter's clothes that'll fit her. Come, come along." Gesturing, the woman led the way.

Michael stared down at Lucy's upturned face. She gazed at

him hungrily, as if she wanted to memorize his face. He grinned, dipping his head to kiss her brow. Wasn't that exactly what he had been doing?

Bliss! Oh bliss! Lucy kept her eyes closed, her head sinking into a lumpy pillow and another lump in the mattress poking at her back. Ah, but it was heaven, absolute heaven, compared with lying on cold, hard ground!

A weight settled onto the bed with a firm purpose, so Lucy knew it wasn't one of the local women come to check on her. She opened her eyes and smiled up at Michael.

She'd slept through the remainder of the day and the room had fallen into darkness, the only light coming from the freshly stoked fireplace. The odd light cast deep grooves into Michael's face, making him even more forbidding in appearance.

If Lucy didn't know of his tenderness, nor the reason he had come to her bed, she might have been afraid.

He leaned over her, brushing back wisps of her white-gold hair. "How do you feel?" he whispered.

"Much better," she replied. It was true. Her arm still ached and bandages covered the bangs and scrapes she'd received being pulled out of the water, but she no longer felt quite so waterlogged. "How is Jane?"

"Developing a nasty cold, I think, from all that water she swallowed. Why on earth did you go in after her?"

"Because I can swim, and I didn't want to wait to see if anyone else had noticed. A delay and she may have drowned."

"She nearly drowned you both." His voice sounded flat and emotionless.

Lucy reached out to him, her hand falling upon his forearm. He wore his redcoat, and the rough wool felt oddly soothing to her. "But she didn't."

"You hardly knew her, I don't understand . . ." Michael frowned at her, his dark brows shoving together.

"Beside yourself, she is the only one who has shown me any kindness. In any case, I would have done it for anyone, had I been the closest. Which I was."

He shook his head at her, his sensuous lips curved into a smile. "I never thought the gentry'd rescue common folk like us."

Lucy's cheeks warmed. "There is not so much difference between you and I . . ." She paused, her hand clasping his. "Although I find I do prefer sleeping in a bed."

His lips pursed and he chuckled. "It's a rough life. Not like yours, at all."

"I have not complained." *Much.*

He bent over and kissed her, an innocent kiss, on her lips. "No, you have not. I have been grateful for that."

"Good." Her arms twined behind his neck. "Care to show me how much you have been grateful?"

He didn't draw back, nor did he take her up on her invitation. "Don't you need rest?"

She laughed softly. "I have slept for hours. What I need is you, Sergeant Michael Hall, to reassure me that I am indeed among the living."

Michael chuckled at that. "Oh, you are. Have I created a monster who craves me in her bed?"

"Hardly," she replied. "Don't you long for a soft pillow, an actual mattress? What must I do to convince you?"

"Very little, I promise." His tight, desire-filled voice confirmed his words. "Are you cured of your horrible memories? Is my work done?"

She didn't miss the teasing in his voice. "I am. But why can't I still have you?"

He took a sharp breath. "Lucy, dear Lucy. If there weren't this separation of class between us . . ."

"But there isn't." Lucy tightened her grip behind his neck.

"You can have no expectations of me. A woman of your class . . ."

Lucy glared at him. "Will you stop talking of 'class'? Michael, I want you and only you. If this lasts only until we reach London, so be it. I would rather treasure the memory of our time together than live a lifetime of regret because we let class get in the way of enjoying each other."

Michael's eyes darkened into a now-familiar look of desire. He kissed her again. Kissed her until her toes curled with the pleasure of it. His mouth invaded hers, moulding her eager lips to his.

She arched her body into his, the quilt covering her a sudden, unwanted impediment. "Michael," she murmured against his lips, in almost a groan. "Please."

He stripped back the covers and picked her up, still kissing her with fervent abandon. Kneeling before the fire, he settled her onto the worn rug, his fingers going to the buttons of her borrowed nightgown.

"I want to see you naked," he whispered, his voice hoarse. "I have never seen you bare before me."

Lucy joined in the struggle to remove her nightgown. She wadded it up and put it behind her head for a makeshift pillow. Her forearms remained covered with thin bandage strips, the rest of her visible for him.

She cupped her breasts, showing him how her hardened nipples ached for him. All of her ached for him. Wanted him with an abandon she never expected she possessed before this change in her life.

Her thumbs smoothed over her pert nipples, bringing them into even more prominent life. Her hands trailed down over her ribs and back to her breasts, teasing them so her nipples swelled and grew.

When would he touch her? Show her how much he wanted her? Couldn't he see she longed for him?

She skimmed a path down to the golden patch of hair between her legs glinting red in the firelight. She slipped a finger in between her cunt lips, teasing her little clit into life.

All the time, she kept her gaze on him, watching his thigh muscles flex through his tight overalls, watching his cock thicken and harden behind the breech flap.

"Do I get to see you without clothes?" she asked, her voice husky. She licked her lips.

"Woman, is it possible you are insatiable?" In haste, he unfastened his wide belt and stripped off his coat. His shirt followed soon after.

"You will have to find that out, won't you," Lucy teased, feeling laughter rise in her throat. His haste showed his banked hunger, despite all his earlier protestations.

He hauled off his boots and faced her while he unbuttoned his overalls. His cock sprung free, already weeping.

Fire shot through her, from cunt to head, a burning flame melting all in its path. Watching him strip naked so eagerly made her want him even more.

She admired Michael's naked figure. On his knees, he faced her proudly. His pale thighs, covered with a scattering of black hair, flexed and his cock bobbed in response.

His cock. Oh, his magnificent cock. She had never seen one. Touched one, yes, had one impressed deep inside her, yes, but available for her inspection? No. Michael's thick cock had two veins curving along its thick trunk before disappearing into his bulging tip, a smooth, glistening mushroom cap with a hole weeping his lust.

Lucy licked her lips, wondering at its taste.

Her ogling gaze rose higher, past the flat stomach with the line of dark hair rising to his navel. Black hair matted his chest, the pale skin an odd contrast to his sun-darkened neck and face. She stared into his eyes, darkened with desire and almost impenetrable. His sensual lips curled and he crawled toward her on all fours.

"You look beautiful," he whispered, slipping the black ribbon from his hair. He shook out the simple queue, letting it fall in a black curtain across his shoulders. "Very wanton."

His words blazed a trail from her head down to her cunt. Her fingers slipped in a sudden rush of liquid. "So do you," she replied, almost breathless.

"I saw you stare at my cock," he continued, between peppering kisses across the tops of her breasts. Lucy bit down on her lower lip. Just him saying the word "cock" gave her a rush. "Did you want to taste it?"

"Taste it?" Lucy echoed, her eyes wide. Did he test her?

He grinned down at her. "I long to taste you. Not just your pretty, pouty lips but your wet cunt." His hand slid down over her belly and pressed between her legs, tangling with her own fingers there.

"There?"

"There," he affirmed. He probed deeper, his finger sliding into her slick hole.

Lucy's breath hitched and she licked her lips.

Michael grinned. "Just don't bite and I promise I won't either."

He pivoted, straddling her head. His scent filled her air, hot, male, and aroused. A dirty scent. A sexy scent. His cock bumped against her chin, smearing his juice across it.

Tentatively, she flicked her tongue against his cock, striking the underside. His cock jerked in response. Michael's breath blew hot against her thigh, followed by the pressure of his mouth against her cunt lips.

His tongue slid across her wet clit and Lucy cried out, Michael's cock sliding across her lips. His tongue continued with a light swirling, around and around her clit until she glowed from the inside. A gorgeous light threatened to burst forth from her belly and coat the stars with her coming. She jerked her hips upward, but Michael's hands held her down.

"My cock," he said, his breath bouncing off her juicy cunt. "Taste me, Lucy."

She reached up, hands cupping buttocks, her fingertips brushing the base of his balls. He groaned, his mouth pressed against her wet slit.

He licked her, making her pant, and she returned the favor, her eager tongue wetting his cock with her saliva. She tasted him, rich and salty upon her tongue, upon her lips.

"Take me in," he groaned. "Take me in your mouth."

Lucy obeyed, kissing the tip and letting it fall between her parted lips. The sensation of nubbled texture vanished the deeper it went, her teeth grazing its gravid heaviness.

Just like that, he filled her. She gave an experimental suck. His cock pulsed and sent her trembling with need. Still licking her cunt, he slipped one finger in, maybe more, stretching her the same way his cock stretched her lips.

His hips flexed, pumping into her mouth, in time with his delving fingers. She bucked against him, fingernails digging into his thighs. She moaned, vibrating his cock, wanting more and more. Wanting the release his mouth teased at. The slightest touch made her erupt.

She wanted more.

He fucked her mouth, her cunt, in earnest. He slid in and out of her lips, pressing against the back of her throat but going no farther.

At any moment, at any intake of breath, Lucy would explode, her body a mass of raw sensation, of bursting light.

She cried out. She came and came into Michael's mouth, her body twisting and tense. She flung her head back and forth on her nightgown pillow, his cock slipping from her lips. Her orgasm washed over her and over her again.

Michael pivoted, crouching between her parted legs. Lucy

held her breath. He slid up her body, his cock nudging into place against her still-spasming cunt. He claimed her mouth in a wet kiss and she tasted herself and her sweet juices. She licked at his lips and chin until his mouth devoured hers again.

His rough hands encircled her breasts and she moaned into his mouth. She wanted him to suck on her nipples until she begged him to let her come. She wanted him inside her, fucking and fucking her until she revisited that glorious release again.

"Want . . . you," she managed to gasp.

He growled, dipping his head to nibble at her vulnerable neck, sucking at her pulsating pulse point before claiming her mouth again. His hands imprinted themselves upon her sensitive, soft skin. He plucked at her nipples until their fire grew too much to bear and even then, Lucy wanted more.

He hauled her upright, like a sagging rag doll in his strong grasp. Her legs wrapped about his waist as he drew her in close.

His cock, wet with both their juices, rubbed at her belly. He rocked against her and she squirmed against him, wanting him inside her but hardly knowing how, in this position.

His hands grasped her narrow waist, lifted her, and slowly, ever so slowly, drew her down upon his thick, delicious cock. He sank into her overstimulated flesh. She sobbed her pleasure. He stretched her, making her moan. He filled her and tears blinded her.

She writhed against his invading cock, twisting upon his shaft, her muscles convulsing around him, sucking on him as her mouth had done, drawing him in, keeping him in. Always in a constant, fevered motion, she rocked against his cock, rotating her hips so that his bulbous head coursed across every part of her soaking tunnel.

She gripped his shoulders, head flung back as she ground down against him. *Heaven, absolute heaven. No better perfection than this.* He dipped his head and suckled upon her tender breasts, arteries of fire rushing through her.

Lucy squeezed her cunt about him hard, and harder again, feeling the delicious tension rise. Could it be? Could she experience that bliss twice in an evening?

Michael groaned between her breasts, his every muscle radiating tension. He had to be close. Somehow, his cock felt huger inside her than it had before.

Oh God! Oh God! Clinging on to him, she rammed her groin hard against his in a thousand sharp thrusts, her release flooding her senses.

His hands dug into the tender flesh of her back and he held her in place, his cock pumping in and out of her, gushing his salty fluid deep inside her in time with his long, almost agonized groan.

Lucy clung to him, her body shuddering with each attempt to get air into her lungs. Michael sheltered his head against her shoulder, also gasping. Lucy didn't want to ever move again. She wanted to remain at his side for a lifetime and beyond. She had almost lost him today, almost lost her life, making their wild joining ever more precious.

Michael stirred at last, cupping her face in his hands and kissing first her nose and then her forehead. She leaned into him, letting him pepper her with kisses for a long time.

His cock greasily slid free of her sated cunt. "Michael, you could have bedded me in that bed. Instead, we are on the floor!"

He burst out laughing. "Oh, I am so sorry, duchess! I just wanted to look at you naked. The light isn't near as good in bed." He leaned forward and captured her lower lip between his lips. "What say I bed you there now?"

She linked her fingers behind his head. "I thought I was the insatiable one."

He laughed again and rose, swinging her up in his arms. He laid her on the bed and crawled in after her, pulling the covers up over them.

Lucy snuggled into his arms. Now this was bliss, utter bliss. Far better to share one's bed than be alone! His heartbeat thudded in her ear, still accelerated from the sex.

She nestled closer. No man had ever given so much of himself to her before. Admittedly, her experience before Michael came to a total of one man, who gave only enough so that he could take more.

Michael, Michael was different.

"I thought we were going to . . ."

His dry chuckle sent a delicious shiver through her. "Give me a minute to catch my breath, love."

Lucy caught hers. "Love"? Did he mean that?

He stroked her hair, silky once more thanks to the warm bath after her dunking in the dirty river water. She loved the feel of him touching her like that, so at odds with his tough demeanor.

She woke some hours later after a second bout of great sex to find Michael spooned behind her, his hands upon her breasts and his hot breath huffing at her ear. It reassured her that she wasn't alone in the world.

Lucy held her breath for a moment, realizing that his cock nestled between her buttocks. Not hard, nor soft either. It roused her from her dreamy contemplation. Even in his sleep, Michael wanted her.

An answering heat grew deep within her belly. Her nipples hardened under Michael's sleeping palms. Would he fuck her in his sleep? Lucy wondered what it would be like, his cock sliding into her and moving out in a slow, slow motion, rocking against her bottom.

She couldn't help it. She wriggled against his waking cock, smiling to herself when it roused further, prodding at her soft, mounded flesh.

Lucy squirmed some more, small movements so as not to

wake him, only to wake his cock. He lengthened and hardened behind her, the nubby head poking into her.

Daring to shift position, Lucy raised her upper leg, hooking it casually back over his muscled calf. His hand flexed over her breast, a quick pulse that had Lucy almost leaping out of her skin.

Had he woken? She stilled, holding her breath. Michael nestled closer and let out a soft snore.

Lucy relaxed. She wanted to play out this fantasy, to take him without his being aware. She bent forward, reaching between her legs for his cock.

Hot and hard in her hand, with a little wriggling and direction, she had his cock nestled against her cunt lips. Just one flex of her hips would plunge him inside her, but she refrained.

Licking her fingers, she toyed with her clit. Sexual heat rose from that almost-joining, flushing her body with need. She bit back a moan, wanting more than anything to have him inside her.

She couldn't resist any longer. Pushing back against him, his hard cock slid ever so slowly into her wet cunt. Her breath hitched, her fingers slipping down past her clit and across his hard cock bent inside her. A vein pulsed against her featherlight touch.

Tracing the rounded curve back behind her to his balls, she had to bend forward, her breast slipping from his sleeping hold.

"Where are you going, miss?" Michael nipped her shoulder, curling around her and reclaiming her breast with one hand. He tweaked her nipple.

Lucy cried out in pleasure. "You weren't asleep."

"You think I'd miss this?" His hips flexed and he thrust deeper into her. Lucy gasped, gripping the sheet before her.

He held her there, buried deep inside her, ignoring her squirms against him. His rough hands gave her breast a light squeeze before tracing along her curves, caressing her with a lazy gentleness. Lucy wanted him to fuck her hard now. Right now.

Or no. Nice and slow and endless. Conflicted, she gave herself over to the sensations he aroused in her, wondering where next his touch would go.

He brushed over her hip and down her thigh, holding still all the while. His path curved inward, finding the sensitive skin of her inner thigh before curving out again. He retraced their path, fingering through her wiry curls, finding her parted cunt lips.

His cock pulsed inside her. He roamed from her clit to her filled hole, his touch disappearing and returning again. His sticky hand smoothed over her thigh, leaving a smeary trail. He hitched her leg higher over his and held it.

His hips swung back until the head of his cock almost threatened to slip out of her and he drove his cock ever slowly back in. Her muscles clutched at him.

God, it felt so good to have him inside. She arched her back, wanting him in even deeper. Her head pressed against his shoulder, nestled beneath his chin.

Michael kept the pace slow, nibbling at her ear. He hooked his knee under her upraised leg, lifting it even higher and driving himself even deeper into her hot core.

He slid a hand under her writhing body, snaring a breast from below, his fingertips plucking at her soft mound. He found her nipple, much neglected compared to the other one, and brought it into rousing life, a hot point pressing against his fingers and the cool sheets below.

Lucy turned her head, pressing her mouth against his cheek, his chin. His slow pace drove her wild, each rhythmic thrust rocking her into sweeter and stronger tension.

Strung tight, a bow ready to be plucked, her release poised to soar to the heavens like an arrow. Poised on the brink of firing, Michael's gentle strumming sent her higher and higher.

Barely able to breathe, she gasped out pleasured moans and cries, rocking against him.

Michael ignored her begging squirms, keeping the pace steady. She burned, her skin hot and flushed. Michael became a fever possessing her, and the only freedom lay in giving in to his command, to his mastery over her.

He nipped her shoulder to remind her of it, soothing the bite with an openmouthed kiss. He thrust in hard at the same time, grinding his groin against her bottom.

A soft wail burst from her throat. The action of his cock against her tender tunnel drove her ever higher. Her cunt tightened about him, squeezing hard, and Michael lost all control. He bucked into her, his cock driving in and out. She clamored for more, her body going rigid while he pounded into her.

She came in a rush, gushing around his hammering cock. He shuddered behind her and joined her in her coming.

Slipping out of her, Michael released her leg, caressing and smoothing out the ache of having it elevated for so long. He kissed her shoulder, his cock wet and slimy at her back. Sweat coated both of them and their panting breaths clouded the cold night air.

"Michael?" Lucy whispered into the night, glad for once she couldn't see his handsome face. She had to let him know. She couldn't continue to be his lover without him knowing the truth.

He made a contented, inquiring mumble.

"Michael, I think—I think I am falling in love with you."

He tensed behind her and she cringed. She had said the wrong thing. She'd feared it might be the case, but she'd had to say it, the words burned on her lips and in her heart.

"You are mistaken." His voice lost its soft edge and he gripped her bicep too hard. He relaxed his grip, leaving the echo of his fingers in her flesh. "This isn't love."

"Isn't it?" Lucy blinked away a stray tear.

"What you feel is an attraction to me, to be with me, but it is because of the great sex, it has nothing to do with me."

Was he right? "But it does have everything to do with you. You have been kind to me, sheltered me, protected me, saved my life twice now. What is there not to love?"

Michael rolled onto his back. Lucy missed his touch at once and wished again to unsay the words she'd had to speak.

"The way I live my life," he replied roughly, "I have chosen not to take a wife for that reason. My life is too hard, too uncertain, to bind it up with responsibilities and burdens."

Lucy sucked in a pained breath. Not his lover, but a burden.

He continued, oblivious to her pain. "In my world, I might die at any time. At any time, the line might be overwhelmed by the enemy. Any woman I called wife might be captured or killed.

"The men under my command are my prime concern. It is my job to get them and my officers home again, to their wives and children. I cannot be distracted by that."

"I am not useless baggage," she grumbled.

"I didn't say that," Michael replied testily. He swung out of bed.

Lucy sat up and watched him don his clothes. This was not how she wanted this night to end.

He fastened the buttons of his coat and looked at her for the first time since getting out of bed. His features softened. "Lucy, lass. I don't want to hurt you, but if you fall in love with me, that's what will happen. I'm taking you home, but there cannot be a life for us beyond this journey to London. You must see it is impossible."

Lucy refused to admit it. She glared mutinously at him and then flung her head down into the pillows, covering her head with her arms.

The door clicked shut behind him.

He was gone.

6

Caroline rose and dressed before Radbourne even stirred, not looking at him once. Her head pounded with the aftereffects of last night's wine, but she did not want to be found half-naked when Radbourne woke.

She had trouble enough dealing with her own traitorous body without Radbourne's lascivious looks adding to her confusion.

In the process of pulling on her gloves, Caroline turned to find Radbourne awake. He sat up in bed, his forearms propped on his knees and his hands loosely clasped before him.

He reminded her of a ruffled golden lion, sleepily regarding her as his next meal. "You are dressed already?"

"Of course." Her cool voice carried her disdain to him. "I have no intentions of being seduced this morning."

"You? Being seduced?" Radbourne barked a surprised laugh. "You were a willing partner."

He'd cornered her, confronting her with last night's act. She didn't want to acknowledge it. She couldn't. She mimed outrage. "A willing partner? You bedded me last night?" She clutched her head. "Oh, my head. What did you put in my drink?"

His jaw dropped. He rose, draping the coverlet about his hips. The bandages about his head fell loose over his eye and he pushed them off his forehead. "Do you mean to tell me you don't remember?"

"Remember what?" She tried to recoil as he approached instead of leaning toward him. In the morning light, he glowed with magnificence. She saw how he'd turned Lucy's head.

He reached her and touched her cheek. She leaned into it for the barest second before jerking away. His voice dropped very low. "The best sex I've ever had in my life."

She gasped. Did he really mean that? She let out a soft moan, wishing it didn't sound so much like the cries she made last night. "Oh, I am ruined."

He stepped back and tried to assume his dignity, considering his seminakedness. "Caroline, nobody need ever know."

Caroline drew herself up to her full height and stared him in the eye. "I forbid you to use that name. I am Miss Waverton to you, sir."

He glowered. "I don't know what game you are playing at, Miss Waverton, but I'm in no mood for play this morning. If you will allow me to dress, I will join you downstairs for breakfast."

She made her escape before he cast off his flimsy covering and she feasted her eyes on his cock. She descended the dark and narrow inn stairs, shaking her head. She had to get control of herself. No more lustful thoughts and no more acting on those thoughts.

She entered the small and empty dining room. At least she had this moment of privacy, away from the general populace in the tap room.

Crossing to the window, she stared out of it. At a lower elevation, it still brought back memories of the previous night.

How he'd cajoled her for another kiss and how they had exploded into such passion that even now it stole her breath away.

Unbidden, she touched her breast, fingering the nipple through the thin folds of her gown. It reacted at once, puckering and hardening. Caroline sucked in her breath, half-closing her eyes.

She hoped, oh how she hoped, that they found Lucy today. Could she keep her hands off Radbourne for one night?

Why *had* Lucy run from him?

A floorboard behind her creaked and she spun, her hand dropping to her waist. Radbourne grinned at her. "I did not think you to be the innocent, Miss Waverton."

She turned up her nose. "Just checking the damage. I appear to be unusually tender." She silently cursed her breathless voice.

"Now that I am dressed and shaved, I am in a better humor," Radbourne announced. Someone had also restored his bandages. "Why are you playing this silly game? I know I am not your first. I know that you want me."

Caroline twitched her head back toward the window, trying to steady her breathing. "I don't know what you speak of. You should be grateful I have not run crying rape."

The few paces between them vanished and he grabbed her arm. "It was not rape," he got out between gritted teeth. "I'll allow the wine made you incautious, but you were not so drunk as to be insensible of what you were doing."

She glared at him. "Was I not?"

"You were not," he affirmed, his head bending down towards her.

She ought to wriggle free before he kissed her. Frozen, she stared at his approaching face, not even daring to lick her lips.

He kissed her with initial tenderness, the kiss rapidly deepening until she clung to him in an echo of last night's kiss.

Breaking it off, he gazed at her, not even a hand's breadth from her face. "What are you afraid of, Caroline?"

Everything, she wanted to say. *Everything and nothing*. She backed off a step, unable to stay so close. "This is wrong, Radbourne. This is very wrong."

He opened his mouth to speak but she held up a quelling hand. "Do not butter me with reassurances that if it feels right, it must be right. It is not right. You are to be my sister's husband. It's wrong even on a Biblical level."

"I am not her husband yet."

Caroline's chest tightened with anger. "So you will leave her ruined in order to have me? Or will you cast me off when the next pretty filly comes along?"

He gaped at her and then turned his back. "Woman is ever unreasonable," he grumbled. He directed her to the table. "Come, eat. We will catch up with your sister."

Caroline settled opposite him and picked at the cold breakfast left out for them.

They ate in silence.

Radbourne cleared his throat. "Caroline, I expect you are right, but I do hope you'll keep the memory of last night as a positive one, not something to be ashamed of."

She regarded him, her fork poised midway to her lips, a slice of ham dangling from it. "I rather think that is up to me, don't you?"

He stared at her, his dark blue eyes seeming to penetrate her very soul. She ducked her head and continued eating.

Cloaked in silence, they journeyed south over green hills and reached the next village. Caroline strolled the main street, searching for her sister, while Radbourne and his coachman went to make further inquiries.

She rejoined them at the carriage.

"Nothing," Radbourne told her. "It is like she has disappeared." He slumped against a carriage wheel, ignoring the mud on it.

"Where is she?"

"Why does she head south? She'd reach safety at your home far sooner than heading to London."

"And if she heads for London, why does she keep off the main road? Is she hiding from you?"

"She ran away from me, stands to reason." He cursed, pushing himself off the dirty carriage wheel and kicking it. "We should have headed inland. Those people she's fallen in with, if they're off to the Peninsula, then they'd be taking the most direct route to Dover."

"The Great North Road would be faster, at least until they reach London."

"Not if you're walking and can't afford to take the mail coach." He stroked his unshaven chin, the dirt clinging to his blond bristles. "No, we'll have to go further inland and see if our paths will cross. If she lives."

Caroline shivered at his last words. "Don't say that! Don't think it or even wish it."

His brows lowered. "My dear, I would personally track down and wring the man's neck who stole her life. I do not wish Miss Lucy dead."

"You must not call me 'my dear'," Caroline said, her voice shaking.

"I'll call you what I like," he snapped. "Now, get in the carriage. We must be on our way."

She didn't want to accept his hand to help her up into the carriage, but it was that or fall flat on her face. She chose the dignified route and settled inside, facing forward.

He gave orders to his coachman and joined her, brushing the drying mud off his arm. He studied her for a long moment, until Caroline couldn't bear it any longer and turned away, staring out at the rolling green hills.

There had been nothing heated in his gaze. Had their altercation in the morning killed any desire he felt for her? Her well of sadness surprised her. Hadn't she expected this? His expression held only concern.

Caroline wished her desire for him had been killed too. She still wanted him. Every movement he made grabbed her attention, even the slightest shifting in his seat. He breathed and Caroline knew the intake of each breath.

Oh this was a disaster, an absolute disaster. How could she live, knowing that her sister was married to this man? How would she endure their visits, knowing his hands and his mouth as intimately as she did?

She swallowed and blinked back tears. She would manage. She had to.

They reached another village, a tiny hamlet with a giant wool church of golden sandstone.

"Stay here." Radbourne got out.

Caroline leaned out the window, watching him and his coachman stroll into the inn. A few moments later, they exited, Radbourne shaking his head at her.

She leaned back against the leather bolsters and waited for him to get in again.

He didn't, choosing to ride with his coachman.

She frowned, folding her arms. *Well, fine. If he was going to be like that!*

The carriage wheeled out of the tiny village. Above, the sun struggled to break through massing gray clouds. Caroline gazed up at them, biting her lower lip. Rain meant the washing away of tracks, although how they'd ever be expected to find them coming at them from this angle, she didn't know.

They stopped at village after village, crisscrossing the countryside on narrow dirt trails, trying to find a clue that Lucy might have passed by there.

Evening fell early and twilight had transformed into night by the time they rolled into the next village.

This time, Radbourne opened the door and helped her descend. "We'll stay here tonight." His gaze swept over her from head to toe, possessive and yet dismissive at the same time. "We'll get two rooms. I'll say you're feeling unwell, so please do me the honor of coughing frequently."

"As you wish."

She suffered his arm going about her and she leaned into him, smelling his manly scent. God, he smelled good enough to eat.

They passed under the inn's low threshold and she coughed, turning her face against Radbourne's coat. He gripped her shoulders tight, steering her through the patrons and to the innkeeper.

"Have you two rooms?" he asked without preamble. "My wife is sick and I would prefer not to listen to her cough all night."

Caroline waved a hankerchief she had slipped from her sleeve cuff. "It's just a cold," she gasped out, pitching her voice low and speaking through her nose.

"Bloody tiresome cold, if you ask me," Radbourne grumbled. "Well, sir?"

"Your lordship, we have plenty of rooms this night. I shall lead you to our two finest. I trust madam does not wish to be disturbed?"

"Just a little broth," Caroline gasped out, although her stomach gurgled, not having had anything since breakfast.

The innkeeper nodded and led the way. They ascended the stairs, Caroline relishing the heat of Radbourne's body pressed against hers as they went up the narrow staircase.

At her door, he bowed over her hand. "Do feel better, dear," he pronounced in bored tones. Despite his nonchalant air, her senses thrilled at the sound of his voice. "Sleep well," his low voice burred. "Think of me in your bed, pleasuring you until time stops."

Somehow she thought he wished her to the very devil instead. Her cheeks flushed. He chuckled, stepping away to be led off somewhere else. Somewhere not with her.

His absence came as both a relief and an aching pain. In short order, her luggage arrived in her room and she sank back on the bed, staring up at the wood and plaster ceiling.

A young maidservant came in, bearing a tray with a steaming bowl of soup and some hunks of bread.

Caroline covered her mouth with her handkerchief and waved at the maidservant to set it down, coughing to emphasize her point that it would be best if the girl made a quick exit.

The maid did so, and Caroline sat up, reaching for the tray. It was not broth, but vegetable soup, with bright orange carrots and translucent green celery bobbing in it.

Caroline ate hungrily, dunking the hard bread into the soup and devouring the whole. When she had finished, she placed the tray by the door and prepared for bed.

She didn't expect any midnight visits from Radbourne. He'd made that clear. She slid the bolt across the door and placed a chair against it for extra measure.

Just in case he had second thoughts.

She'd only packed one nightgown and it smelled of last night's sex: a heady, almost dirty scent that recalled the events of the previous night as if they had just happened. She hadn't realized they'd fucked on the neatly laid out garment until afterward.

She crawled beneath the faded quilt coverlet, drawing the covers up to her shoulders. Sinking into the down pillow, she squeezed her eyes shut. She would sleep and in the morning, they would find Lucy. Radbourne would marry her, they'd go off on their honeymoon and move to his country estate, and have lots of babies.

Lucy ought to be grateful. She'd been ruined by an aristocrat who promised to make good. At least it had not been a footman or a street sweeper.

A tear slid from beneath her closed eyelids. She shouldn't have thought of that, not of him who she'd so steadfastly tried to forget all these years.

Think of anything else but him, she told herself. *Anything. Anyone. Radbourne.*

She lifted the folds of her gown to her nose and inhaled. The first stirrings of wanting swirled in her belly. She lay curled up and replayed their liaison, the fight for dominance. What would it be like if they were in perfect accord?

He'd suckle more upon her breasts, Caroline decided, fingering a nipple through the unbuttoned neck of her gown. Trailing her touch back and forth, she pinched the puckering bud between her fingers. She rolled the nipple back and forth and stifled a moan.

He'd worship her breasts, kissing them and teasing them and tugging on them, until her nipples grew large and round.

Rolling onto her back, she pulled up the nightgown, bunching it up above her breasts. She tweaked the tight buds, pulling on them until her chest flushed and swelled with heat. Her hands smoothed over her hot flesh, her hard tits radiating a hotter temperature, almost fevered.

She gathered the weight of her breasts into her hands, cupping and squeezing, pulling them up as if they were trapped in a pair of revealing stays, pushing them together to reveal a deep cleavage.

He'd lick that crevice, she imagined, running a wetted fingertip along it. *He'd lick her bosom.* She swiped a wet finger across her nipples.

His hands would be all over her body, caressing and exploring. Her hands smoothed along her belly, curving around her waist and hips and back again. Her fingertips brushed the tops of her thighs, skirted her golden verge, and slid down her outer thighs.

He'd dug his hands into her haunches when he'd fucked her

from behind, and she could almost feel the indentations of his fingernails. All memory, of course, only light red half-moons remained when she'd checked that morning.

Her legs parted, encouraging exploration along the tender flesh of her inner thighs. She wanted him to touch her hot center, wanted to touch herself, but she knew the game of teasing and waiting.

Her hands roamed elsewhere, teasing her nipples, tracing her curves, warming her body more effectively than the coverlet. His hands were smooth, the hands of an aristocrat, not a working man. Only light calluses marked where the reins rubbed at his hands when he rode, calluses soothed by cream.

She bit her lower lip. *What would it be like to have him rub cream over her and then lick off the sticky confection?* She'd return the favor, dolloping the sweet, heavy cream on his hard cock and licking every part of it off.

She missed that.

Think of Radbourne.

He'd need no enticement to go down on her, to lick her cunt, creamy with her juices. She couldn't resist: her fingers dipped into her soft pubes, parted her cunt lips, and brushed lightly against her clit, already poking from its hiding place.

She skimmed past it, delving deeper, finding her reward of slippery wetness oozing from her fleshy hole. She slicked her juices along her crevice, getting closer and closer to her clit with each upward movement.

Brushing her clit again, Caroline let out a little sigh. It tingled, a fast, delicious thrill that promised a more heady throbbing later.

With a very gentle touch, she teased her clit, wetting it again and again with her own juices. The tiny tingle at the tip of her clit expanded, taking over her whole cunt and spreading deeper.

Oh, how she longed for something, anything to plunge into her cunt. She blinked her eyes open, examining the tapers from where she lay on her bed, and resigned herself to going without. The room looked like it hadn't been cleaned in ages and she wasn't about to shove a dusty candle up her quim.

She shuddered in distaste and closed her eyes. In her envisioning, Radbourne hovered over her, his blond hair golden from the dancing candlelight.

Then he'd slide down the length of her body, ever so slowly, peppering kisses until he reached her juicy quim. There, lying between her legs, he'd part her lips and let his tongue flick over her clit.

She shivered at her fingertip's brief touch.

He'd lick her clit, making it swell and grow ever more sensitive until she couldn't stand it any more. Caroline rubbed at her clit, her hips rising and squirming against her own touch.

Oh, she was growing close, ever so close. Her heart pounded, her body tensed. A roaring sounded in her ears and she cried out, curling around her hand still pressed against her pubic mound.

She lay there, curled on her side, hand trapped between her legs. Oh, she had needed that. Now she wouldn't succumb to Radbourne, to any man, and when her sister was found, she would go back to her cloistered life. She'd made her choice. There lay no temptation, no man to fantasize about, no man to expel from her tangled desires.

At dawn, a knock on Lucy's door woke her. She struggled awake, sitting up in the rumpled bed. Michael hadn't come back. She'd waited for him, hoping he'd return, but she'd eventually dozed off.

"Come in!" she called.

The innkeeper's wife entered, bearing an armful of dull gray and brown clothing. "These are my daughter's," she said. "Take what you like."

Lucy slid out of bed. "This is too generous of you. Why?"

The woman's face crumpled. "Because I lost my Emma in that river last winter. You saved that poor woman when you both could have been lost. I gathered from your sergeant that you had no other clothing and I have no use for these." She patted her expansive girth.

"I am so sorry." Lucy fingered the woolen cloth. "These are very well made, thank you."

She looked up to see the innkeeper's wife examining her. "What did happen to your clothes? The river didn't do all that damage."

Lucy smiled ruefully. "This has been my week for misadventures." She held up a high-waisted brown woolen gown with long tapered sleeves. Once she would have scorned such a common item, but the wool would keep her warm. "I don't know how I can ever repay you."

The innkeeper's wife patted her on the shoulder. "No need, no need. Gave you and that poor girl rooms so you can at least sleep in comfort for once. My sister Mary was a soldier's wife and I know how hard it can be on ye."

Lucy thought to protest she wasn't the sergeant's wife, but the woman barreled on.

"For all you've been through, thought it be nice for you and your man to have some comfort and privacy. Wouldn't want you catchin' your death of cold after surviving that."

Impulsively, Lucy hugged her. The woman was redolent of the kitchen, of beef gravies and boiled leafy vegetables. Lucy's stomach rumbled.

The woman laughed. "I'll leave ye to dress and come straight on down to breakfast. Your sergeant is talking about moving out."

Lucy speedily dressed. She scratched her hip, unused to the shift's coarse material.

She met Jane in the hall. Jane had a blue woolen shawl

wrapped around her shoulders, and her nose was quite red. "How are you, Jane?" Lucy asked.

"Stuffy," came Jane's response. "I feel like my nose is holding half of the river." She reached out and hugged Lucy. "Thank you. I don't know what my Joe would do without me."

"I'm sure he wouldn't know what he'd do either," Lucy replied, hugging back. "I'm starving. Are you?"

"Oh yes."

The two women descended the dark, narrow stairs of the inn, arm in arm. The bustling ruckus took them both by surprise, but Jane recovered first, dashing across the taproom and into her husband's arms.

Lucy looked about for Michael, but didn't find him.

"He's out with his men, lass," the innkeeper said. "Take a seat and I'll get ye breakfast."

Sitting with Jane and her husband, Lucy kept looking toward the main door. Did Michael plan to ignore her for the rest of the journey south? What would she do if he decided he'd had enough of her? Would she have to make the rest of the journey herself?

The innkeeper's wife settled across from them, folding her beefy arms and leaning over them, giving them a view of her expansive bosom. "Have ye heard the latest news?"

Joe Jones tore his gaze away from Jane. "What news? The war?"

"Oh no, lad." The woman waved off his suggestion. "Nothing like that. It's Society gossip."

Lucy raised an eyebrow. She had no idea Society was of interest to country folk.

"Another one of them Society girls has run off, eloped, with a notorious rake. Some are saying she's been abducted."

Lucy ignored the Joneses' focused gaze. "I'm sure she's well-married by now."

"Aye," the woman said. "You'd think so. But a chap came in from Wingdon, which is east of here, and said a handsome, well-dressed aristocrat type was asking questions about a blond woman." The innkeeper's wife narrowed her eyes at Lucy, as if she had just put it all together.

"And they don't know what happened to the girl?" Lucy asked.

"Not at all. Of course, this gentleman had a woman with him, also asking questions and as blond as you please, so it must be all some sort of silly jape."

"I imagine so." Lucy's mind spun at this latest revelation. A blond woman with Radbourne? Who was it? That Danielle whose name he called out? And why would he continue to look for her if he'd already found her replacement?

Unless . . . unless . . . Caroline's honey-colored hair leapt into her mind. But surely she'd have nothing to do with a man like Radbourne. No, no doubt he'd picked up some doxy and used her to warm his bed while he looked for her.

There could be no other explanation.

The innkeeper's wife still stared at her. "Where did you say you were from, lass?"

"I didn't," Lucy replied acerbically. Then she remembered how kind the woman had been. "Up north," she added truthfully.

Jane came to her rescue. "We all live in Burnswick. Up by the Scots border. Do you know of it?"

The innkeeper's wife shrugged. "Never been more than a mile from here, and that's a fact." She rose from the table, still casting suspicious glances at Lucy. "Best of luck to ye, and mind ye stay dry!"

Jane promised she would.

Lucy followed the other two outside, blinking at the bright morning light. Any trace of the previous storm had vanished, with the occasional white puffy cloud scudding across an azure sky.

It made the men's uniforms seem a brighter red and their freshly clay-piped crossbelts even whiter. The others had already broken camp, the last stragglers exiting from the stables. The innkeeper's generosity had not extended to quite everyone.

Michael's gaze passed over her and he barked the order to move out.

"Enjoy your night of luxury?" Maggie snarled, passing them by and not waiting for their answer.

"Bitch," Jane muttered under her breath and exchanged a sympathetic glance with Lucy.

The act heartened Lucy. That one of Michael's people would like her enough to say so gave her hope that perhaps she could fit in. She didn't want to go to London now. She wanted to stay with Michael.

However, it looked like she wouldn't get her wish. If Michael didn't want her, what could she do about it? She fell into line next to Jane. Her husband Joe left them after a few moments to take his place farther forward.

Michael didn't deign to notice her until much later in the afternoon. They'd stopped for a rest, the women sprawled out on the green grass under the shade of an alder tree. The soldiers crouched closer to the roadside.

Michael came and sat next to her, stretching out his legs before him. "There were rumors back at the inn."

She didn't look at him, choosing to gaze at the sheep in the field opposite. "I know. I heard them."

"Anyone suspect you?"

"The innkeeper's wife, but I don't think she knew for sure."

"What is certain is that if your rake finds that village, there are dozens of people who will say they have seen you. We made quite a stir back there."

She shot an angry glance at him, catching him off guard. His brooding gaze quickly shuttered. Had that been desire in his expression? Did he still want her?

"Firstly, he's not *my* rake. I want nothing to do with him. What are his chances of catching up with us?"

"He has horses, we don't. The chances are pretty good if he stumbles across our path. Who is the woman with him, do you suppose?"

Lucy shrugged carelessly. "I don't know and I don't care." Probably that woman whose name he cried out when he should have been calling for her.

Michael leaned closer. "Lucy, what's wrong?"

She tried for a smile. "Nothing. Why do you say that?"

"You looked very angry just now."

"More annoyed." Lucy decided not to tell him the reason why. "Why does he insist on pursuing me? If the gossip has reached the country, there's no point in attempting to preserve my reputation."

"Maybe he's trying to save his."

"Ha!" Lucy snorted softly in scorn. "He's the worst of rakes. There is no reputation to save."

She withstood his penetrating gaze.

"I have heard of this man," Michael drawled, each word said with careful consideration. "He has not stooped to seducing unwilling virgins before."

Lucy raised an eyebrow. "There is a first time for everything."

Another pause. "You—you were a virgin?"

She glared at him. "I should slap you," she snarled. "Of course I was!"

"It is—well, I have been thinking . . . Your enthusiasm for the sport is not that of a virgin's."

"That's because he took it from me and you have taught me to enjoy it."

"I think *he* taught you to enjoy it, not I."

Lucy gasped, but didn't draw in air. For a moment, she thought she might never breathe again. How had he guessed? "What?"

"Why else would he pursue you? He wants you in his bed."

"I don't know why he wants me," Lucy snapped, "but your theory rests on his enjoyment, not mine."

"Do you mean that? That you didn't enjoy him."

Lucy chose to look at the sheep again.

"Lucy?"

If she kept silent, he would get up and walk away and she'd never have the chance to win him again.

"It—it wasn't awful. He was kind to me." At least, until he revealed he'd been thinking of some other woman.

"A rapist, kind?"

Lucy glared at him.

"There's that fierce look of yours again." This time, Michael spoke gently. "Was he that bad?"

Lucy wanted to lie. Oh, how she wanted to lie and tell Michael anything except that it had been a wonderful, freeing experience, one that she intended to continue to enjoy with him.

"No, he wasn't. I just—just feel very foolish." Her confession choked her voice.

"So . . . it wasn't rape?" Accusation ran in an undercurrent in his voice.

Lucy couldn't look at him. "I knew nothing about relations between a man and a woman. It didn't feel like it does with you." She sniffled. "I didn't—didn't—" A sob escaped her.

"He forced you. I understand." Michael shifted. He sat behind her, his muscled legs on either side of her and hugged her from behind. "Lucy love, don't cry."

She didn't dare to contradict him. She leaned back against him, tears vanishing with his protective embrace, the happiest she'd been all day. "Michael, where do we go from here? I know you don't want me in your life—"

"The problem is, I want you too much." His lips found the back of her neck. "But you don't fit in my world, Lucy. You would be miserable, and given the hazards of my life, probably dead."

Lucy sighed. "I no longer fit into my world either. I had hoped to avoid scandal and shame, but it appears to be my lot." She covered his arms with hers, placing her hands over his gloved ones. "Michael, I am happy with you. I never thought I'd be happy trudging across the countryside, but it doesn't matter when I'm with you."

"But, lass—"

"I know. I know. You've made your feelings on the matter clear. But you still want me." Indeed, his cock had hardened since he changed positions and it pressed against her lower back. "May we not stay together until you're shipped to the Peninsula?"

"It will be harder to part then."

"It is hard enough to part now. I will leave and make my way back home to Durham, if you wish it, for I cannot travel with you and not be yours."

His arms tightened about her. "What will you do . . . after?"

After he left her. Lucy shivered at the thought that he couldn't bring himself to say the words. Did his feelings for her run deeper than the desire they shared?

She glanced down at the fresh white clay mark on her second-hand gown, hoping it would never come off. "If my father gives me the choice, it'll either be exile from my family and Society, or I'll be cast out and forced to whore to survive."

7

"No." Michael's broad hand covered her mouth. Looking down, she saw the dark hairs sprouting from the back of his hand. When had he removed his gloves?

After a moment, he released her. "No, you cannot do that."

Relief that he couldn't see her face washed through her. "I embroider well. Perhaps I could find a place embroidering clothes or hats or scarves or something."

"Your father is likely to throw you out?"

Jane, seated a short distance away, snuggling with her husband, looked over at that. "You're welcome to live with Joe and me."

Lucy flushed. "You're going to the Peninsula with Joe."

Jane bit her lip, her eyes shining. "Only if I win a ticket aboard the ship. Joe and I know I'll have to find my way back home else. I'd be happy for the company."

Lucy didn't know what else to do but thank her.

Smiling, Jane returned to the attentions of her husband.

"Exile," Michael murmured, keeping his voice low so that

they wouldn't be overheard by anyone else. "But exile with a friend. And when I return from the war—"

"If you return," she corrected, hating to have to say such a thing. "And how long will you be gone? You wish me to live alone and loveless, pining for you like some Penelope? What if you don't come back? You want me to spend the rest of my life without love?"

He nuzzled at her neck. "I would very much like a Penelope, whoever she is. It'd give me something to come home for." His grip tightened momentarily. "You won't find love as a whore, Lucy."

She didn't doubt that. "What if Jane does win a ticket, what then?"

"I don't have all the answers, Lucy. However, I will not see you become a whore."

"Why not? Haven't I become quite good at it?"

Breath hissed out between his teeth. "Is that what you think we've been doing?"

"No," she admitted honestly. "But if I were fallen before because of . . ." Her voice trailed off. "Then I am doubly fallen for having chosen to sleep with you, with no prospect of marriage in the offing."

Tension seeped out of him. "Aye, there is that. But I didn't force you to have sex with me."

"No, you didn't. I wanted it too. I still do."

There was a long silence. "As do I, lass. As do I."

She ran her hand along his outstretched thigh. "Then we will stay lovers?"

"I cannot promise you a future that's not mine to give." Michael unwrapped himself from about her and moved to her side, kneeling back on his heels. "I refuse to put you in danger and that is any place beyond these shores."

He took a deep breath. "Unless circumstances drive us apart, I'd be honored to be your lover until we reach London."

"I'll come with you to Dover. Another day or two will not make any difference now."

He nodded, a sensual grin spreading across his face. He leaned in and kissed her. The kiss took her breath away: his lips curved over her own, rapidly possessing her willing mouth, kissing her long and deeply.

When they parted at last, Michael settled on the ground next to her. He didn't seem to mind her putting her hand over his.

"What about your family?" he asked. "We should send word to them that you are alive and safe."

"That would mean heading back to the mail routes and getting caught by that man."

"Not necessarily. We surely could send a message from the next village. It might take a little while longer . . ."

Lucy smiled, feeling a weight lift from her shoulders. "I would like that very much," she murmured, leaning into him. "My sister will be worried about me."

"Your mother too."

She shook her head. "No mother. Just my father and my older sister. No brothers, even, to come to my honor's defense."

He managed a grin. "At least I don't have to worry about that, then!"

Something about his unfettered grin made her smile. "No, indeed not."

He paused, concern etched upon his forehead. "Lucy, you didn't have a brother who died?"

Taking pity on him, she shook her head. "I would have told you, if so. You need not worry that you've insulted the dead— or me."

He bent forward and kissed her lightly on the cheek. "I'm glad." He rose to his feet and held out his hand, helping her up. That she ended up in his arms, pressed against his chest, was an added bonus. "We need to start walking again if we're to make Dover by the end of the month."

Lucy nodded, pulling out of his embrace and taking his hand instead.

He shouted out to the others. "Let's get moving!"

With a grumble, the women rose, dusting off their skirts and hoisting bags of possessions onto their backs. A lot of items were in the donkey cart, which had survived the river crossing unharmed, but even a donkey could bear only so much weight.

They trekked across the field, away from the road, following one of the ancient pathways that crisscrossed the country, used as such for centuries and still available to all.

Lucy fell in beside Jane, who at once tucked her arm into hers and began discussing Lucy coming to live with her. Lucy had never seen her so excited.

The idea did not thrill Lucy: living in an isolated northern village, unmarried and friendless except for Jane. Jane's company would do much, but Lucy reckoned the two of them would be dead miserable in those first months after the men departed.

"Do you think the sarge will marry you?" Jane asked. "He has a place of his own in a farm not far from ours."

Lucy knew "not far" meant anywhere from within shouting distance to a couple of miles. "Tell me about his farm."

"It's the family's place. His parents are still living and the oldest brother runs the place, but I know the sarge will always have a home there." Jane smiled. "So how about it? Are the two of you getting married?"

"I doubt it very much, Jane. It's not like that between us." Lucy didn't want to mention Michael's belief about the dangers overseas. She didn't want to upset Jane.

"But I've never seen him so smitten by a woman!" Jane exclaimed, a tendril of dark hair escaping from her simple bonnet.

"How can it be some casual liaison? He's never put that much attention into one before."

"Perhaps because he feels some responsibility toward me. He found me and is determined to bring me home in one piece."

"No, it's not that. He's got a responsibility to all of us and he's never mooned over a single one."

Lucy laughed. "I think the men'd have something to say if he started casting sheep's eyes at their wives, or at them!"

Chuckling, Jane had to agree. "But you know what I mean." She went on to explain before Lucy demurred. "He's too handsome not to have women for company, but he doesn't keep women. Ever. He's not had a steady girl since he was a young lad."

Of course, living in the country, everybody knew everybody else's business, right back to the cradle. However, this bit of news made Lucy curious.

"Has he not?"

"Not that I've heard tell. So it's strange, that with you . . ." Jane trailed off, an expectant look upon her face.

Lucy looked away, gazing upon Michael's strong back and broad shoulders. The tails of his redcoat hid his rear, but Lucy remembered enough about it to have a fair idea how it would look if she could but see it.

"It is strange," Lucy admitted. "But I am sure it is like I said. He can hardly leave me behind when he's promised to get me home."

Jane turned thoughtful, pursing her lips. "And you? D'ye love him that much?"

"How much?" Lucy directed a startled glance at her companion.

"It's writ clear on your face that you want him."

Lucy blushed. "I had no idea I was so transparent."

"Well, it's no secret. There's no privacy to be had with this lot."

"Speaking of which," Lucy said, deciding to change the subject, "did you enjoy your room last night?"

Jane's pale cheeks flushed redder than her nose. "Oh aye. Raised the rafters we did, Joe and I." She giggled at Lucy's blushing. "There's no chance of a night like that again until we reach Dover. We have to be so quiet and furtive out here on the road."

Lucy agreed, making a sympathetic noise. Michael made her forget the outside world until only he and she existed in it, but a tiny part of her had always been aware of their shared company while they had sex.

After a night of relative luxury, they returned to camping out. Lucy settled by the fire, arms wrapped around her bent knees, watching the other women prepare the evening meal.

She felt useless, worse than useless. Not even Jane asked her for help after promising to show her how things were done. Did they think she wasn't able to cook? Jane waved her away, telling her to sit, every time she made a move to help.

Michael sat next to her. "Why are you scowling?" He arranged his limbs comfortably in front of him, soaking up the fire's heat.

For a moment, Lucy almost refused to answer. Her shoulders sagged and she sighed. "Just today, Jane wanted to know if we were going to be married—" Lucy ignored the abrupt choking noise coming from Michael. "And yet, they won't let me help with a simple thing as fixing a meal. How can I be a good soldier's wife, if I am always waited on?" She added hastily, "Of course, I informed her that we weren't even considering marriage."

Michael drew her into a one-armed embrace. Relieved he didn't seem angry at her, she leaned into him, nestling her head upon his shoulder. He nuzzled her hair. Did she imagine that he placed kisses in her hair?

"Lucy," he said at last, "a soldier's life is not for you. They know that. You deserve so much more than living rough in the countryside. How could you want that?"

"Have I uttered one word of complaint so far?" she demanded, elbowing him in the ribs in annoyance. "Given that my future holds hardships almost equal to this, why shouldn't I want to choose one that has you in it?"

"Because, lass, I won't always be in it. If I'm not marching ahead of you by a mile or so, I'll be in battle, or I'll be dead." He took a deep breath. "Out on campaign, a soldier's wife usually marries right away after her husband dies. It's the only way she can survive. Without a husband to protect her and answer for her, there are no rations, and she is stranded in a foreign country.

"You're pretty enough to find someone who'll marry you in a heartbeat. You might even be able to attract an officer's attention if you still have your looks—life on the campaign trail is rough, make no mistake. But those will be your choices: marry a man you don't know, or scrounge for survival. Would your family send you the money to bring you home?"

Lucy thought, tears welling in her eyes. "Caro will, I'm sure of it."

"We'll reach the next village tomorrow. You can write to her there." Michael took her hand into his. "Matters may not be as bad as you fear."

Lucy sighed. "Oh Michael, there's no question I am ruined. It is as bad as it can be, except for you finding me. I might be in an even worse place by now, if not for you."

He hugged her roughly, one-armed. "Don't even think of it. You're safe now."

"With you," she murmured, leaning into him.

He paused, the silence stringing out between them. Had she said too much once more? She kept still in his loose embrace. What did he think?

"With me," he said at last, a kind of wonder in his voice. The timbre changed, with his next words going flat. "Until Dover." While they walked, he didn't leave her side, seemingly content to leave his arm slung casually around her shoulders. Lucy should have felt offended that he'd so impinged on her personal space, but the truth was it was a casual expression of his possession of her.

His presence gave her a prickly sensation down her spine, a shivery mix of ice and fire. If they hadn't been walking, she'd be melting into a puddle on the narrow trail.

Maybe—her mouth curved into a secret smile—maybe, if they didn't have all this company, she'd pull him off the dirt path and to the nearest shaded patch of grass. Kissing him all the way, she'd unbuckle his belts and shove his coat off over his shoulders, thrilling at the way he loosened the tapes of her gown so it practically fell off her.

She longed to see his bare chest in daylight. It had been thrilling to see him naked by the fire, transformed from dusty sergeant to something even darker and more magnificent.

Michael leaned in and whispered in her ear. "You're blushing. Am I embarrassing you?"

"No, no!" Lucy hastily reassured him. "I was . . . thinking."

His sly grin widened. "I don't need to guess about what. May I ask for specifics?"

Her cheeks burned brighter. She edged nearer, slipping her arm around his waist, her head almost bumping against his. "I was wondering what it would be like to see you naked during the daytime," she murmured, hoping that her little fantasy wouldn't be overheard by the others.

Michael cleared his throat. Lucy glanced up to see his own cheeks redden. "I see. Dare I ask for more?"

"You may ask," Lucy playfully allowed, "but I fear you interrupted me before I could go much farther in my daydreaming."

"Hmm." It sounded like he didn't believe her. "It is a tantalizing idea. I will have the others go ahead of us when we reach the village tomorrow. You can write your letter, have it dispatched, and you and I can take a shortcut to catch up with them . . . and dally a little on the way."

Lucy grinned at him. "Are these wonderful ideas the reason you're a sergeant?"

For a moment, his face turned sour, but he quickly recovered. "There are a lot of reasons, love, but that'll do for now, I reckon."

After a minute or so, Michael excused himself, trotting to the head of the line and spending a long time conversing there. Lucy stared after him hungrily. Tomorrow, she would have him all to herself.

Some of his troupe vocalized their displeasure that their sergeant would leave them for a day. The grumbles increased around the fire that night.

Michael responded to their complaints. "And what will you do, Smith, when I am cut down before your eyes and you have no sergeants on the line? There'll be no time for complaining then."

Lucy went cold inside. Their carefree escapade held a darker message. Time was too limited to waste.

Private Jones perked up. "So this is a test?"

Given that it cheered the man, Michael nodded. Let him think what he will. All his thoughts turned to Lucy. He kept his features shuttered, not wanting anyone in on his private delight.

Lucy surprised him in so many ways: from adapting to life on the road, to her demanding a larger role among the travelers. The sheer bravado of her leap into the river after Mrs. Jones had both petrified and excited him.

Lucy was heedless, reckless, and considerate. A quirky paradox, a lady who should be shining on all from on high. Not mucking about with the likes of him.

And yet she hadn't flagged despite the unaccustomed hardships. And she was undeniably attracted to him, and far less scarred by her horrifying experiences than any girl ought to be, let alone one from Society.

That bugged him, raising suspicions in his mind, but not enough to care about pursuit of the truth. Be she mistress or whore, the woman wanted him in her bed, and he wasn't about to give that up for the sake of the truth.

It didn't explain why the man hunted her, unless he never let any possession escape him without his say-so.

His hands curled into tight fists and he forced himself to relax. Not even a whore deserved to be treated like that. Lucy seemed different from most, having a genuine interest in the others who traveled with him.

He glanced over the fire to where she sat with Jane and Maggie. Maggie laughed at something Lucy said. Lucy's hair shone, its golden sheen not dulled by days on the road. Every morning, he'd watched her brush her hair out, borrowing Jane's brush and then brushing Jane's hair, tying it up in a simple, elegant style for the girl. It had been an oddly intimate feeling, watching them together like that, and each time Michael had to turn away before his cock got too excited at this simple sight.

Tomorrow, tomorrow he'd have her all to himself.

After a day of fruitless searching, Caroline and Radbourne's carriage rattled into a small village. Caroline stepped out, pulling the hood of her cape up over her head, as it had grown cold again. Nearby, she heard the soft rush of water.

She followed Radbourne inside, hardly listening as he made

arrangements for their stay. She scanned the taproom for her sister's face, and not finding it, followed a tiny maid upstairs.

Behind her, she heard Radbourne's voice rumble, only catching the word "blond." Good, he asked after Lucy. She caught the rise of an argument but the turn of the dark stairs blocked the specifics.

On reaching her room, she thanked the maid, who made a hasty departure. Caroline wondered at that, pushing the hood of her cape off her head.

The door creaked again and she turned to see Radbourne standing there.

"She was here," he said, beginning to take off his coat. He had not come on this journey prepared for anything at all and he had borrowed some of her father's things, which didn't fit him well, being somewhat too large. "Probably right in this—"

The door crashed back against the wall.

"You beast!" a plump fury cried, her well-muscled arms raising a heavy skillet over her head. "You animal!"

The skillet came crashing down. His arms trapped in his coat behind him, Radbourne tried to avoid it, but it slammed against his shoulder, knocking him to the ground.

"Bringin' your whore to look for the poor girl!" the woman hoarsely cried, lifting her skillet for another blow.

Cheeks flushing red, Caroline stepped between them, over the groaning form of the Earl of Radbourne. "Please! Don't! I shot him in the head once already. He's had enough punishment for now."

The woman took a good look at him and his bandaged head and then at her, her brown eyes widening. "Gracious! You look just like her! Does he have an inclination for blond women?"

Beneath her, Radbourne shifted and Caroline stomped on his calf. Radbourne cursed under his breath. Her action didn't go unnoticed by the woman, who snorted with amusement.

"I am her sister," Caroline told her. "This fellow has promised to marry her to make up for his dreadful error of judgment and to save her reputation."

The woman snorted. "Too late for that. The young lady's taken up with a sergeant."

"Taken up?" Caroline's eyes grew round. "Please, come and sit and tell me everything."

"What about him?" the woman pointed at Radbourne on the floor.

"He won't bother us." She spotted a sofa in the room and led the woman there. "Who are you?"

"My name's Anne. My husband runs this establishment. That's how I know."

"Know?" Caroline prompted, sounding clueless. Alas, she had all too good an idea as to what the innkeeper's wife had meant when she said Lucy had taken up with a sergeant.

"M'lady, you seem awfully naïve to be traveling with such a notorious fellow. I mean that she and the sergeant are lovers. You should have seen his face when he carried her in from the river—"

"The river!" Caroline exclaimed, truly alarmed.

"Ah, your sister is a brave girl. One of the camp followers had fallen into the river and your sister went right after her, from what I heard from the men. We dragged both of them out of the river."

"Is she—was she badly hurt?"

"Cold and shaken up. Gave her and that poor girl two of our rooms. I saw at once the sergeant was mad for her. He never left her side once."

While it heartened Caroline to know someone had taken care of Lucy, she asked in a faint voice, "A soldier?"

"Aye, he's not high-and-mighty like yourself, if you'll pardon me saying, but he's a good man. Reliable. His men sing his praises."

Caroline covered her mouth, staring across the room at Radbourne, who'd dared to sit up and rub at his shoulder. His blue-eyed gaze met hers, and she couldn't quite read what message they held. Relief? Disappointment? Renewed desire for her?

"Miss Waverton must have told you about her abduction from London for you to attack Radbourne so," Caroline prodded, changing the subject.

"Nay, I got it from one of the other women, and the sergeant too while we waited for her to wake up. Fainted from the cold she did."

"Did they say where they were going?"

"I'm not sure I should say." The innkeeper's wife cast a dagger-filled look at Radbourne. "M'lady, why are you with him? Why do you support him? He raped your sister!"

"He what?" Caroline leaped to her feet. "Hand me that skillet," she said, her voice turning flat and deadly. She stormed toward him.

"I did no such thing!" Radbourne cried, holding out his hands defensively. "She was willing, I swear it! Hell, she even enjoyed it!"

"Liar!" Caroline swung the skillet and he ducked under it.

"Caroline," he pleaded, watching her every move, dodging her. "Put the skillet down. I do not force anyone to have sex. For all my bad reputation, *that* has never been laid at my door."

"There is a first time for everything," Caroline snapped.

The innkeeper's wife shouted advice. "Over your head, m'lady, and down!"

"Caroline," Radbourne coaxed. "I'll admit I seduced the girl, but not once did I do anything she did not wish me to— aside from the initial abduction, of course."

"I prefer to believe my sister, sir." Caroline raised the skillet. The pan was extremely heavy and her arms trembled with the effort.

"Is she likely to boast that she enjoyed it? Do you suppose she'd get much sympathy for that?" His gaze bore into hers, almost as if he willed her to stop fighting him.

Despite the great effort, Caroline held the skillet high. What she had feared had happened. Her sister had fallen as low as she. There must be something corrupt in their blood for Lucy to make the same mistake as she without knowing Caroline's history.

"Swear it," she whispered. "Swear you did not force her."

"I swear," Radbourne vowed, his hand over his heart. His voice dropped to a whisper. "Her release was incredible to experience and not something she faked. There is no enjoyment to be found in rape."

Her arms shaking, Caroline lowered the skillet to her side. Behind her, the innkeeper's wife squawked in protest. "How can I trust you?" Caroline whispered.

"I don't know," he replied. "You have thus far."

Caroline stepped back. "Anne, you better take this and go."

Anne rose, still protesting.

"This man is my only chance to find my sister. I'll discover the truth when I speak with my sister myself."

Anne dropped an abbreviated curtsey. "I hope you know what you're doing, m'lady." She left them, slamming the door shut.

Radbourne relaxed, his shoulders sagging. He winced and grabbed his shoulder. "I think she broke something."

Caroline knelt by his side, helping him take his coat the rest of the way off. She probed his shoulder with her fingers, ignoring his hissing breath. "You have a certain knack for infuriating women."

"Lucy must possess some quality that makes even women leap to her aid."

Caroline paused, gazing at him. He had to be blind not to

see the transparent worry on her face. His face moved closer. Close enough for a reassuring kiss, but she wasn't sure if she wanted that, not knowing what she knew now. "When we find her, you must take care with this sergeant fellow."

He rubbed her back, a soothing action that made the last of her tension drain away. "She is surviving, Caroline. If she's bewitched this man, she is that much safer."

She leaned against him, resting her head on his sore shoulder. The bandages on his head scraped her forehead. "What will happen when we find them? What if she thinks she's in love with this man?"

"You worry too much." He kissed her temple. "It will sort itself out."

Caroline pulled away slightly, meeting his unruffled gaze. She wanted to tell him things, fears she wanted to express, and desires too . . . but not now. To speak now would make her vulnerable, too vulnerable.

She rose, shaking out her skirts. "I have some more bandages. We should wrap up that shoulder and check the wound in your head as well."

He grinned up at her, his smile not quite at full force. Perhaps he guessed she pulled away from him more than just physically. "You just want to see me with my shirt off."

"But I've seen you already," she coolly returned. "Why should I care to again?"

He rose, crossing to the bed and sitting. With a groan, he removed his shirt.

"At least we know it isn't broken," Caroline said, viewing the purpling bruise while Radbourne flexed his arm. "It must not have been a direct hit."

Radbourne glanced over his shoulder at her. "Considering that she aimed for my head, I'm lucky it ended up as a glancing blow."

"You should keep it still until the muscles recover from the shock. Just for a day or so." She wagged her finger at him. "And no getting drunk to dull the pain. I need you to be sober."

"Will you make it worth my while?" He dragged her against him with his good arm.

Caroline hung on to the roll of bandages and tried not to touch him. She gazed down at his upturned, smirking face. "You would like that, wouldn't you."

"Very much," he affirmed, his smirk transforming into a boyish grin.

"Have you no shame?" she accused. "You think I would—be swived by you now?"

His grin disappeared into a thin line. "I never hurt her or forced her. Not Lucy, not anyone. I won't even force you."

Caroline jerked away from the pain in his eyes. "I need to bandage your shoulder."

He released her, staring over her shoulder while she bandaged him. His silence did more to relieve her tension than any further protestations. It allowed her to review what she knew of the man. He hadn't forced her to do anything she didn't want to. Lucy hadn't had her experience, as far as she knew. Had it all been too overwhelming for her?

She gazed down at Radbourne's bent blond head. She had reasons enough for not pursuing him, but his intriguing mix of honesty, honor, and sexiness drew her nearer.

"Caroline," he murmured in a delicious burr.

She paused in her work, closing her eyes. With one word, he beckoned her. In speaking her name, she wanted to bend down and kiss him and be kissed. She wanted to push him down onto the bed—no, she wanted it to be her beneath him—and have him fuck her, long and slow, so that she might believe it would last forever.

"Caroline," he repeated, brushing a strand of blond hair back from her cheek.

She took a deep breath, shaking off his voice that hinted at fantastic sex. She knotted the bandages and stood back, out of reach. "I suppose now that you are without a shirt, you'll have to sleep here. I'll move to the other room."

"There is no other room."

Caroline blinked at him. "What?"

"The inn is full tonight. I had planned to sleep in the dining room tonight, but you certainly cannot do so."

She shivered. "No, I cannot." Again, thoughts rose of the two of them entwined. "You can put your coat back on. I'll help you." She bent to gather it up. "I'll loan you my cloak to cover the rest." She spun away to look for it. "Hardly anyone will notice."

"Caroline," he murmured. She looked over her shoulder at him. He hadn't moved at all from his place on her bed. "Do not fight it."

"Is this what you said to Lucy?" she snapped, trying to break the mood.

"If it is the only way to deliver proof that I'll not take a girl until she is completely willing, then yes, I am sure I must have said something similar to Lucy. Mind, I had also proposed to her by then."

That gave Caroline pause. "And she accepted?"

"Not at that moment, but later, after we—" His cheeks actually reddened and he cleared his throat. "She didn't say anything, but I thought all was right between us."

She arched an eyebrow. It was unlike him to confess to such vulnerability. "Perhaps she let you take her in order to survive."

"Let me?" His blond brows drew together. "She was an active participant. Shall I tell you how it went in precise detail?"

Caroline turned away, rolling her cloak into a tight ball. "I do not think I want to hear it."

"I think you ought to, Caroline. I will not have this ghost between us."

"What difference does it make? You're marrying my sister, remember?"

Silence. And in that Caroline believed she had her answer.

8

_____

"Why do you deny yourself?" Radbourne made himself more comfortable on the bed, reclining against a pile of pillows. His head rested against the headboard.

Caroline folded her arms. "Because it is the right thing to do."

"You weren't so concerned about that the other night."

She sucked in her breath. "That was a mistake."

Radbourne shifted, easing his arm into a different position. "What you are doing is unfair to both you and me." He took a deep breath. "Caroline, I'm not going to apologize for something that didn't happen. However, it's you I want."

Ire and desire rose within her. She chose to stick to the former. "Me? That is too bad. You're marrying my sister. Already I will not be able to face her with what I've done."

"Is that all?"

Caroline shot him a shocked look.

"Caroline, Lucy won't care whether I bed you or not. She ran away. She's having an affair with a common soldier. I am well within my rights to back off and give up the idea of marrying her because of her current behavior. I knew her to be head-strong—but this!"

He shook his head, running his undamaged hand through his short blond hair. "But I'm not going to do any of those things. I promised you I will marry her, and I will."

"You will?" Caroline hated her voice sounding so small. His words gave her an unwanted glimmer of hope. She might have him for herself and abandon this guilt that burdened her.

"All we have right now is gossip. It may not be true."

She relented, approaching the bed with slow steps. "I never pegged you for an optimist."

He grimaced ruefully. "There is a lot you don't know about me."

She wrapped an arm about the plain bedpost. "But you were going to reason that if Lucy could have an affair, so could we."

He cocked his head. "Are you reading my mind?"

"I am not as naïve as our hostess thinks me. There are things you don't know about me either."

His blue eyes sparked. "I know. I wish you would tell me."

She snorted. "What would be the point? After we find Lucy and you marry her, you will never see me again."

"'Never' is such a strong word," he chided.

"Hardly ever," she amended.

He propped his head on his hand, the elbow lost in a mound of pillows. "What is in your future?"

"I am not a soothsayer," she retorted. "But I don't expect much change in my life."

"So this is an adventure," he practically purred. "An opportunity to explore beyond your usual bounds."

"I've already done that," she snapped, letting go of the bedpost and retreating a step. "I will leave you to rest and I will bid you good night."

She spun, snatching up her wadded cloak and heading downstairs to the private dining room. Thankfully, there were no other guests occupying it. She stretched out on a bench, covering herself with her cloak and propping her head with a folded arm.

She'd hardly closed her eyes when the door opened and a throat cleared. She looked up to see Anne, the innkeeper's wife, bearing an armful of bedding.

"I doubted you," she said. "What with you traveling as his wife and sharing one room, but I see he tried to bamboozle you too."

Caroline struggled to sit up. "Bamboozle me? You mean there are vacant rooms in this inn?"

"Lord, no," the innkeeper's wife confessed. "But he hardly handled it in a gentlemanly manner."

"It was my fault." Caroline clutched her cloak about her neck. "I did not linger long enough to find out there was one room."

"You need to be more careful." Anne handed her a pillow.

Caroline agreed. "Tell me more about my sister. Do you think she's really in love?"

Anne sat on a stool and shrugged. "Hard to tell. I know they had an argument in the wee hours of the morning. The sergeant came downstairs and sulked. But he bedded her good and thorough beforehand. Two or three times in my estimation."

Caroline gaped. "How do you know?"

"I changed the bed linens afterward. In my line of work, you get to know."

"Well, she wouldn't do that if she didn't like him," Caroline mused aloud. She had the sneaking suspicion that Anne would make it her personal mission to check Radbourne's room tomorrow after they left.

"What's on your mind, lass?"

"If it would be a horrible, unsisterly thing to just let her go. She doesn't want *him*." She stabbed her thumb overhead and sighed. "If only she had written, letting me know her plans . . ."

"She's doomed to be hurt, if you ask me. These aren't militia she's with but active soldiers. If she follows them to war . . ."

Caroline joined Anne in shuddering. "I will have to catch up with her, save her from herself."

"And that mighty-fine-lookin' sergeant of hers." Anne smirked and rose. "I'll let ye get some rest."

Left alone, Caroline lay down, staring up at the plaster ceiling etched with dark gray smoke rings. In the firelight, she could barely make them out.

Should she really make Lucy marry Radbourne? No matter how honor drove the situation, Lucy had sought happiness elsewhere. Caroline frowned. How would she herself feel if her affair from years ago had been discovered and she was forced to marry in order to save her reputation?

She had to find Lucy, no question, and rescue her from this dangerous scrape. But make her marry the man she'd escaped from?

Caroline sighed. Weren't these just excuses to sneak back upstairs and into Radbourne's bed? To enjoy him as she had done before?

Why shouldn't she cast caution to the wind? Lucy's escapade had forever blackened the family's reputation. What did it matter if the spinster sister got a little joy before Society closed its doors forever?

Her mind made up, she slid out from under the old quilt, donning her cloak once more. Opening the dining room door, she peered out. The inn had settled into sleep for the night, but every creak would be heard.

Who would be awake to hear it? Probably Anne, the innkeeper's wife.

She eased the door closed behind her and headed upstairs, feeling her way in the pitch darkness. Counting the doors with her fingertips, she came to one where light still shone out from under the door.

Opening the door a crack, she peered in. Yes, that was her luggage. She slipped inside the room, closing the door behind her.

Her gaze went at once to the bed. Radbourne lay sprawled in the middle of it. Legs apart, eyes closed, he'd unfastened his pantaloons and stroked his cock with his good hand.

Holding her breath, Caroline crept farther into the room. Her gaze flickered between his face and his hard cock and the broad fingers pumping it.

Another step and she reached the bed. She watched his hand massage his cock in a steady up and down motion. He didn't touch the bulging head, already dark and red. He released his cock, and caressed his balls instead, dusted in golden hair. His cock rose stiff from the dark golden curls.

She shot a nervous glance at his face, relieved that his eyes remained closed.

"I know you are there, Caroline," he murmured, his voice hoarse with lust. "Are you enjoying the show?"

Caroline stumbled back, her hand rising to her lips. "How— how did you know it was me?"

"Educated guess. If it were one of the maidservants, she'd have been all over me by now."

"Don't think it didn't cross my mind," Caroline snapped, flushing when she realized what she'd just said.

His eyes opened then and he chuckled. He patted the bed. "Come here."

Gingerly, she perched on the edge of the bed. He looked so magnificent lying there, like some foreign potentate waiting for a girl to pleasure him. The bandages lent an odd touch of vulnerability, stirring her heart. How easy to give herself to him in that fantasy.

But she wasn't that girl any more, if she ever had been.

"Look at me."

Unwillingly, her gaze dragged itself to his face. His eyes

were alight with desire, the rosy stain of arousal marking his fair skin.

"Touch me."

Her hand remained clasped in her lap. "I am not a maid-servant to order about, sir." She forced herself to relax. "I would be interested in hearing about how you seduced my sister."

Radbourne frowned. "That story will end in argument and very little pleasure for either of us."

"Then tell me how you would seduce me in that situation."

"You are as different from your sister as night is from day. Indeed, the only characteristics you share are your fair coloring and your deep need for passion."

Caroline drew back. "Are you trying to flatter me or insult me?"

"Flatter you, my dear. Have you any idea how gentle I had to be with your sister, so she wouldn't take fright?" He sighed. "And it seems I was not successful even in that, in the end."

Caroline turned his words over in her mind. Being gentle didn't coincide with rape . . . She did believe him when he said he hadn't forced Lucy. Even the worst of rakes had some code of honor.

Her gaze traversed from his face to his bare chest, while she mused on him. Sprigs of golden hair shone on his upper chest. Across the flat of his belly, a darker golden line trailed to his groin and his still-hard cock.

"Then," she said at last, having looked her fill of him, "you must tell me how you would seduce me, right now. Your first attempt to order me into your bed hasn't worked. What's next?"

He chuckled again. "It's hardly seduction if you know about it ahead of time. It will give you time to prepare your defenses. A man does not give away his secrets."

"I think you protest too much." Caroline sniffed and rose. "Perhaps I should return to my bench downstairs."

He reached out and grabbed her. "No need for that." He

tugged on her wrist and she sat again. He drew her hand up to his lips, making her lean forward. His gaze focused on her décolletage and he kissed the back of her hand.

"I would start here," he murmured, lifting his eyes to meet hers. "And then here . . ." He flipped her hand and kissed her palm. "And here . . ." He pressed his mouth against her wrist.

Her pulse raced. His heated gaze slid along the pale underside of her arm and then to her face. "Radbourne . . ." she murmured, not even knowing herself whether she protested.

He sat up, his face ending close to hers. "Kisses are the sweetest of seductive tools." His lips brushed her cheek, light as a butterfly. Another kiss landed closer to her mouth. The third kiss captured her lips.

Any thought of resisting fled her mind. In truth, she only played at resisting. They both knew why she'd returned to the room.

She returned his kiss, opening her mouth before his lips even parted. She opened her eyes to see his glinting back at her, eyelids sleepy with desire. Even so, he did not take her mouth as she'd expected.

Impatient, she flicked her tongue against his lips, twining her arms around his neck, hands sinking in his golden mane. Eventually, she pulled back, linking her hands behind his neck. "Why aren't you kissing me?" she demanded.

A blond eyebrow quirked upward. "I thought I was doing the seducing, not the other way around."

Caroline tilted her head to one side, regarding him. "You wouldn't care to be seduced?"

His lips twitched. "Are you offering?"

Breath caught in her throat. Such an opportunity! "Would you give yourself over to my command?"

"Not command, cajoling," he corrected her, just as she had corrected him.

She smiled in acknowledgment of the hit. "Would you give

yourself to me?" she whispered, her hands slipping from his neck to cup his face. "Would you submit to me?"

"I'm not the type that submits to a woman," he growled playfully, ducking in to nibble at her lips. He caught her lower lip between his teeth and gave it a teasing tug.

She let him place a soothing kiss upon his play bite. "You may have noticed I'm not the type to submit to a man."

He grinned. "But you have, and rather gloriously, I might add."

She flushed. "And so have you, as I remember it. That was also rather glorious."

His grin deepened into a smirk. "So it was. There is no reason why it has to be all one and not the other." The smirk dimpled his cheek. "Do you not agree?"

An unexpected golden glow seemed to fill her being. He understood. "I agree wholeheartedly," she replied, her voice husky.

He met her embrace with equal enthusiasm. At once, it became a laughing battle for dominance. In the end, neither claimed defeat, but Caroline hadn't felt such lightheartedness for a long time.

She started out on top, straddling his torso, burying his cock in the folds of her gown behind her. He fumbled with the ties of her gown, pulling apart the bodice flaps. He drew her down, kissing her exposed flesh. Her lack of stays rendered her breasts visible and available. He flattened his palms over them, stroking them.

She captured his face between her hands. "I want you," she purred and pressed her mouth against his. She kissed him hungrily, pushing him back against the mattress.

She wriggled out of her gown, the various pieces of her bodice falling to her waist. His hands combed her arms, fingering the back of her neck before dancing down her spine.

He cupped her breasts. She grinned down at him. His thumbs

swirled over her nipples. Already tight, they hardened and warmed under his touch.

Caroline tilted her head back, enjoying the gentle waves of arousal surging through her. Radbourne knew just how to touch her, how to elicit the deepest excitement.

She fell forward, raking her fingernails down his chest to the high waist of his pantaloons just visible above her skirts. She bent backward, her back arched, her fingertips flitting over the linen pantaloons and reaching the top of his leather boots.

Sitting up, she grinned down at him. "Did you intend to wear those to bed?"

He inclined his head. "I had nobody to help me undress."

She grinned. "Now you do." She scrambled off him and the bed, her gown and shift puddling to the floor. Almost at once, she wanted to cover herself, and a hand even went to cover her much-teased breasts.

"No need to be shy," Radbourne murmured.

Caroline let her hand fall back to her side. "I'm—not used to being so naked with a man." Realizing that comment revealed more than it should, judging by the quizzical crinkle of Radbourne's forehead, she ducked her head and focused on the removal of his boots.

That done, she swiftly divested him of his pantaloons. It took some tugging, because the finely tailored pants clung to his thighs like a second skin.

Radbourne didn't seem shy of his nakedness; all of his muscled form reclined at ease. All of him, except one muscled part: his cock, big, thick, red, and hard, bobbed in greeting. Caroline recalled the last time he'd buried that magnificent muscle inside her, and shivered in delight.

Clambering back on top of him, she slid back until his cock nestled between her buttocks. She pulsed her groin against him, feeling his length rub back and forth behind her.

He groaned, echoing her own excitement. He rose up, palms

sliding along the outside of her arms. His penis was buried beneath her and against him and he groaned again. "I have an idea," he murmured against her collarbone, between peppered kisses. "Would you be willing?"

She smiled down at him, her eyes alight with laughter, even as a deeper need flamed within her. "I think I have proven my willingness already." She squirmed against him to prove her point. If he wanted to take her from behind, shove his cock into her arse instead of her cunt, she had no objections.

Radbourne sucked in his breath. "Some other time," he murmured, reading her mind, and her movements, aright. "I have something else in mind for tonight."

He reached behind him, to the mound of linen on the bedstand. His cravat. He retrieved it, and made a heavy knot in one end.

Throwing the knotted end in the air, he caught it again. Caroline looked over her head, to see he'd accurately aimed it such that it draped over the lengthwise slats of the four-poster bed.

While she examined this, the slither of fine linen caressed her wrist. Her gaze shot there to see the knotted end of the cravat wrapped about her wrist. She lifted her eyes to his.

"May I?" he purred, his voice deep and breathless.

She had said she was willing. Caroline gave a reluctant nod.

He tied a knot about her wrist and reached for her other hand, wrapping the cravat around her wrist just once. He kept the longer end firmly gripped in his hand.

He pulled on the long linen end. The cravat tightened about her wrist and slowly drew her arms upward. He kept hauling on the line until her hands were over her head. He didn't pull so hard as to raise her body off of his, but her shoulder sockets groaned at the potential of his doing so.

Bending forward, Radbourne flicked his tongue across a nipple. Caroline gasped. Immobilized, her back arched, presenting her upturned fleshy mounds to him. Held in place, she had no choice but to offer herself to him.

As if she hadn't done so already. She smirked, and Radbourne caught the expression, his gaze warming.

"I thought you would like it." He brushed her lips with his. She leaned into him, but he retreated and his stiff grip on the cravat linen kept her in place.

"My arms will grow weary," she warned him, unable to resist flinging him that challenge.

"I will make you forget that," he vowed, his sandy eyebrows quirking. He leaned in once more, bruising her lips in a punishing kiss that she returned with fervor.

Bending lower, he laved her breasts, tugging on one with his teeth and twisting the other between thumb and forefinger. She squirmed at his touch, the sharp sensations rippling out from the pinpoints of her nipples, throughout her chest, making it difficult to breathe, and down to her belly and the swelling wetness of her cunt.

With a sharp tug on her bonds, he hauled her upward, his tongue slithering off her breast and down her stomach. Caroline set her teeth, struggling to get her feet under her to take her slender weight.

He shifted, fingers teasing at her blond nether curls and along her wet slit. His lifting her enabled his cock to slide from behind and nestle against her cunt hole, a delicious pressure that promised much.

She whimpered, wanting him to fill her, wanting him to lower her, dammit, onto his eager cock.

He lifted his wet hand to her lips, filling her nose with her intimate scent, sweet and musky. He brought them to his lips and licked them, one by one.

With each finger, he let the linen length slip from his other hand. Bit by bit, finger by finger, his cock pressed harder and harder against her opening before breaching her and sliding inside her. Her flesh stretched to accommodate him and she moaned, her cunt muscle clutching his invading cock.

He released the linen completely, and with relief, her arms came down and she hooked them over his shoulders. She sat on his lap, squirming there to wrap her legs about his hips instead of kneeling on top of him.

Her moment of submission over, Caroline took control, rocking her pelvis against his, trying to get her little clit to spark and catch fire with arousal. His cock had little room to move, pulsing in and out of her, but always more in than out.

The tension on the white linen length grew tight and Caroline fought it. She wasn't ready to give up yet. She clasped her hands behind his neck.

Radbourne nipped at her collarbone and gave her bindings a sharp tug. "Relax, Caro."

Gasping, she relaxed, her arms rising above her once more. He raised her until only the head of his cock remained inside her. Caroline pressed down with her feet behind his back, anything to ease the pressure on her arms.

Almost at once, he lowered her again, his cock carving his way along that well-known path inside her. She rested her forearms on his shoulders, leaning her forehead against his.

He dipped below, catching a kiss from her lips, holding the kiss while he again shortened her lead, lifting her again.

He released the linen and she thumped down against him, his cock thrusting inside her, deep inside her until their groins ground together.

She rocked her hips against his for a long moment, until she felt the tightening of the linen about her wrists. It would be so easy to unravel the cravat from about one wrist, for it was not knotted or bound, but Caroline had another way to prevent Radbourne from renewing the ache in her shoulders.

Shifting, she knelt over him, raising herself up and down, his cock going in and out of her in short bursts. The linen went limp.

She bounced on his cock, reveling in each deep drive into her, and the way his hands gripped her back, digging into her flanks, holding on for her wild ride.

Pushing him onto his back, she rose even higher on her knees, bending over him, her breasts brushing his chest, her aroused nipples sparking at the wiry hair rubbing against them.

He caught the back of her neck, holding her there, while he kissed her, their tongues tangling, while his hips thrust up into her immobilized cunt.

It felt so delicious that she broke the kiss, meeting each thrust with one of her own, each thrust punctuated by a panting gasp.

His hands slid to her hips, flexing occasionally but otherwise holding her lightly. "Fly for me," he whispered with breathy hoarseness. "I want to see your release."

How did he know that the tension rose in her, cresting? Closing her eyes to his intent gaze, she stayed on that crest for as long as possible, rocking herself against his slick cock, hearing their sex juices slap and suck with each penetration.

Her whole body felt flushed with the release, as if it sought any outlet. Her heart raced, her flesh throbbing in time. A moan escaped her lips, and then another and another.

She flew into her release, her senses soaring around her. She sat up, grinding her convulsing cunt about his cock, the white heat of release taking her breath away.

Her moans erupted into a keening cry as wave after wave of release swept through her. For a time, it felt like she would never stop coming, that this blissful, agonizing state would last forever.

It didn't and she slumped against him, burying her flushed, panting face against his neck.

His cock still pulsed within her, had not diminished in its hardness, but Radbourne let her catch her breath before murmuring in her ear. "That was beautiful, my dear."

She pressed a kiss against his neck. To her surprise he surged inside her. Had he not found his own release? Again and again, his cock thrust into her still weakly convulsing cunt, until at last he let out a deep groan and stiffened beneath her, filling her creamy cunt with his jism and wetting her thighs with their mingled juices.

They lay together, panting, their bodies sticky with sweat. Radbourne's broad fingertips smoothed over her shoulder and then kissed it.

Caroline kissed him and then dismounted, rolling to lie at his side. She stared up at the ceiling, at the cravat linen still draped over the struts of the bed, twisted now that she lay the other way. She unwrapped her wrist and undid the tight knot on the other.

Radbourne gave his end a tug and watched the linen fall, spiraling in on itself. He rolled onto his side, but Caroline's eyes were already fluttering closed.

He gave a rueful grin that nobody saw. Kissing her cheek, he pulled the coverlet over the two of them and relaxed into sleep himself. He oughtn't be surprised, for he'd given the girl quite the workout.

impressed it a
recognize th
"Why
up to the
Luc
"This"
she

Michael sat opposite her, his presence in the inn's half-shadows distracting Lucy from her writing. They'd left the rest of their group to walk on.

Lucy's tongue poked out at the corner of her mouth. She tried to stop when she realized it, but neither the quill, ink, or paper was of very good quality and her letter was spattered with scratches and splatters.

She found the letter easier to write than she first thought. She'd always been honest with Caroline, but this letter might be seen by anyone. Michael watched her write, but he didn't ask her to read it to him when she'd finished. She shook sand onto the paper and then poured it back into the jar.

"All done."

Still, he didn't ask to read it. Did he trust her that much? She hoped Caroline would be able to read between the lines and not come chasing after her.

She folded the letter and tipped some of the rough tallow wax over the folds to seal it. She slipped the pendant, a small locket shaped into an ornate heart, from around her neck and

gainst the wax. Lucy hoped that Caroline would
e clear impression in the cheap wax.

id you do that?" Michael took the letter and held it
light, examining the wax seal.

put the necklace back on and fingered the pendant.
was my mother's. If she's in doubt who wrote this, then
know for certain that it is I if she sees that mark."

Michael nodded. "Why don't you write another? If your
ster is looking for you, she might come here."

"I doubt it." Lucy shook her head. "Michael, she has no idea
where I am. Even if she knows that I've left him, she won't have
any idea where I was when I escaped or that I haven't taken the
Great North Road home."

Michael slid the letter back to her. "Very well. It's your
choice."

"Besides, what if *he* finds it?" The very thought of it made
her tremble. "Then he will know where we are and will be
waiting for us in Dover."

"You told her that?" Michael cocked his head.

"Yes. I asked her to send money to me there. At least I can
repay you—"

"I don't need payment, Lucy. Don't ever think I do."

"But it will be my way of thanks. If you and your men had
more money with you, you could get better provisions and—"

"How do you know about provisions?"

Lucy smiled shyly. "My father has quite the military library.
I've never lived the life until now, but I've read about it."

Michael shook his head in admiration. "You never said . . ."

"You never asked." Lucy rose and crossed to the innkeeper.
In moments, she'd consigned the letter to the mailbag, ready
for the next mail coach that made it through the district.

Lucy and Michael strolled outside. He slipped his arm
around her waist and she didn't protest. Why would she? It
was a gorgeous sunny day and she had a handsome escort.

They left the last of the village cottages behind. Michael leaned closer. "Tell me," he murmured, his breath tickling her ear, "that fantasy of yours again."

She'd whispered it to him the night before, embroidering on the tale until the two of them had squirmed together, although Michael had refused to consummate their desire, promising that waiting would make it all the more sweeter on the morrow.

"Have you forgotten it already?"

He chuckled. "Every word is seared into me, Lucy love. I thought it would amuse us until we find the right location to fulfill your fantasy."

She pulled away from him, feeling her cheeks warm. "I'd rather just find the right location. Besides, if it is seared into you, then I don't need to say anything."

He chuckled and, taking her hand, led her off the dusty road and across an open, green meadow. "Then let us not tarry." He tugged on her hand and made her run after him, stumbling on the uneven ground.

Laughing, she followed, catching up her skirts before she tripped over them. Almost parallel with the road, they crossed one field and then another, until finally he slowed, and stopped.

Panting, Lucy stumbled to a halt beside him. Midway into the next field, a giant old oak spread its lowering branches across a wide expanse, leaving all beneath it in shadow.

Lucy never thought she'd be so happy to see shade, but perspiration beaded her brow and no doubt marked her clothing. "That's perfect," she murmured.

"I thought so too," Michael told her, and, tugging on her hand once more, led her across the field. No sheep or cows or their dung dotted their path. For some reason, this land had been left fallow. Off to the left, trees marked the winding line of a creek.

They reached the shelter of the tree, Lucy sighing at the immediate drop in temperature. Michael let go of her hand and took off his jacket, spreading it between two large roots at the base of the tree.

He gestured to her. "Come here."

She stayed where she was at the edge of the shadows. "I thought you had my fantasy seared into your brain? Did you forget that I wanted to undress you?" She pouted.

"Not at all." He attempted a mollifying smile. "Isn't it the gentlemanly thing to do to lay down one's coat for a lady?"

He had such an adorable little impish dimple that Lucy forgave him at once. "It is," she said, stepping toward him and into his embrace.

He crushed his lips against her, cupping her face in his rough hands. They swept back from her face, burrowing into her thick golden locks and scattering pins.

She twined her arms behind his neck, responding to his kiss. Her legs trembled with her need. She clung to him, pressing her slight form against his body, reveling in his power over her.

Lifting her up in his strong arms, he spun her around, carrying her the short distance to his spread-out coat. Laying her upon the ground, he joined her, collapsing into her welcoming arms.

Lucy scrunched the fabric of his shirt, hauling it upward in fistfuls. She wanted to see his bare chest in the daylight. It had been gorgeous to watch him in the firelight. The sun would hide no secrets from her. Seeing him thus was her fantasy.

To her surprise, he reared back, before she had even removed his shirt from his overalls. He captured her hands, drawing them down to her side.

She frowned up at him, puzzled. "You know I want to see you."

He gave an abrupt nod. "And you will, just not right now."

Her frown deepened. "Why not? I want to see you, Michael."

He gathered her hands in front of her, his rough palms

pressing against them. "There is something I need to tell you first. I've had a rough life."

"I know," Lucy interrupted.

"No, you don't know." His sharp voice brought her out of her dreaminess. "This life on the road is hard but it's not like . . . it's not like being at war or even working from before sunrise to after sunset. You don't understand any of that."

Her chest compressed as if tears threatened to escape her. She wanted to cry, but she didn't dare, for Michael looked so fierce. She feared if a single tear fell, he would be lost to her.

"You are correct." Her voice broke, and she sucked in her breath. "I'm sorry." Unbidden, a tear tracked down the side of her face and melted into her hair.

Michael wiped away the tear track. "I didn't say that to make you cry, lass. It's—Not all of me is pretty."

Lucy recovered, snorting a brief laugh. "You're hardly pretty."

"I have—I have scars . . ."

"Is that all?" Lucy shook her head at him. "Don't you think I have felt them already?"

"They are not something you should see."

Lucy sighed. "You think they will insult my sensibilities? After all I have been through with you thus far? Don't be absurd, Michael. Take off your shirt. I'll still love you afterward."

His expression darkened for a moment, but a rueful smile broke in the corner of his mouth. "I never reckoned myself to be vain until now."

Her lips twitched, returning his infectious grin. She'd rarely seen him smile like that, so unfettered.

Michael pulled his shirt off over his head, tossing it to one side and gazing down at her with a partial frown, as if he still worried she might not like him after seeing him naked and in the light.

What was not to like? Michael had the broad shoulders of a working man, tanned from being in the sun. Lucy surmised he hadn't been shy about his scars before. Dark hair covered his upper chest, the occasional thin white scar cutting a line through the hair.

Lower yet, the dark hair trickled down into a narrow line, across a flat, hard stomach. There were odd red marks here, as if some large insect had bitten him and the bite wound had stayed swollen.

Lucy smoothed her fingers over them, finding them glossy to the touch. "Were you shot?" she asked, puzzling over them.

Michael reached for his shirt. "Burns."

Lucy shivered, but grabbed a hold of his shirt, preventing him from covering up. "How horrible for you, Michael, but they are not so bad to look at, nor to touch."

His dark gaze regarded her. "Really?"

"Truly." Lucy essayed a smile. It echoed on his lips, sending a shiver of pleasure through her. She released her grip on his shirt and let her fingertips walk up along the dark line center of his belly.

He sucked in his breath, his abdominal muscles trembling beneath her touch. His hot gaze fastened upon her, and she didn't dare look at his face, preferring to focus upon his skin. When would he allow her to look at his face like this again?

Her fingers feathered out across his chest and he lowered himself, making her explorations easier.

"You're beautiful," she breathed.

He chuckled, kissing her nose. "Now who is being absurd?"

She grinned up at him, not regretting her words in the slightest. "You are more man than any I have ever known."

"Lass, compliments like that will go to my head," he joked. "Be careful."

Her arms slunk around his neck, drawing him even closer. She captured his lips with her own, ending talk of scars or compliments. The moment their lips touched, a conflagration of need sparked. Michael hauled her up against him, his powerful arms at her waist and shoulders preventing her from falling back onto the earth.

He ravished her with his mouth and she surrendered to him utterly, letting her tongue tangle with his. She breathed him in: the dirt, the sweat, the very maleness of him. She wanted him with every fiber; every part of her thrilled at his touch. This is what she wanted: absolute surrender.

Shifting his grip, his hand plunged into her hair, holding her head just so while he continued to kiss her. Lucy blinked at the dappled light casting specks over them. She gripped Michael's back, reveling in the flexing of his muscles.

Michael broke off the kiss, hauling her up from the mossy ground, straddling her lower body. "I'd like to try something. Will you let me?"

Blinking at him, still breathless from his kisses, Lucy nodded. He rose, taking her hand and helping her stand also. Her knees trembled and threatened to give way.

Unaware, he let her go, grabbing his jacket and laying it over a root bulging from the ground. The size of a small tree trunk, the gnarled root twisted out of the earth from the old oak and sank back into the black, loamy soil.

He patted the rough wool of his coat, gesturing for her to sit. She did, looking expectantly up at him. "Now, lie back."

Lucy looked over her shoulder behind her. It suddenly seemed a long way back.

He grasped her hands. "Here, I'll hold you."

She bent backward over the tree root, her descent slow and graceful. The world turned upside down, the blood rushing to her head.

Unseen, Michael flung her skirts up over her waist and she batted them away from her face. Parting her legs, he puffed a breath of warm air against her exposed groin.

Lucy repressed a shiver. She realized his purpose: to view and taste her cunt in full daylight. Her vaginal muscles squeezed in anticipation.

"Ah, lovely," Michael sighed. He licked along her exposed slit, tasting her already oozing sex.

The very tip of his tongue flicked against her clit. Lucy gave voice to the shock of sensation rocking through her, a high-pitched cry that echoed in the shady space beneath the oak tree.

Another long lick, and another. Lucy, giddy from all the blood rushing to her head and then off to other parts of her body, wordlessly moaned her begging for him to kiss her clit again.

His tongue slid over her clit again, the delicious warmth of his mouth soon following. He suckled her there, lightly swirling his tongue around and around the hard, fleshy nub.

Breath escaped her, shudders wracking her body, giving into a small release that had sufficient strength to blank her mind.

When she came to herself again, Michael peered at her over the rise of her pelvis, his face glistening with her juices. He grasped her hips, drawing her closer, for she had slipped away in finding her release.

The blunt end of his cock pushed against her wet slit. He held her steady and then slid all the way into her still convulsing cunt.

The new angle wreaked fresh havoc within Lucy. She knew, as surely as she knew her name, she belonged to him forever. This branded him upon her, from the scratchy wool and bark beneath her bottom to the pounding of her heart in her ears.

He slid in and out of her, almost casually, letting her feel the full length of his cock. She embraced his flesh with her own, aware of every corded vein in his cock, the compression of its bulbous head against her flesh.

His thumb found her clit, rubbing it against her pelvic bone, his cock thrusting faster into her.

She keened her pleasure, knocked into a fresh release. A release unceasing, for he still pounded into her, a wild bucking that held no rhythm, just hard and fast. His thumb slipped off the clit, found it again, and was gone.

Above her he groaned, driving his cock in hard and deep and holding there, pulsing inside her. Her cry joined his, her mind filled with nothing but him and his cock inside her.

At length, he slid out of her and allowed her to collapse over the other side of the tree root, her legs curling beneath her. He joined her, gathering her up in his arms and holding her close.

She sensed his trembling and wondered if it had been as incredible for him as it had been for her. She opened her mouth to ask him—

A disturbance in the twittering peace surrounding them broke her thought process. Rolling away from Michael, she peered over a large tree root toward the sound.

A carriage rolled along the road, heading south. Lucy caught her breath. "Michael."

He stirred, lying alongside her and taking a look. "It's only a carriage."

Lucy didn't even look at him to reply. "It's *his* carriage. I recognize the insignia on the door."

The breath hissed out between Michael's clenched teeth. Lucy saw him reach for his rifle, but it lay among their discarded piles of clothing on the other side of the tree root. "I'll kill him," he growled.

Lucy started in alarm. "You will do no such thing."

He twisted to stare at her. "Why not? He hurt you, Lucy!"

"But I am safe now." She placed a reassuring hand on his forearm. She wished now she hadn't overdramatized her predicament, but how to undo it?

Michael turned to watch the carriage vanish out of sight. "They will overtake the others," he muttered.

Lucy shot a worried look at him. "Will they be all right?"

"It depends on whether he survives the meeting. They know enough about what happened, Lucy, to take revenge for you." He bared his teeth in a horrible grimace.

Lucy swallowed, her gaze falling upon the tiny dust cloud left behind by Radbourne's carriage. "I hope they don't. It will get them into trouble."

"Is that all you're concerned about?" Michael's gaze fixed hers, searching her features as if for a clue. Lucy hoped she presented a suitably worried expression.

"Of course." Lucy pushed off the tree root and rose, returning to their makeshift love nest. She started sorting out their clothes. She looked up from her work. "I wouldn't want to see you hanged, Michael."

That seemed to mollify him for he relaxed, if only slightly. "There's no way we can catch up with them, Lucy. And I don't want Radbourne to catch you. But we'd best hurry all the same. Let's hope they have better sense than to get into trouble."

Lucy nodded and began to dress, Michael coming to her assistance.

10

Caroline gazed at the passing countryside. They'd gone through another village without success. It was as if Lucy and her companions had disappeared off the map. She kept reassuring herself that they had headed south to Dover. At least there, she'd catch them.

Their carriage slowed. Radbourne pounded on the ceiling making Caroline jump. "What's going on, man?"

The coachman flipped open the small trapdoor in the ceiling. "Looks like we found 'em. They're on the road ahead. I didn't want to startle 'em like."

Radbourne sank back onto the seat. "Good man. Take it easy and let us know if you spot Miss Lucy."

"Righto." The coachman closed the hatch.

The traveling group split into two, stepping off the narrow country road to let the carriage pass. As they passed, Caroline looked at each face. Not one of them lifted their eyes to meet her searching gaze.

They passed the last of them, two soldiers standing to attention, but who didn't salute. Caroline met their frank gaze. The eyes of one of them widened on seeing her.

The carriage slowed to a halt and the trapdoor flipped open. "She's not there."

Radbourne cursed. "Then where the devil—"

"Alex." Caroline laid her hand on his coat sleeve. "I think we have a bigger problem."

A thud on the rear of the carriage punctuated her statement. "Let 'er go!"

Radbourne frowned in confusion. "What—"

"Let me handle it," Caroline murmured, almost unheard over the coachman's bellowing and whip cracking. She unlatched the door and leapt to the ground before Radbourne could act. "Stay there."

He gaped at her. "Stay—"

Caroline raised her voice. "Gentlemen, you have mistaken me for my sister."

The angry faces curled into confused ones. "Her sister?"

"Look at 'er." A buxom woman stepped forward, red hair flying from her improvised bun. "She's dressed too fine for our Lucy."

Caroline met her gaze, recognizing in her a force to be reckoned with. "Where is she?"

"Ain't with us, miss." The buxom woman folded her arms.

A smaller woman, dark-haired with a pinched expression stepped forward. "She was with us," the woman supplied. "The sarge's gone and taken her to York."

The buxom woman started to protest but got a sharp elbow from the smaller woman.

Caroline frowned. Did she tell the truth? It didn't make sense that Lucy'd go to York. "Doesn't she know the scandal that's raging? She'll be humiliated!"

"Funny sort of family not to accept their own," the buxom redhead remarked.

"You may as well go home, or on to York," the smaller woman said. "Do not be concerned. She is well and in good hands with the sarge."

Caroline rested her hand on the carriage door. "Yes, and that liaison will ruin her twice over." She regretted her sharp words immediately.

The crowd bristled. "The sarge is a good man. She could do a lot worse!" protested the smaller woman.

"I'm sure," Caroline replied, feeling panic well up in her stomach, "but she had the choice of better men." She darted a glance into the interior of the carriage where Radbourne watched her, fists clenched on his knees. He looked ready to spring out.

Caroline nodded to the women and men. "Thank you for your help. I wish you all a safe journey."

Somehow she managed to clamber back into the carriage and settle next to Radbourne. The carriage jerked into motion.

Radbourne grabbed her arm and hauled her to him. "What the devil did you think you were doing?"

Her heart pounding, Caroline strove for a calm voice. "They thought I was Lucy. That's why they yelled what they did."

"But you didn't have to— I could have—"

"They would have torn you apart. If the innkeeper's wife knew the story of her rape, you can safely wager her traveling companions also know. You are Lucy's only hope for restoration to Society, and I can't risk the chance of getting you killed."

He'd glared at her until the last and he sobered. "Is that all I'm good for?" he drawled.

Caroline drew away, shaking her head. She didn't want to talk about their affair any more than she feared he did. "You know it is not." And she didn't say that in a playful manner.

She turned her head to look out the window, refusing to have any more conversation with him.

"Do you think she's really gone to York?" he asked after a short silence.

Caroline shrugged. "Honestly, I don't know if they were trying to hide her from us, or be helpful because I am her sister. In any case, she isn't with them and neither is that sergeant fellow."

"We'll head over to the Great North Road. If she's on it, we'll find her. If she's not, she's either headed home to Durham or London. Write to your aunt and warn her that Lucy might be returning to her."

"Yes! Auntie wouldn't dare turn her out if she knew Lucy had a husband waiting, and perhaps she could also start mitigating some of the damage." Caroline heard the false enthusiasm in her voice and restrained from wincing, wondering if Radbourne saw through her guise.

She knew why she hadn't sent a letter to London before now. Doing so made the engagement practically official and then she'd lose Radbourne forever. Easier to forget that future lay ahead and enjoy his company in the here and now.

Radbourne didn't seem to have noticed her sudden pensiveness, continuing to plan in a jolly voice. "And in case those camp followers were lying about her not going to Dover, we should make directly for the port and wait for them there. No more of this flitting about across the countryside."

Caroline had to agree. There would be more comfortable rooms, if not fashionable, to be taken in Dover. "I wish we could find Lucy before then, but you are right. We are certain of at least two destinations. It would be foolish to continue to comb the countryside for her." She sighed. "I just hope she's all right. That woman said she was well."

"Then she is. There'd be no reason to lie about that. If Lucy were in difficulty and needed assistance, they would say so."

"If they believed it best for her," Caroline murmured, gnawing on her lip. Perhaps she should have stayed and demanded more information from the women.

Radbourne slid over and slipped an arm about her shoulders. "We will find her, Caroline." He tilted her chin up so that she looked him in the face. "You want this very badly, don't you?"

Caroline could flirt and say she wanted other things more, with a come-hither flutter of her eyelashes, but they talked of her sister. "She's my only sister. I've been responsible for her my entire life."

He made a noncommittal noise, which Caroline took for simple agreement. Knocking on the trapdoor, he ordered his coachman to make for the nearest village.

She rested her head on his shoulder, not even the jolting of the carriage bothering her. His warmth, his reassurance, calmed her. He would take good care of her sister, and make her happier than she ever expected.

Caroline knew this firsthand.

The sun had set by the time Lucy and Michael caught up with the others. Maggie didn't waste any time. "We saw your sister today."

Lucy gaped in astonishment. "Caroline?" Could she be the blond woman Radbourne escorted? She truly hadn't expected Caroline to go looking for her personally. They had plenty of staff to spare for that and Caroline hadn't gone beyond Durham in years. "Was she alone?"

A chorus of responses of "yes," "no," and "dunno" left Lucy even more confused. She looked at Jane, who shrugged, and back at Maggie who was adamant Caroline hadn't been traveling alone.

"Quiet!" Michael bellowed, and even Maggie took heed. "How was she traveling?"

Lucy dashed an astonished look at him. Caroline would have had to borrow a carriage from someone, perhaps hire one from the inn in town. Servants they had aplenty, but their father had taken the only coach with them on his hunting trip.

"Big fancy coach," said Maggie.

"Closed berline," said one of the soldiers who had been a stablehand once and knew his equipage.

"Any marks on the door?" Michael asked.

A number of them shrugged, some of those muttering that there had been something on the door, but what . . .

One of the privates spoke up. "I saw it when it passed. It was old and fancy lookin'. Had a swan's neck and a shield with some stars or something on it. Hard to tell, it was all muddy."

Michael and Lucy stared at each other. He drew her to one side. "What is your sister doing with Radbourne?" he asked in a slow, menacing voice.

"How did—" Lucy stopped.

"One of the regiment officers belongs in the family. I know the crest. What is your sister doing with him?"

Lucy held her hands up in protest. "How should I know? He's probably spun her some crazy tale to make her help him." She hoped that would be sufficient to calm Michael's suspicions. "You heard the gossip as well as I did. Surely my sister must have also heard it."

Michael turned to the others gathered by the campfire. "Was there anyone else?"

"Just the coachman, I saw," offered one of the soldiers. More than one person agreed with him. "Just two in the coach—"

"—berline," interrupted the former stablehand.

"Just two, if that."

Lucy shook her head. "That cannot be right. Caroline is very proper about appearances. She never travels anywhere without her maid."

"Perhaps we just didn't see her," Jane Jones tried to mollify Lucy.

It bothered Lucy on a deeper level. Had her sister become so upset by Lucy's action that she'd dashed off with that rake before even thinking of where that might lead her?

"It is not even certain there was someone with her. Maid, man, or otherwise." Michael gave her shoulders a rough hug. He called to Maggie. "Maggie, is there anything left to eat? I'm famished!"

Amidst much joking and laughter at the reason for his hunger, Michael led Lucy closer to the fire and to sustenance. The group settled down after that, murmured speculation still rife as to how many rode within Lucy's sister's carriage.

Michael nudged her with his elbow. "You're not eating."

Obedient, Lucy scooped up a mouthful of stew, chewed, and swallowed. She stared into the fire, puzzling over why Caroline and Radbourne traveled together.

"Don't worry about your sister," he murmured in her ear.

She turned on him. "How can you say that? She's in grave danger if she's with *him*!" Tears rose. She almost believed it herself. Radbourne would ruin, had probably already ruined, her sister.

"We can't do anything about it," he said, rather callously, Lucy thought. "They are in a carriage, we are on foot. We don't have money to get a roof over our heads, let alone purchase a horse—and do you think I'd let you go after them alone? Do you think I would even leave you alone for a minute to go after them?"

Lucy ducked her head, her voice much fainter, less angry. "You wouldn't leave me alone?"

"No, I wouldn't," Michael's voice came low and fierce. "If they come back, we'll face them together, but I'm not about to hand you over to him. Not without a fight. Not after what he's done to you."

"How will you stop him?" Lucy whispered. "How will you stop him when you have sailed for war?"

His hug tightened. "We'll work something out."

Lucy nestled against him, relieved the subject turned from Radbourne. "I suppose I could look for a situation in Dover and wait for you to come back. Especially if Jane gets to sail with her husband . . ."

"If she does not, will you return home with her? The way will be hard with no money."

Lucy had heard of the indigents harassed out of each parish they entered. "We will manage—and if I can reach my sister without Radbourne knowing, I may have the funds to afford to travel in a little style."

"Would that be possible? If she's with him, it's unlikely he'd let her out of his sight."

Lucy made a face. He'd brought *him* up again. "Is it? I'm the one he wants, not her."

Michael snorted. "You sound jealous."

"Oh, believe me, I am not!" Lucy replied, folding her arms. "I've no doubt that if he can, he will take advantage of her, if he hasn't done so already. That's the kind of man he is. But he's on this search with her, and that makes me think his prime interest is me."

"I also," Michael agreed. "There will be no time after the wives' lottery is drawn for finding your sister. They board us at once after that."

"I will manage." Lucy tried to sound confident, but everything hinged on her somehow getting money. Surely her sister would see reason? Even being settled in the remote countryside would be better than being married to Radbourne.

Lucy grimaced. Caroline didn't give up on a person easily.

Michael kissed the side of her forehead. "Maybe there are some arrangements we can make in Dover ahead of time."

Wrapping her arms around him, Lucy gave him a squeeze. "You are sweet, Michael, but there is no need to sugarcoat the pill for me. I made my decision and I'll stand by it, no matter how hard it becomes."

Like that other decision? her conscience mocked. *The one conceding marriage as the only option with Radbourne?*

Lucy swore silently this would be different. She nestled her head on his shoulder and listened to Jane and her husband sing a little ditty while someone played on a cheap tin whistle. The crackling fire warmed her front and almost made her forget the cold at her back.

Michael had not forgotten and draped a blanket about her, snuggling with her beneath it.

Under the concealment of the blanket, Lucy reached for the buttons on his breeches. Michael shifted position at once, giving them a little more privacy.

Her hand slid into the gap and found his cock, already waking into life. Running her fingertips over his cock's nodding, bulbous head, she trailed her fingers down his wrinkled length and below, cupping his balls. She felt the faint traces of hair upon them while she stroked them, lifting them toward her to feel their weight. She marveled that his balls weighed heavy in her hand, given the sex earlier in the day. Did man never run dry?

Michael moaned under his breath, kissing her hair. She released him, her hand traversing the distance back to the head and finding he had lengthened and hardened.

"Witch," he whispered, his voice filled with suppressed urges, "what am I going to do with you?"

"Whatever you want," she whispered back, smiling across at Jane, who smiled back and started to rise. Lucy signaled her to stay.

Jane took one look at her and Michael and laughed, sinking

back down next to her husband. Lucy watched as Jane leaned into her husband, artfully casting her shawl across his lap. The two women shared conspiratorial grins.

Michael nuzzled at her neck, his fingers fanning across her collarbone. They crept up the side of her neck, making her shiver, a rough fingertip brushing her earlobe.

She bit down on her lower lip, intent on continuing to rouse him. His cock lay hard in her hand and already she had swiped a tiny bit of moisture from the end, making her palm sticky.

Stroking the length of him, she held him in her palm, letting her fingers trail along the upper side of his cock. He moaned again, burying his mouth in her hair, muffling the sound.

Rock-hard, his cock strained against her hand, twitching at her lightest touch. "We need to move," he whispered into her hair, "back into the shadows. I have to have you, lass."

How could she complain about that? They rose, the blanket strategically placed. Muffled laughter rose from the others and her cheeks turned hot. Thankful that the dark hid her embarrassment, she continued to back away.

Michael stopped her in the outer circle of their encampment, still too close in Lucy's opinion, but the other option was to stumble about in complete darkness. He rearranged the blanket and drew her down on top of him.

"Sit on top of me," he directed, as she slid off his lap. "That is, if you're ready. Perhaps I should check."

Lucy swallowed an embarrassed giggle. She started to straddle him, but he stopped her. "No, lass, the other way."

She swiveled, facing the fire instead of Michael. A cold draft of air told her he'd lifted her skirts. His cold hands caressed the backs of her thighs. She shivered at his touch on her warm skin.

"Michael," she murmured. "They'll see me . . . see me . . ." How to describe the rapture she felt when she reached that divine release?

"Lucy love, there is no privacy in the army. If we were on

the Peninsula, we wouldn't even get this much privacy to ourselves. Forget them. Think only of me and how you're going to milk me dry, empty out my balls of all their jism."

Gasping at his hot words, Lucy closed her eyes, bowing her head.

He reached her heated mound, fingers probing between her lips. The moment he touched her there, she realized she was soaking. More than ready for him.

She heard him make a grunt of satisfaction, his fingers smoothing the liquid up and down her slit, until she thought his hand must be drenched. She almost burst with excitement, his fingers doing delicious things, rousing her even more than her furtive fumbling with his cock.

With his other hand he drew her down onto him, her back arching as she came into contact with his eager cock. It slid along the length of her wet crack, slipping past her hole. She squirmed against him, trying to get it back into the right place. She loved the feel of his great bulk against her sensitive slit, but he felt so much better inside her.

Gasping and bent over at an angle, Lucy achieved her goal. Michael's cock nudged against her tight opening and pushed inside. She sank down onto him, panting for breath. This new pressure elicited fresh, intense delights.

Michael held her hips steady, holding her in place when she had completely engulfed him in her cunt. Rocking against him, the swell of enflamed need rose even higher within her. The cold air scorched her lungs with each excited inhalation.

A low keening built up inside her, and she tried to keep it down, flexing her cunt muscles about his pulsating cock. She gripped his boots, trying to anchor herself to earth. His hands encouraged her to rise up on her knees and come back down, his cock sliding along the same delicious path, the sensations increasing triplefold.

Lucy raised her head, staring almost blindly at the fire. Most did not look her way but others frequently did so. She didn't care any more. She didn't care that they saw her reduced to an animal state, humping her mate with a wild abandon.

She bounced on his cock, pumping and squeezing in a sweet desperation to reach release. Michael bent forward, his hands skimming up her sides, reaching her breasts. She reared back against him, letting his hands cover her covered bosom, his cock plunging even deeper.

She cried out, her head falling back against his shoulder. Oh, this was heaven, heaven. One of his hands cupped a breast, the other slid down between her parted legs, scavenging through the folds of her gown until he found bare flesh.

He wasted no time, finding her throbbing mound and her clit sticking out between her hairy nether lips. His fingertip skimmed it once, then twice. He tweaked a nipple, sliding beneath the fabric to tease her bared flesh.

While she rocked against him, rhythmically tightening her cunt about his cock, he rubbed at her clit, sliding deeper every now and then to retrieve fresh juicy essence from their joined bodies.

Lightning shot through her, again and again, and she cried out, not caring that her cry echoed across the small clearing, utterly lost in the maelstrom of coming again and again.

Michael grunted and groaned behind her, his hand squeezing her breast as he stiffened, and she felt his jism pound against her solid flesh inside her.

She sank down, resting her head on her folded arms atop his boots, struggling for breath. His cock still lay buried inside her and she didn't want to give that up, just yet.

"Oh lass, lass," he murmured, his hands smoothing over her covered rump.

After a moment, she raised herself up by her arms and looked over her shoulder at him. Inside, his cock had softened, but even she felt its tiny pulse of reaction at only her glance.

"Come here." Michael beckoned her.

She untangled her limbs and her gown from him and joined him in a modest embrace. He peppered her face with weary kisses, seeking out her mouth again and again until she melted in their combined warmth.

She leaned against him, never wanting this dazed afterglow to end. He lay back, bringing her with him. She curled against him, her head nestled on his shoulder.

"Lucy, rest," he whispered. "We have an early start in the morning."

His remark awakened her curiosity. "We do? Do we not always?"

"We must be abroad earlier than the rest," he murmured. "I think it wise we travel separately from the others for a couple of days, in case your sister decides to retrace her steps and accost my troop again." His arm tightened about her, his hand squeezing her shoulder. "I am not ready to lose you just yet."

Lucy didn't reply, holding her breath. He hadn't admitted so much in all of their short time together. She didn't know where that admission would lead: would he relent and take her with him? Or did it mean that he remained firm, if reluctant, that their affair had an ending at the end of the road in Dover?

Radbourne's carriage rolled onto the Great North Road by mid-afternoon and a short time thereafter they reached a village, which naturally included a stop for the London mail coach.

Letting Radbourne make the accommodation arrangements, Caroline strolled along the street, looking for a place to purchase paper and ink. She had not thought to bring any along with her. The inn had a supply to be had for a price, but Caroline didn't want the owners to get the impression she had gone on this journey without even a portable writing case.

She found the supplies she needed and returned to the Boar's Head Inn, finding Radbourne waiting for her outside. "Well, *wife,*" he said, draping his arm about her shoulders. "It seems we are out of luck again with regard to rooms. We must share."

Caroline gazed up at him through her eyelashes. "This is a bad thing?" she teased. She'd resolved to take as much of him as possible in the short time left to them and then walk away, leaving him to his future with Lucy. She'd be the one to face exile, not her sweet sister.

He chuckled, dipping his head to kiss her upturned lips.

"Really," she murmured, when their kiss had ended after an unseemly amount of time, "I am sure married couples are not meant to act so much in love."

He stiffened and then gave a rueful chuckle. "A wise observance, my dear. A husband soon tires of his wife." His arm slipped from her shoulders and he gestured that they enter the inn, beyond the curious onlookers.

"They do?" she whispered, passing him to go inside.

"So I have heard. So I have seen, if the great number of adulterers I've known, both male and female, are any indication." He led her past the beaming innkeeper and his wife and upstairs to their room.

The coachman had already deposited their meager luggage in the center of the room.

Caroline stepped away from Radbourne, needing to put distance between them. "Will you do so? Will you tire of my sister and take a mistress?"

A frown flitted across his face, but the grin below his crooked bandages was all wickedness. "If I do, I assure you that you will be my first call."

Caroline stared at him, frozen. Become his mistress? The idea both appalled and appealed.

He closed the space between them. He placed one hand on her shoulder and with the other, held her chin between thumb and forefinger. He didn't have to tilt her head back very far for them to look eye to eye. "If your sister is your equal in passion, and I suspect she is, given that she's taken up with a common sergeant, then I assure you it is very unlikely that I will tire of her." He gave her chin a tweak. "I have not tired of you."

"But you will?" she challenged.

A sandy eyebrow quirked. "I do not foresee it, Caro. You have bewitched me." His voice lowered into a delicious dark burr. "It will be hard to give you up when we find your sister."

His pronouncement took her breath away. Did he mean it? Did he want her that much? But what did it matter? It would all come to an end when they found Lucy.

"Your expressions change like the wind," he murmured. "It's as if I can see into your very soul."

"And what do you see there?" she breathed.

"I see that you want me. You want me. Down to the very core of your soul, you want me. You are tired of the loneliness, of your empty bed."

She flinched. "You do not know if my bed was empty before now."

His brief nod acknowledged the hit. "You are right. You have far more experience in bed than any unmarried chit should have. Did I take you from a lover?"

Caroline shook her head, wordless although her eyes were huge.

"I did not think so. You were too eager, too hungry to taste the sweet elixir of sex again." His voice dropped, his blue-eyed gaze twin fires of desire. "I would like to hear that story, some day, of how you came to lose your innocence."

"Perhaps, some day." Never, if Caroline had any say in the matter, and she wondered for a moment what Radbourne would have to do to pry the tale from between her lips.

11

He seemed satisfied with that. "Then let us not think of to-morrow, but of this very moment. You want me, Caroline. You radiate with it. Do you deny it?"

"I do not." Caroline met his burning gaze and it melted her distress of losing him, of the insult of becoming his mistress, his second choice, rather than his first. "I feel you want me too."

"You are observant," he murmured before capturing her lips.

Her hands traversed the small gap between them, finding his pantaloons and the engorged cock trapped within.

"Very," she breathed between kisses.

He kissed her hard, his embrace imprinting her against his body, every line of him, every muscle, every button on his waistcoat. His mouth probed hers, seeking dominance and gaining it. She gave herself up to him utterly, releasing all control to him, her only act to cling to him and return his kiss with fervor.

He broke off the kiss, taking a half-step back, and she sagged in his loose grasp, her legs lacking any strength. He caught her, gazing down at her limpid eyes and swollen lips. "You need to write your letter," he murmured. "We have plenty of time tonight to explore the depths of your wanting."

Just the thought of it made her wet between her thighs. She took one breath and another before she'd recovered sufficiently to pull away from him. Picking up the parcel she'd dropped at some point, she made her way to a small table in the room, silently cursing her wobbly legs and the faintness that threatened to take her.

Unwrapping the parcel and laying out its contents before her, Caroline's senses prickled with Radbourne's continued presence. He stood behind her, out of her line of sight, seemingly content to watch her at work.

She strove to drive him from her mind and started to write. The first letter she wrote to her aunt, explaining her plans for Lucy, and that Radbourne appeared determined to have Lucy to wed.

It pained her more than she thought to write that simple sentence and she halted, pinching the bridge of her nose. It had seemed so easy at first, to search for Lucy and ignore Radbourne's incredible magnetism.

But he'd proven impossible to ignore.

Impossible to ignore even now, for she heard him settle in a chair behind her, the wooden legs scraping against the floorboards.

Sharpening her quill, she dipped her pen into the ink and continued writing. She begged her aunt to take Lucy in, should she show up in London, and noted that they would stop there on their way to Dover in pursuit of Lucy.

"Are you going to be much longer?" Radbourne inquired from his corner.

That made Caroline chuckle. "You never give up, do you?"

"Never." He grinned. "You would do well to remember that."

She returned his smile. "You should recall the same about me."

He opened his mouth to argue, and her recent submission to him, just moments ago, came to Caroline's mind, but he closed his mouth again. "Just hurry and write your letter," he said. "I am aching for you." He pressed his hand along the front of his pantaloons, highlighting his engorged cock, trapped beneath the tight linen.

Sucking the breath in between her teeth, Caroline returned to her writing, her mind burning with the image of that cock, eager for her. She imagined freeing it, sinking it into her cunt until he filled her. Filled her and filled her, for his cock was larger than any she'd ever had. She would ride him until she came, screaming her release.

Ink splashed across her page and she hastened to daub it off, relieved to see it had not masked anything she had already written. Hurriedly, she scribbled down the remainder of her message, again begging her aunt to be lenient toward Lucy, for the girl had landed herself a husband out of this after all. She reminded her aunt that it was possible that only further disgrace would dissuade the earl from marrying her. Even rakes had their limit.

Not this one, Caroline knew, but her aunt didn't need to know that. She signed the letter and took another sheet of paper and started to write anew.

"Caroline?" Radbourne sounded a touch impatient. "Another letter?"

"I'm writing to Lucy." Caroline continued to write. She found it easier to write about Lucy's upcoming nuptials the second time.

"Not about us, I hope."

She didn't even give him the benefit of an indignant stare. "Don't be ridiculous, Alex, but I don't want her running again."

Glancing over her shoulder with a wicked grin, she added, "I'll be sure to sing your praises, if you wish."

He snorted. "Are there any?"

She pivoted in her seat. She hadn't expected to hear that from a man of such confidence. "Of course there are." She smiled slyly. "Of course, I will have to leave out the ones I'm not supposed to know about."

Radbourne grimaced. "I scarcely have a sterling reputation."

She frowned. "I'm not writing about the reputation, I'm writing about the man."

Caroline turned back to her writing. She listed Radbourne's qualities: kindness, generosity, sense of humor (she didn't mention how wicked it was), dedication, resolve. She added she had noticed his handsome looks and reminded Lucy to remember that the reputation didn't give the whole picture of the man.

He's willing to give up his bachelorhood to you, dear sister. Indeed, he seems devoted to enjoying your company as his wife. I cannot guess at what made you flee him, except that perhaps the situation had grown too unruly and frightening, even for you, but I do wish for your happiness and safety. At the very least, please hear the earl out.

She signed it *"Your loving sister"* and dashed sand over it before she could change her mind. Folding it, she dripped wax onto the letter and sealed it with her ring, a signet ring that had belonged to her mother. She enclosed the letter with the one to her aunt.

She pulled another sheet of paper toward her.

"Now who are you writing to?" Radbourne sounded frustrated.

"Home. They need to know I will be in Dover if they need to get a message to me. It's not beyond the realm of reason for Lucy to return home."

He snorted. "Unlikely. That sergeant won't go with her. He's got sailing orders."

"My father will need to know what is happening." Caroline planned to tell him as little as possible. She kept writing.

"You plan to tell him all?"

"I am not a fool."

"I hope not."

Caroline turned to snap at him, but the words vanished, unspoken. "What are you doing?"

Slouching back in the wooden chair, resting his head on the back spokes, he'd unbuttoned his pantaloons. His cock, sprung free from its prison, jerked to purplish attention, its rosy length masked by his lazily stroking hand.

"Whenever you are ready," he cajoled, his features suffused with lust.

She gazed at him with longing. How easy it would be for her to abandon her letter writing and straddle him, riding him with abandon.

She sighed, beyond frustrated. "I have to get these done before the mail comes."

"The one north won't be a while yet."

She raised a slender blond eyebrow. "You want me to go downstairs *twice?*"

He laughed, the sound filling the room with joy. "Finish your letter," he declared, his hand falling away from his stiff cock. "I'll wait."

She turned back to her letter. In the end, all she wrote was that she was on Lucy's trail and planned to catch up with her in Dover at the latest. Let her father think whatever he wanted to. She doubted he even cared.

She sealed it with her signet ring and gathered up the letters. "I will return shortly."

He grinned at her. "I'll be waiting."

Caroline fled the room, hurrying downstairs, almost tripping on the uneven steps in her haste. Breathless, she delivered her missives to the innkeeper, who promised to hand them to the next mail coaches heading north and south.

Thanking him with a brief nod, she dashed back upstairs. She flung open the door, and she looked to the chair by the fireplace.

He wasn't there. She glanced in the other direction, toward the bed, and there he lay, supremely naked, bare of even his bandages. The fire cast a warm, golden glow upon his skin.

She caught her breath. Alex lounged, his hands folded behind his head, showing off his flexed biceps, flattened stomach and thick muscled thighs. His cock rose from the dark golden hair at his groin, like a dark rod of rich velvet.

Taking an involuntary step toward him, she paused. Behind her back, she fumbled for the bolt and slid it home, making sure it fell across the door. She had no intention of being disturbed by anyone.

Caroline gazed upon her golden lover and wondered how she'd ever give him up. Just looking at him set her aflame. She burned for him in the pit of her belly. Not even the surging wetness between her legs could put out that fire.

"Caro, I think you are overdressed."

She stifled a laugh at his impatience. "I am sure of it." She leaned against the door. "And what are you going to do about it?"

"Nothing," came his insolent reply. "I am going to watch you undress."

She pouted, folding her arms. "But I need help."

He chuckled. "The hell you do."

She gazed at him for what seemed like a long time. He looked so magnificent, so virile, that it didn't seem worth fighting him over who got to undress whom. She had surrendered utterly to his kiss earlier.

All she needed to do was surrender to his will again.

She lifted her hands to the tapes on the right side of her gown. Sure he wanted her to strip as quickly as possible, Caroline delayed. Perhaps she didn't want to give up all control. Just yet.

Untucking the narrow strips of material from within the gown, she casually unknotted the ties, and twisted to the left, fishing for the tapes there. She untied them. Reaching behind her for the last set of tapes, Caroline grew very aware how her cleavage showed to even better advantage, the fine muslin of her gown slipping to reveal her chemise.

"Hurry," Alex growled. His hand drifted down across his chest and stomach and his fingers curled around his thick cock.

Her lips twitched. "If I don't take care in disrobing, I'll ruin the gown."

He glowered. "Rubbish."

"Have I worn again the gown you tore off my back the first night?" The first fold of her bodice fell back, revealing her right breast. The light pink areola of her nipple puckered.

Caroline turned back to the other fold that made up the front of her bodice, leaving only her puffed sleeves that continued in gauze to her wrist.

Tugging on the thin green ribbon at her wrist, she unraveled the bow and let the gauze fall over the back of her hand, concealing her signet ring.

She did the same with her other hand and lifted them both to her shoulders, the gauze falling to her elbows. Releasing her sleeves, she let her arms fall to her sides and the muslin and gauze slipped off her arms to the ground.

Caroline kept her gaze on Alex's face, marking each small reaction as she bared more of her skin. Despite his complaints, he appeared fascinated by her slow stripping.

The thick ribbon on her high-waisted gown, bound by a double bow, came next. She didn't dare show him how easy it would be for him to untie the wide green silk band and so she held the ends behind her, watching him feast upon her almost-exposed bosom.

She released her grip on the ribbon, letting it flutter to the floor. With a little shimmy, the rest of her gown followed suit, leaving her standing in her shift.

Oh and her stockings and shoes. She crossed to the chair by the fireplace and propped her foot on it. She rolled up her shift to reveal that her stockings were held up by ivory ribbons. She unraveled the bow and slid the opaque white stocking over her knee and down her calf, looking up through her eyelashes at Alex as she did so.

He seemed mesmerized, his gaze flicking between her protruding bosom and the length of pale leg she now revealed.

She took off her stocking and slipper in the same movement. Switching legs, she repeated the languid movements until she stood in bare feet before the fireplace. The light leapt through her translucent shift, revealing the outline of her legs.

"Don't stop there," Alex murmured, every line of his body tensed.

Caroline paused in her disrobing. "That was not in my plan."

He grinned ruefully. "If I watch you any more, I will explode and you'll miss all the fun."

She sashayed toward him. "Oh, I am sure you know ways of pleasuring a woman without using your cock." She reached the bed, her fingertips trailing over the nubbly counterpane. "Although I profess, I would much rather have that big cock of yours inside me, fucking me until I scream."

Alex groaned. "Woman, you undo me." He twirled his finger. "Finish."

Still, Caroline delayed.

The mattress lurched, Alex rising to his knees, his hands grasping her hips. She looked down at him. Only the thin tie at her shift's neck stood between her and utter nakedness.

His gaze feasted on her. "You are a wonderful, wanton creature," he murmured. He reached out and his fingertip brushed over one nipple and then the other. Her nipples, already hard, tightened further. "Magnificent," he breathed. "Luscious curves." His fingertips trailed from her breast to her hip and returned, the fine linen fabric ruching under his light touch before falling back into place.

She arched her back, presenting her lips and her breasts to him. "Stop teasing," she whispered, her breath catching. "I can see in your eyes you want to rip this shift from my body."

He sucked in his breath. "I thought no such thing. On the contrary, I was thinking how sweet it would be to suckle your breasts through it, but if you'd prefer . . ." He trailed off, his intense blue gaze watching her.

A soft sob escaped her. "Do what you will," she whispered. "I am yours."

Alex hauled her onto the bed in a bear hug. She hung on to his arms, laughing as he pivoted and flung her down onto the bed. "I will hold you to that," he growled.

He pinned her hands onto the mattress, straddling her slight form. He took her mouth in a soul-stealing kiss that consumed her. Nothing else existed but his weight across her hips and his mouth on hers, his tongue plunging inside. The red heat of desire filled her senses. Closing her eyes, all she saw were scarlet shadows.

Alex released her hands, but she left them over her head, feeling his touch drag along the soft skin of her arm and down to her breasts. He hefted the weight of them in his hands, the thumbs exploring across the front, swiping her nipples.

She whimpered into his mouth, his touch trebling the sexual fire that burned her. She pushed her breasts into his palms, arching under him.

His mouth slid from hers, leaving a wet trail over her chin and down the curve of her neck. He nibbled at her pulse point, tasting the wildness of her heartbeat, before continuing to kiss his way to her collarbone.

His hands worked at loosening the gathered cotton tie of her shift. His kisses stopped at the neckline and he ducked his head lower, his lips landing squarely over her taut nipple. He drew it and the linen up in his teeth, before sealing the small torture with a healing kiss that burned where the teeth had seared.

Caroline sobbed for breath, her hands clawing the sheets. He suckled each nipple alternately, occasionally pulling them up between his teeth. Her breasts felt like hot mounds against the cooler wet linen of her shift.

"Alex, Alex, please," she gasped, thrusting her breasts closer to his face. A familiar sweet tension grew in the pit of her belly.

He only redoubled his efforts, twisting one nipple between his fingers while he sucked and bit the other. The heat overflowed from her breasts, seeping down into her belly, turning her cunt into molten liquid. Alex's constant teasing only drove the sweet tension higher and higher, until Caroline thought she couldn't stand it any longer.

She clawed at the sheets, at his bare back, at his tousled head, seeking relief, seeking . . . seeking something to bring an end to this exquisite pleasure.

She stiffened beneath him, crying out as wave after wave of release came, her nipples two fiery nubs in a swirling mass of sensation.

Her release subsiding, she cradled his head in her hands and he raised his head to gaze down at her. Panting, she stared up at him, astonished at what he had wrought in her.

He hardly allowed her to catch her breath, pressing his mouth against hers, swallowing her murmured astonishment. He made space between them, hauling up her shift until it gathered at her waist, slipping his knee between her legs.

She parted for him willingly, moaning into his mouth when

he felt her wet crevice. Moaned again when she heard the liquid sound of her sex lap against his fingers as he slid one finger in and circled the rim.

Two fingers went in deeper and her cunt, still fluttering with the aftereffects of coming, tried to grip him. His fingertips swooped along the walls of her tunnel, finding a particular place that made Caroline jerk against him.

The thicker head of his cock pressed against her opening. She hooked her legs around his buttocks, urging him with her heels to press further in.

He slammed his cock inside her and she bit his lower lip in surprise. He thrust in again and again, an unrelenting pummeling that made her shriek with delight.

After coming with no penetration, hard and fast was how she wanted it. Her whole body jerked with each thrust. He broke off his kiss, sucking in his wounded lower lip and frowning in deepest concentration.

The entire bed shook with his driving into her. Caroline clung to him, reveling in the ride and feeling the delicious, wonderful tension rise again. Would she be able to gain release again before he came inside her?

He pounded harder and faster into her. Each plunge shot thrilling bolts through Caroline. She tried to catch her breath, failing. Her ears roared with her own impending release.

It hit her like a wall and she cried out, her fingernails digging into his back in bloody half-moons. A hoarse cry twisted itself from his mouth and he stiffened, his hips still bucking into her, emptying himself.

He slumped, his sticky forehead pressed against her shoulder. Their breaths rasped loudly in the sudden silence. Caroline held him close, her pounding heart sounding so loud in her ears. It felt odd, and yet right, to be so tender after such a violent session. She stroked the quivering muscles of his back, his skin slick with sweat.

At length, he hauled himself up onto his elbows. He didn't apologize for crushing her (which he hadn't) but only stared down at her, his blue eyes containing a curious light.

Inhaling a fresh lungful of air, breathing in the distinct musky odor of their combined sexes, Caroline returned his measured stare, gazing up at his golden loveliness, wanting to memorize this moment forever.

Radbourne's head gave a little shake and he bent to lightly place a kiss on her forehead. "I'm starved. Shall I see about something to eat?"

Blinking in surprise, Caroline nodded.

In moments, Radbourne had dressed, and, stuffing his shirt into his pantaloons, he unbolted the door and fled the room.

Caroline rolled on her side, curling up, regarding his vanished person. "How curious," she murmured, sternly warning her heart not to break.

In the early gray hours of dawn, Michael nudged Lucy awake. Rubbing her eyes, she struggled out from underneath the thin blanket, getting to her feet. He handed her a large kerchief folded around some bread. "We'll eat later," he whispered. "Come on."

They broke away from the camp, trudging through the dewy grass. Lucy stuck close to Michael, still sleepily seeking his warmth. She stumbled over hillocks of grass tufts but didn't fall.

The sun had risen and they'd left the others three fields behind them. Lucy stretched, standing in a spot of sunlight as it broke over the tops of a distant grove of trees.

Michael grinned. "You're beautiful, you know."

Lucy grimaced. "Looking like this? My hair's all knotted and matted and I haven't had a bath since, well, my dip in the river. If only you could see me at my best."

He smiled. "I'm sure you'd dazzle me to blindness."

She laughed and rapped him on his upper arm. "Such nonsense you speak." She slipped her arm through his and leaned against him, oddly never happier than to be strolling through a beautiful morning with him. "Did you tell anyone of our plans?"

He nodded. "They'll catch up to us by evening." He kissed her temple. "Come on, we need to keep moving." He quickened the pace from a stroll into a brisk walk.

Lucy lifted the hem of her skirts, hurrying to keep up with his long-legged stride. "Why must we hurry?"

He grinned over his shoulder. "So we can find some privacy, lass, before the others catch up."

She laughed, the bright tones ringing out across the sleepy green field. "Race you!" She hitched up her skirts even higher and made a dash for the far edge of the field.

Breathless, she glanced over to see Michael easily keeping up with her. She hadn't run like this since she was a small child. They reached the hedge and Lucy sagged against it, panting for air.

Michael gathered her into his arms. "I suppose you are too exhausted now to walk the rest of the way and I must carry you."

"It would be nice to be carried," Lucy admitted. She flashed an angry glare. "But I am not too exhausted."

Standing, she stalked over to the nearest stile and climbed over the step structure, striding across the next field.

Michael soon caught up, hugging her from behind and planting a firm kiss on her neck. Anger forgotten, she turned in his arms and kissed him back, arms twining about his neck. His lips pressed against hers, teasing them open, deepening the kiss until warmth shot through her from head to toe. She could stand in this muddy field and kiss him forever.

Alex burst out of the inn, the late afternoon sun hitting him square in the eyes, temporarily blinding him. He stumbled into the courtyard and across the cobblestoned space, seeking shade.

Leaning against the wood and plastered wall of the Tudor-style inn, he gazed up at the tiny windows that marked the upper storey.

He had to get away. Had to escape the strange sensations that clung to him even now, like a wraith that refused to let go of life.

Taking a deep breath, he tried to calm down. What had sent him into such a panic? He'd fucked many a woman before now, in much the same way. Why was this time different?

Why the hell did he have to go and feel tenderness for a woman now?

He cursed, kicking at the dirt and straw littering the courtyard. He was to marry Lucy. He'd promised Caroline that he would honor that original proposition. How could he break his word to the woman he loved?

Loved.

The word drained him of all breath. Love? Had his wicked heart betrayed him at last and sought the one woman he could not have?

He rubbed his hand through his hair, staring once again at the upper windows. He wished Lucy would disappear, preferably to the Continent with her soldier lover. If the wretched girl loved the man, she would not honor her marriage vows to him and he didn't want that.

But that condemned the girl to a hard, short life, and he couldn't do that to Caroline's sister. His only hope lay in convincing Caroline that in due course, she would become his mistress.

No man would love his mistress more.

12

Shafts of early afternoon sun slanted through the overhanging foliage of nearby trees. Lucy and Michael skirted the edge of the ancient grove.

Lucy noticed Michael's silence had turned watchful. His eyes always turned toward the farmhouse whose field they edged around and the hayloft that lay midway between them and the house.

His gait had changed into the stealthful gait of a predator, or of prey that did not want to be caught. She opened her mouth to ask him a question, but he shushed her to silence.

The twittering of finches and other birds in the trees above seemed almost deafening. Michael halted her and Lucy strained to listen for what he had heard.

She heard the wind travel over the grass in an almost silent hiss of pleasure. A contented cow lowed from the next field over.

The hoarse cry of a woman, almost at once muffled, made Lucy almost leap out of her skin. She shot a concerned look at Michael.

He shushed her again before she could even ask. With his finger, he beckoned her to follow him. He headed for the hayloft in a loping crouch and Lucy tried to follow suit, her gaze searching every which way for whatever it was that Michael feared.

They reached the hayloft, the ancient wooden structure leaning to one side. The walls, made of broad slats of wood, had shrunk with age, leaving gaps.

Michael peered through one of the holes and after a moment, beckoned Lucy to do the same.

If a woman was in danger, why did they watch instead of going to her rescue?

On one side of the hayloft, the side best protected from the outside elements was heaped with last season's hay, a musty dusty smell that made Lucy want to sneeze.

Just out of sight of the large doorway, a man and woman stood, locked in a tight embrace. The woman's simple bodice had come loose, her bosom riding high against the taller man's chest. His hands held up her skirt, the hem hovering above her knees, his hands groping her buttocks.

Lucy pulled away from the peek hole and looked at Michael in wordless astonishment.

He tilted his head to glance at her with a wicked grin and pulled her close to him. He'd put down his rifle, leaving his hands free to fondle her breasts.

Another gap afforded Lucy a view of the embracing couple. They staggered back toward the hay until the man pulled the clinging woman out of his arms, hoisting her into the air and tossing her into the hay.

The woman shrieked in fright and delight, her large, freed breasts bobbing. She lifted her arms at once to her lover. He fell upon her, tugging and shoving at her clothes until the woman's pasty-white thighs were visible.

She didn't wait for her lover to finish disrobing her. The woman's hands busied themselves with the fellow's breeches, freeing the man's cock in an instant and tugging on the man's engorged flesh with healthy eagerness.

Almost behind Lucy, Michael's breathing quickened, and Lucy realized that the sudden flush of heat within her had little to do with embarrassment and everything to do with arousal.

Through her cotton gown, Michael teased one of her nipples into life, but a quick glance revealed that his attention was wholly on the scene playing out before them.

Lucy swallowed a gasp, not wanting to be heard, or caught spying. It didn't seem to matter: the two lovers talked in urgent voices, too low for Lucy to hear what they said. They seemed utterly oblivious to anything but each other.

The man tweaked his lover's nipples, pulling harder than Lucy would have thought comfortable. Michael proved her wrong, mimicking the man's actions with a sharp tug of his own upon both her nipples.

Lucy bit back a whimper, arching her back so that her breasts pushed further into Michael's hands. He teased her nipples mercilessly, pausing to palm them as if to soothe the torture he'd inflicted.

She never thought she'd be so aroused to watch two other people have sex. In traveling with Michael's troop, she'd heard the muffled sounds of lovemaking coming from different parts of the camp and it had made her warm to think of what they were doing and what she had just done with Michael, but this . . . this was different.

Watching the two lovers turned the place between her thighs into liquid and she knew that if Michael wanted to, he could take her right now, pressed up against this wall, and she wouldn't utter a single word of protest.

Michael pressed against her hip and she felt the fleshy hardness of his cock rub against her. She held her breath, knowing he wanted her as badly as she wanted him.

Within the hayloft, the man lifted the woman's hips, aiming

his cock at the dark hairy triangle at the top of her thighs. The woman's legs parted eagerly, revealing her glistening red crack.

Lucy sucked in her breath. That's what she looked like to Michael? So wild? So wanton? Her hand slid down to cover her mound, watching the woman slide her fingers up and down her juicy flesh.

Lucy pressed her fingers against herself. What would Michael say if she displayed herself like that to him, touched herself the way he touched her? Her lips compressed around a moan. Michael must have sensed something, for he leaned in, nibbling at her ear, his tongue curling around her lobe, making her shiver with his silent promise of pleasure.

The man bore into the woman beneath him. He didn't spare her, barreling hard and fast into her, their grunting cries filling the closed space of the hayloft. Lucy heard their flesh slap together, a wet smacking sound like waves slamming against a pier.

At length, the man pulled out and Lucy saw his cock, hard and glistening with the woman's juices. The woman sat up, licking her lips at the sight. The man pointed to the floor and she scrambled to kneel on all fours, presenting her rounded arse at him. Her heavy breasts hung loose and the woman lifted one hand to tease a nipple into a tight bud.

The man knelt behind her, cock in hand. His other hand pressed down on her lower back, making her bend like a bow. He eased himself against her and then started to thrust wildly against her buttocks.

Mouth open, Lucy gaped at the scene. She'd seen farm animals take a similar position, but Radbourne had introduced her to the way of human lovemaking and disabused her of the notion that humans fucked like animals, except perhaps in the absolute abandon one had as one approached release . . . Lucy's thoughts tumbled in confusion, her heart pounding so hard she vibrated with it.

The woman's breasts joggled with each powerful thrust, the woman giving a joyful yelp with each hard penetration. The man bent over her, reaching for the woman's breasts and massaging them.

Michael's hands flexed, giving Lucy's breasts a light squeeze. She wriggled against him, against his trapped cock, telling him without words that she wanted him to do this to her.

The man gave a hoarse cry, rearing up and plowing even faster into the woman. Beneath him, the woman keened. Lucy thought she must have imagined the liquid dripping from their joined parts. The man bellowed once more and collapsed atop the woman. The two of them slumped onto the dirt floor.

Michael didn't cease his teasing though, his hand sliding down to lie over hers. Lucy panted with need. She'd almost thought she'd come with the woman. Michael's probing finger would set her off and she wanted to come when he was inside her.

Inside the hayloft, the lovers rose, reassembled their clothing and hastened out of the barn, the man smacking the woman on the rear. The woman giggled and hurried toward the farmhouse. The man strode off at an angle.

Michael stood still, once again alert to possible discovery, Lucy quickly realized. She remained motionless, waiting for Michael to relax.

He whispered in her ear. "Let's go inside."

"Inside?" Lucy breathed.

His dark sexy voice sent shivers through her. "I want to bed you in all that hay." He paused. "It doesn't make you sneeze, does it?"

"No more than anyone else," Lucy replied. She caressed his thigh behind her. "Will we . . . will we do what they did?"

He turned her, drawing her in, his hand firmly on her bottom and his trapped cock a thick bulge pressed between their bodies. "You would like that?"

"It was . . . it was very exciting," Lucy confessed in a quiet voice.

"Then follow me." Michael stole along the side of the hayloft, casting off his bright red telltale jacket and turning it inside out.

Hardly breathing for the anticipation, Lucy followed him around the barn and inside the open door. He led her out of sight of the farmhouse, tossing his gun aside. He gathered her in his arms and kissed her passionately, driving her back toward the hay.

His mouth devoured hers, stealing her breath and making her more alive at the same time. Her world constricted to only him: his mouth, his warm body, and his arms holding her. She focused on the throbbing of her groin and his hard cock pressing through his overalls and against her.

She wanted him free, wanted him in her hand, wanted him inside her. She forced her hands between them, reaching for his breech buttons. Michael refused to make things easier for her, grinding his hips against her. She laughed into his mouth, her eyes closing in concentration.

One button flipped free and then another. A third and he popped out of his constriction into her waiting hand. She wrapped her hand about his cock and pumped him, not bothering with gentility because the lovers they'd watched had not been that way.

Michael growled at her, lowering her to the wadded pile of hay. Lucy let go of him to haul her skirts out of the way, presenting an easy path into her quim.

He wasted no time, sliding into her smoothly. He groaned. "My God, you are so wet."

Wrapping her arms around his neck, she asked, "Is that so wrong?"

He shook his head, claiming her mouth with his. He thrust into her wildly, reigniting the excitement Lucy had felt watching the lovers and trebling it. She flexed her hips, meeting each of his thrusts with one of her own. His cock slid in and out of her, each delicious filling followed by a transitory ache. He kept the pace up so fast, she hardly noticed the ache, already straining toward the next joining.

"Oh God," he groaned, "I'm going to explode."

Lucy knew exactly how he felt. When he withdrew, she eagerly fell upon the dirt floor on her hands and knees. Looking over her shoulder, she saw the line of his straight hips and the muscles of his belly. She faced forward, feeling his thighs press against hers, his cock nestled in the crack of her bottom.

His rough hands smoothed over her rounded bottom, separating the buttocks. His cock dipped lower, sliding past her eager opening. He pressed down on her lower back, her hips angling back to meet his.

He toyed with her for a moment, rubbing his cock against her crack. She wriggled against him, wanting him inside her. His cock, now slicked with her wetness, at last nudged against her hole and slid in.

She moaned, the bulk of him filling her. The bulbous head pushed in, its ridges marking her in new ways. Circling her hips, Lucy wanted to have the feel of his cock against every part of her cunt.

Grunting, he grasped her hips, eased out, and slammed back in.

It shocked the breath out of her, a red hot bowshot shooting through her. "Yes!" she gasped.

His grip tightened, his short nails digging into her soft flesh. He thrust into her, deep and hard, again and again. Lucy's delighted staccato cries echoed through the hayloft.

Each hammering thrust was a raw delight, and although she'd experienced the same sensations a dozen times before, it never failed to feel brand new and take her breath away.

Her cunt fluttered about his cock, wanting to hold him,

wanting him to fuck her even harder. The glorious tension rose, higher and higher, until her lungs seemed emptied of air.

All of a sudden, Michael froze, his cock buried deep inside her. She squeezed him with her cunt, gripping him and sucking him in. When he didn't move, she ground her hips against him.

"Still," Michael whispered, placing a spread hand on her lower back.

Lucy didn't want to keep still. She was so close, poised on a crest. Every moment of inaction lessened her chances of reaching release. She moaned in protest.

"Trespassers fuckin' in my barn?" A gruff voice snarled, shadowed with menace.

Twisting to look over her shoulder, through a curtain of her long blond hair she saw a man pointing Michael's rifle at them, not the lover she'd observed earlier. His light brown hair grew long, graying at the temples. Years of hard work had ravaged his brown face, leaving deep creases and not a few missing teeth.

He hawked and spat onto the ground near Lucy. "Now, mister," he said. "Why don't you move out of 'er, nice and slow."

Cold washed over Lucy, feeling Michael's cock slide out of her. "Michael?" she whimpered.

"Hush, lass." She felt the sweet abrasion of his palm over her rear before his warmth left her entirely.

"Don't you move, missy." The hard point of the rifle prodded her buttock. "Patrick, you keep an eye on 'im."

Lucy twisted to look on her other side and saw the male lover, grinning and leering at her, an old flintlock, primed and ready, held in his hand.

Near her, Michael crouched, the flap of his overalls against his thigh. He hadn't bothered to cover himself. "What are you going to do?" he asked, his voice calm and steady.

"Finish what you started."

It took a moment for the words to sink in. "No!" Lucy squealed, scrabbling forward on the dirt floor.

"I said don't move!" The farmer prodded her with the rifle. "Or I'll blow your little cunt to kingdom come." He brayed a laugh.

Lucy stilled, shooting a despairing look at Michael. How could he not act? Why didn't he save her? He was a trained soldier. These men were not.

"How would you like it, missy? To have your lover's rifle stuffed up inside you?"

Lucy's back straightened and she glared over her shoulder, flicking her hair out of the way. "You do not know who you are dealing with."

His eyes widened. "A posh one! Well, it doesn't matter whose gentleman's daughter you are. You're in my barn with a common soldier. Your father knew of that, he'd disown you. There'd be nobody to take you, except me." Missing teeth and blackened gums made his grin hideous. "You're naught but a common whore, missy."

Lucy ducked her head, feeling tears sting her eyes.

"Go on, Pa," grated the other man. "Give 'er a good one and then I'll have a go."

Michael started, but stilled again.

Lucy screwed her eyes shut, beginning to despair of being rescued.

The rifle barrel slid down between her legs. Its hard edge prodded against the lip of her hole. Lucy swallowed a cry of pain, her body stiffening.

The rifle withdrew. The farmer practically purred. "Look at that, son! She's drippin' wet. Ripe for you and me."

He probed her with the rifle barrel, this time the cold metal inching into her cunt.

"You're ruining a perfectly good rifle," Michael remarked, his voice calm and casual.

"Quite right." Lucy heard the smack of steel against flesh.

Glancing at Michael, she saw he lived, and that the farmer's son now held both guns.

The farmer shoved her forward onto the floor. She sprawled, the impact knocking the breath from her for a moment. "On your back, whore," the farmer demanded. "I want to see them titties."

Trying not to sob, Lucy obeyed, moving slow. She closed her eyes. She didn't want to see this. She didn't want to feel this.

The farmer pushed her legs apart. Leaning over until the manure stench of him almost made her gag, he grabbed her breasts, mashing them.

She cried out in pain, tears spilling.

"Such fine titties," the farmer approved. "Now let's taste that juicy little quim of yours."

Lucy swallowed bile. Was he going to lick her with that horrid mouth?

Worse. He lowered his weight onto her and his cock pressed against her thigh. She turned her head, looking away from him and from Michael.

"Get off her now!" Private Jones yelled.

The farmer reared back, giving the startled Lucy a perfect view of Private Jones and three others of Michael's men, pointing their rifles at the farmer and his son.

"It's trespassin'," grumbled the farmer, fastening his rapidly wilting cock into his leather breeches. "I can do what I want."

Lucy scrambled away from him, until a mound of hay at her back stopped her. She fumbled with fixing her bodice.

Michael had also buttoned himself up and had retrieved his rifle. "We'll be leaving. Just be thankful I don't blast off your balls for messing with my woman." His voice, so calm before, now filled with suppressed anger. "Back to the house."

Grumbling, the two farmers quit the field, and Michael stepped forward, thanking his men for the rescue. "What made you come to this barn?"

Private Jones blushed. "We'd caught up some. Saw you and Miss Lucy go into the barn. We were still some distance away, but when we saw those two, we figured you were in trouble."

"*You* figured," said one of the other privates, giving Private Jones a friendly nudge.

Lucy curled up into a ball, hugging her legs against her chest, making sure her skirts covered every part of her. Her senses deadened. Why didn't everyone just go away and leave her alone?

Michael strode toward her, extending a hand.

Lucy shrank back. "No," she sobbed. "Don't touch me."

He halted, shock draining his face. "There was little I could do, lass, without getting one or both of us killed."

She shook her head, burying her face against her knees. He touched her shoulder and she jerked away.

"Lucy, we have to go." Michael's voice burred beside her ear and she heard the frustration and anger in it.

She rose, disdaining any assistance and walked out of the hayloft, head held high. The sunlight warmed her face, but it had no strength against the ice inside.

Lucy walked into the center of a protective circle. Ahead, Michael spoke in a low voice with Private Jones, just out of earshot. They walked through the woods and came out the other side to find that the rest of the group had set up camp for the day.

Private Jones beckoned his wife forward and Jane came running. "Is she all right?" Her gaze went beyond her husband and fastened upon Lucy's face.

Tears welled again and at once Jane was by her side.

"Are you hurt?" Shorter, she cast a reassuring arm about Lucy's waist. Lucy shook her head, wordless. "Let's get you cleaned up. There's a stream nearby." Jane attempted a grin. "I promise not to fall in."

Unable to manage even a smile, Lucy nodded and allowed

her friend to lead her away from the main camp. Sitting her by the stream, Jane wet a cloth and washed the muck from Lucy's face and hands. At Lucy's mute raising of her skirt, she washed her knees and shins as well.

Finished, Jane sat back on her heels. "Lucy, what happened?" she murmured.

Lucy pushed her hair back from her face. She thought of letting it fall back again but worked on twisting her hair into a makeshift knot. All she wanted was for time to roll backward.

"Michael and I were . . . ahh, being intimate, when we were interrupted." A sob broke from her. "They held us at gunpoint, Jane, while they . . . while they . . ." She covered her face with her hands. "Thank God your husband showed up when he did. It might have been worse, far worse."

Jane patted her shoulder. "Then we are even. He saved you as you saved me. Let's go back and have some tea. You've had quite a shock."

Numb, Lucy let Jane take her back to camp and allowed herself to be waited on hand and foot by the young woman. The tea, more adulterated herbs and tasting of dirt, did warm her inside, at least for a while.

Michael approached her, hesitation in every step. He sat beside her, careful not to touch her. "Lucy? It's all over now, lass."

She refused to cringe away from him, but her entire body tensed. "Over for you, perhaps."

"He didn't . . . he didn't . . ." Michael's voice trailed away.

"Penetrate me?" Lucy said harshly. "Not unless you count the rifle, Michael. No, he didn't. But I still feel . . ." How could she describe what she felt? And would he even understand?

Putting down her empty mug, she curled up again, folding her arms about her knees. "I just need to be alone for a little while, Michael."

From the corner of her eye, she saw him curtly nod, rise, and move away.

* * *

They were a day outside London. Michael gave terse orders to make camp, and wandered back down the line to the women. Lucy averted her gaze at once, wrapping a shawl tighter about her shoulders. Jane walked beside her and Michael caught her eye, directing her further back in the line with a sharp nod of his head.

He collected Maggie and they stood on the perimeter of the camp. Lucy sat before the pile of wood soon to become a fire, while everyone else bustled around her.

"I am concerned about Lucy," Michael began without preamble. "She is not herself."

"She was raped," Jane chided softly.

Michael shook his head. "I was there, lass. I won't argue that she wasn't violated in some way but the oaf didn't rape her. He never got the chance."

"But she—" Jane broke off. "She never said, I just assumed . . ."

"Never mind, Jane lass." Michael managed to smile although he didn't feel like it inside. "I just don't understand it. She came to us, fresh from abduction and rape, and she couldn't keep her hands off me."

Maggie's lips twitched. "You're a fine figure of a man, Michael Hall. Who wouldn't feel that way?"

He ignored her teasing. "She won't even let me touch her." He gave breath to his worst fears. "I'm beginning to think she wasn't raped in the first place at all. That what we have in our midst is some rich man's doxy who wants her back."

"That doesn't explain her sister," Jane put in. "You didn't see her, sarge. She looks just like Lucy, almost. Respectable too. That just doesn't fit."

"These high-class courtesans look respectable, Jane. It's possible her sister is also a whore. Perhaps they are both in the employ of this earl."

Jane shuddered. "Lucy doesn't seem like that."

Michael inclined his head. "Once, I would have agreed with you." He knew his cheeks burned. "She's eager, but inexperienced in bed. Not an innocent, mind . . ."

"P'raps she's decided it's not the life for her and did a runner," suggested Maggie, "and she concocted up that story about abduction to get your sympathy."

Michael hardly heard her, nutting out his problem. "She didn't behave like this when I first found her. Oh, she was frightened and crying, but she suggested the best cure for ridding her memories of rape was to lie with me."

Maggie muffled an outburst of laughter. "And you believed her?"

His cheeks turned redder. "I wanted her." He broke eye contact for a moment, casting his gaze back to Lucy.

"Then all you have to do is remind her of it, make the suggestion, and we'll see whether she's telling the truth or not," Maggie suggested. "If it's trouble you've brought among us, sarge, no disrespect but—"

He held her off with an uplifted hand. "Maggie, I know. If she's lying, we'll leave her to make her own way to London. It is not far."

Jane gnawed her lip. "You can't test her like this. We don't know all the circumstances."

"But we should." Now that he'd made a decision to follow Maggie's advice, he resumed the appearance of the efficient sergeant. He delivered a curt bow. "Thank you for your help."

He strode toward the flickering fire, anger and frustration consuming each stride. Two days without her sharing his blanket tore at him. He dropped to the earth next to her.

Lucy gave him a startled look, which became wary.

No doubt his determination was writ all over his face. "Lucy lass, I have recalled something that may help you." His heart almost broke at the eagerness in her face. "I am sorry for what happened, but this helped last time."

"What?" she breathed in a scared little whisper.

"First, let me hold you, so you feel safe again." Gingerly, he draped her arm around her shoulders. She didn't move, but she didn't relax either. "Lucy, rest your head on my shoulder."

A wave of relief washed through him when she did so. He'd missed her warmth more than he thought. "I missed this," he murmured.

"Oh, Michael, I'm so sorry." He couldn't see her face, but her voice sounded full of tears. She almost pulled away from him, but he tightened his grip, just a touch, and she subsided against him.

"Do you remember," Michael began, his voice cajoling and soft, "when you wanted me to bed you that first time?" She stiffened and trembled in his embrace.

"I—I remember," she whispered.

"Let us do that again," Michael continued, keeping his voice calm. He couldn't show his eagerness—for her response or her denial. "You said before it would make you feel better."

This time she pulled out of his embrace, staring at him. "Nothing will make me feel better," she said, looking quite ethereally wild.

His breath caught. "But this time, it wasn't even rape."

Her blue eyes grew rounder. He saw dismay, fear, and anger flit across her transparent expression.

"No. No, I can't." She got to her feet, heading toward the Joneses.

He caught up, grabbing her arm and twisting her around to face him. "It wasn't rape that first time either, was it?" he hissed.

13

Lucy froze. Somehow, Michael had figured it all out. That she had lied to him at the very beginning. For the first time since the incident in the hayloft, the ice cracked and her emotions flowed.

She hadn't cared if Michael never touched her again. Now, in the face of his accusation, she feared to lose him. *I can feel.* Fear squashed her joy of rediscovery.

She tried for a delaying tactic. "You do not believe me?"

"How can I believe you?" Michael snarled. "When you were raped before, you couldn't wait to get into my bed. Now you've been molested and you won't come anywhere near me. I should have known when you never gave me a straight answer to my question. Explain it to me, Lucy. Explain how this can be."

He strained to understand her, Lucy suddenly saw. What to tell him? "The earl was not a stranger to me, like the farmer. He hurt me, but he was not cruel. He forced himself upon me, but he said sweet words, not coarse insults."

She took a deep breath. "I have never been more humiliated in my life."

Michael shook his head, frowning in puzzlement.

Frustration rose in her, choking her. "If you cannot believe that, there is no point in my remaining with you. London is not far." With those words she risked everything, but to tell him the truth would have the same end result. She'd lose him.

She pointed her finger at him. "What is your protection worth now anyway? You did nothing to stop it." A low blow, a killing blow, but her every sense screamed with hurt.

"I couldn't risk getting you killed." With those words, he dragged her away from the fire and from the others.

She let him, seeing his features twisted into some sort of torment. Could they find a way back, to unsay the things they had said?

Concealed by darkness, he stopped, turning so she could make out his face from the distant firelight. "I couldn't risk getting you killed, Lucy." In the dark, he found her hands and clasped them in his. "I admit it, I froze. I don't know if there was a chance for me to save you and for us to get out without getting killed, but I couldn't even stand the thought of you being injured . . ."

"And what that man did . . . ?" Lucy let anger seep into her voice.

"I hated every minute of it, but it kept you alive, and you were not greatly wounded when the earl—"

"I explained that." The anger made her voice sound flat.

She heard his breath huff out. "This is why we can't stay together, Lucy. You were right. I can't protect you because . . . because I care about you too much."

The anger vanished in an instant. It had been largely manufactured, anyway, to protect herself from his truth-seeking. "You—you do?"

"Aye, lass." His hands skimmed up her arms, Michael moving closer to her. "I'll see you safe to London, but there is no future for us."

His words sent a chill through her, and a very real fear. He didn't want her any more? She clawed at the front of his jacket. "Michael . . . Michael, I'm sorry! I didn't mean it when I said you couldn't protect me. You can and you do! You have! I'm sorry for everything!" She sobbed between her words. "I do not wish to lose you! Not yet, I mean."

"Hush, lass, hush." Michael drew her into an embrace, patting her back.

She hugged him back. "I have missed you," she murmured against his chest and through her tears. "I just didn't know how to tell you."

"And I didn't want to face what I'd done," Michael murmured into her hair. "There's nothing I want more than to bed you again, Lucy love, but if you're not ready . . ."

She tilted her head back to look up at him. "Wipe the memories away, Michael. Like you did the last time."

Lucy knew she'd bear the scar of that afternoon in the barn forever, but her healing had to begin now. Her humiliation wasn't worth losing Michael, and she so nearly had.

He tilted his head. "Are you sure?"

"Yes," she breathed. "Right here, Michael. I want it to be just you and me."

They sank onto the grass, already wet with fallen dew. Lucy lay back, drawing Michael down beside her. His fingers feathered across her cheek, followed by the puff of his warm breath, and at the last his mouth.

His lips, cool from the night air, brushed across her mouth. She responded, arching her back to be nearer to him, parting her lips.

His tongue slipped in, a gentle caress. To Lucy's astonishment, it overwhelmed her as much as his previous, more powerful kisses.

She slid her hand along the nape of his neck, not wanting his ardent kiss to end. Warmth seeped from their joined mouths to her frozen heart. Tears gathered at the corners of her eyes and she blinked them back, feeling happiness well inside.

He was hers again.

They exchanged long, lingering kisses for what seemed like an age, Michael apparently content to hold her and kiss her and nothing more.

He shifted, tracing the outline of her bosom so lightly that Lucy thought she might have mistaken it. His tender, reverent touch smoothed over her curves, warming her against the chill of night.

Thumbing over her bosom, he awoke the sexual spark she had thought forever extinguished. She sighed into his mouth, curling her fingers into his hair, unfastening the ribbon that held back his hair.

Michael took his time, caressing and rousing her until she glowed with his tender love. Oh, there was no question about it. Michael loved her. A man who didn't love her would not have frozen at the moment of crisis, would not make love so tenderly.

His mouth slid from hers, kissing her chin before dipping to press kisses against her neck. She tilted her head back, offering that vulnerable place to him, feeling her heartbeat pound in her throat.

Loosening the drawstring of her bodice, he dipped lower, his mouth making a gentle trail along her skin. She felt aware of every part of him, aware in a way she had never been before. Every kiss, every touch, was a reverence, a silent proclamation of the care he felt for her—no, not care, *love*. Although he had not spoken the words, Lucy knew.

She didn't deserve this. She had lied and lied to him, making him believe her, love her. All this would vanish like the morning mist once he knew the truth.

But push him away? Deny him? Loss lay ahead, so why not live in the present? Her arms slipped around his shoulder, drawing him closer.

"I need you," she whispered against the dark falls of his loose hair.

His hand smoothed down over her belly to her upper thigh, and started hitching up her woolen skirt. Her plain petticoat came up with it, baring her legs to the cold night air.

She shivered and he paused. "It's just the cold," she reassured him, stroking his arms through his coat.

Michael shifted position, settling in between her parted legs. Lucy reached down between them and unfastened his overalls. His cock sprang out, warm and hard into her hand. She stroked it, forgetting all her fears.

Bending to kiss her, Michael groaned, his hands clearing a path for entry. He probed her cunt lips, his fingers slipping in with an ease due to her being ready for him. He moaned approvingly in the back of his throat, and Lucy lifted her hips to meet him.

"Please," she whispered, "I want you inside me now."

He needed no further urging, pressing his hard cock against her cunt hole.

She stiffened; she couldn't help it. He sensed it at once, pausing again. Taking a deep breath, Lucy banished the memory of Michael's rifle in her twat and let out a slow, calming breath. "Go on," she whispered.

Michael slid in, slowly pushing his way in, heating her and filling her, so unlike the invasive cold metal that Lucy's quim convulsed around him, hugging him in.

Rocking his hips, Michael slid in and out of her, peppering her face and breasts with kisses. Each move was smooth, liquid, folding into the next seamlessly.

Desire awakened, spreading through her like weed along the

riverbed. She wanted more. She raised her legs, wrapping them around Michael's waist, drawing him in deeper.

He groaned at that, striving harder against her, increasing the pace. His groin rubbed against her swollen clit, and she moaned, writhing against him with the need to have him touch her there again and again.

The familiar tension built inside her, rushing water heading toward tumultuous falls. She soared off the edge, crying out and twisting beneath him, her quim grabbing on to him as her only anchor, never wanting the sweet release to end.

Above her, Michael grunted, his hips spasming, his own climax joining with hers.

He rested upon her for a moment, his sweaty forehead smearing her cheek. "Ah lass, that was sweet." His cock slipped from her and he rolled to one side, twitching down her skirts.

Lucy agreed. "Thank you, Michael." Tears rose again in her eyes. He had done everything for her. Everything. And what had she done for him?

"Lass, there's no need to cry." His knuckle brushed away a wet trail on her cheek.

She sniffed. "I am happy, Michael, truly."

"And I, lass." He bent over her and stole a quick kiss. "I'll cherish your memory always."

"Michael . . ." She had no words to say. She didn't want them to part, but she had lost the right to insist on staying. She exhaled a slow breath. "May I still come to Dover with you?"

"Would London not be better?"

"I want every moment we can have together. Every moment. Surely you cannot begrudge me that?"

He caressed her cheek and kissed her again. "To Dover, then." His lips founds hers and this time the kiss lasted for a long time.

London, one day later.

After much discussion, Caroline and Alex agreed to time their arrival in London for the early morning, when fewer of the *beau monde* would be abroad and comment on the earl's return to the city.

They stopped first at Caroline's aunt's. Caroline glanced aside at Alex. He'd abandoned the bandages for good, a light red scar remaining on his temple.

With trembling fingers, Caroline lifted the hood over her head. If someone noticed them, she wanted them to think of her as Lucy, returned to her aunt in a married state. The last thing the Waverton reputation needed was a fresh scandal.

Alex helped her out of the carriage, his expression unusually wooden. Caroline wondered what he thought. Did he fear facing her aunt as she did?

Her aunt's butler anticipated them, opening the door and ushering them into the atrium. He bowed. "My lady is not yet out of bed," he murmured.

"We will wait on her there," Caroline assured him.

He bowed again and vanished upstairs. They cooled their heels while they were announced.

Caroline tossed back the hood of her cloak. "Don't worry," she murmured. "She won't bite your head completely off."

Alex grimaced and said nothing.

The butler reappeared, beckoning them forward. He made them wait again while he entered Caroline's aunt's bedchamber. From within, Caroline's aunt's voice rose. "It's not Miss Waverton it's Lady Radbourne!"

The butler's response went unheard. Alex's worried frown deepened. The butler hastily ushered them in before they exchanged any soothing words. At once, they separated, unwilling to appear as a couple to her aunt.

Caroline's aunt sat up in bed, bolstered by a profusion of cushions, her magnificent décolletage covered by a riot of lace. To her credit, the woman didn't faint on seeing Caroline instead of Lucy, despite the fact she already lay down.

"Caroline," her aunt murmured. "This is a surprise."

Caroline bobbed a respectful curtsey. "Ma'am. I take it my sister has not yet arrived."

"She has not." The older woman, her hair quite white, stiffened in outrage. "And what are you doing associating with *that man?*"

"Lucy ran away—" Alex attempted.

"I heard. Shameful that she elope with you, sir, and then have the gall to run away." Caroline's aunt picked up her lorgnette and surveyed him through the round eyepiece. "Although perhaps she recovered her taste."

"Aunt!" Caroline exclaimed. "Lord Radbourne is still willing to marry Lucy. We have been looking for her."

"And you, miss." Caroline's aunt pointed at her with her lorgnette. "Where is your chaperone? What on earth were you thinking, gallivanting about the countryside with *that man?* You have yet to answer me."

"I thought a sister's persuasion might help Lucy to see reason." She paused. "Have the gossips associated me with Radbourne?"

"No, you're fortunate, thank the heavens. Our family prides itself on our respectability, I'll have you know, sir." Caroline's aunt settled back against her pillows. "Unless someone saw you enter—"

"If they did, they would mistake me for Lucy," Caroline put in. "Who else would be with the earl? It would be assumed he had finally captured her."

"That's a lot of assumptions," Caroline's aunt said dryly. "And you, sir. What do you have to say for yourself? Ruining both my nieces?"

To his credit, he didn't color. Caroline hoped the warmth on her cheeks would be taken for embarrassment.

Alex stood stiffly to attention. "Madam, I assure you I have done everything in my power to amend my errors and right this unfortunate scandal."

"Errors?" Caroline's aunt regarded him through her lorgnette.

"Aunt, we need your help," Caroline hastily interjected. "Worse has befallen Lucy and we need to save her."

"Worse?" The old lady's voice trembled. "To little Lucy?"

"She has fallen in with a group of soldiers." Alex spoke in his calmest, most reassuring tones. Caroline saw how easily he'd cajoled Lucy to marry him. Even if she had changed her mind. "From what we have heard, she has formed an attachment to one of them."

Caroline's aunt's eyes narrowed. "This is all your fault, sir."

He gave a short bow of acknowledgment. "And one I am trying to rectify."

"We think she might skirt London and go straight on to Dover if she is truly infatuated with this man," Caroline put in, wanting to relieve Alex of her aunt's fury.

Caroline's aunt nodded. "If she has any sense, she'd know the trouble she's in and come straight home." She sighed. "Alas, she is not the wisest of souls."

"You knew this, and yet you let her gamble?" Alex's ire rose, visible in his clenched fists and stiff posture.

"The child gambled?" Caroline's aunt affected surprise. "I had no idea."

"She was paying a debt to me, not eloping with me as the gossip has it."

"With her body, sir?"

Alex shook his head. "No, of course not. I wanted merely to scare her . . ." He trailed off, his gaze going across the room to Caroline.

She offered him a sympathetic smile, burying it when her aunt turned her way. "I do not blame you, aunt," she said. "Lucy was ever a handful with me in Durham. I had hoped she'd settled."

"It appears not." Her aunt folded her hands. "Sit, the two of you. You're no longer under interrogation. Caroline, do ring for tea. Now," she said, while Caroline did her bidding, sitting on a narrow chair next to her bed and Alex sitting stiffly on the edge of a sofa chair across the room, "what do you plan to do about it?"

"Recover Lucy first," Alex said, ticking off the plan on his fingers. "Persuade her to marry me, with your help, madam. If she doesn't come to London, Caroline and I will continue on to Dover and find her before she catches some officer's eye."

"I shall come as your chaperone," Caroline's aunt declared.

Caroline started. "Oh, we could not discommode you. I am sure that if I find her, I can convince her of the right thing. Besides, what will people say if they saw you driving off with us to Dover? That you were packing us off to the Continent?"

"Don't talk such nonsense, girl," Caroline's aunt reproved. "Honestly, I thought you were the sensible one of the pair, but perhaps you have not learned from the mistake of your salad days."

"Mistake?" queried Alex, shooting Caroline a contemplative look.

"Some little indiscretion within the household," said Caroline's aunt, passing it off as of no great consequence. "An isolated incident."

Caroline gazed at the dark floral rug at her feet. It had not been an isolated incident. She pushed the memory from her mind. She turned to her aunt, avoiding Alex's inquisitive gaze. "Very well, aunt. Of course you must come. I shall have to continue my masquerade as Lucy, alas."

At last she lifted her gaze to Alex's. "Could you send a man ahead to Dover to secure us all rooms? Just in case Lucy doesn't return to us of her own free will."

"You think she's being coerced by this common creature?" blurted Caroline's aunt.

"Surely not," Caroline murmured, patting the older woman's hand. "I meant that she might want to stay with her soldier."

Her aunt clucked in disapproval.

"As for Dover," Alex said, "I cannot promise much in the way of accommodations. If there are troops preparing to embark for the Continent, it will be a squeeze, and the town does not have much in the way of fine establishments."

"Are you trying to get me to change my mind, young man?" Caroline's aunt asked archly.

"I am merely making you aware, madam." Alex conceded the point.

"If you need me to persuade her, then I shall attend. Especially as Caroline seems to lack the sense to procure even a maid for a chaperone."

Caroline flushed. "Aunt, I did not expect to be so long on the road."

"You packed for it."

Caroline sucked in her breath. "Aunt, my actions are of no consequence. May we focus on my sister for just a little while?"

"None of your cheek, my girl." Caroline's aunt looked down her nose at her. "Does your father know?"

Caroline met her aunt's gaze directly. "He is off hunting."

"I thought he was ill," blurted Alex.

"He has the hunting sickness," Caroline's aunt remarked drily. "Although I am quite sure that's not what Caroline meant." She turned her attention back to Caroline. "You hope to have the matter entirely cleared up before he hears about it?"

"I hope to. Unless the gossip reaches Melton Mowbray, which I fear it might for we encountered it on the road. But if the matter is resolved by the time he finds us . . ." Caroline let her voice trail away. She'd rather take her father's punishment than have it inflicted upon her little sister.

"Very well," her aunt concurred. "I shall have a chamber made ready for you."

"It is unfortunate," Alex agreed, "but I am afraid that I must intrude further upon Miss Waverton's good graces."

"Explain yourself," her aunt snapped.

"By now, someone will have spotted my carriage outside this house and assume I have come to gain your blessing for marrying Lucy." Alex gave an apologetic shrug. "If there is not a blond Waverton seen arriving at my townhouse, noses will start sniffing for a new turn in the gossip."

Caroline's aunt frowned. "Is this necessary?"

Alex turned his palms face up, spreading his hands. "*My* reputation can handle the scandal . . ."

"I will send a maid with you." Her aunt glared at Caroline, a silent look that demanded answers to questions Caroline hoped she wouldn't ask.

"Thank you, aunt." Caroline inclined her head. "It will only be for a day or two until either Lucy arrives or we ascertain she's skirted the city and headed for Dover instead."

"And then you will further leave yourself open to disgrace," her aunt mused. "I cannot say I am happy about this, but it seems we must take a small risk to save our family's reputation."

"Precisely," Alex agreed with a perfectly straight face. He rose and bowed. "Now, if there is not anything else, I think we should be on our way. There is much to organize. I need to obtain a special license, among other things." He gestured to his borrowed coat, apparently unaware of the sinking feeling in Caroline's stomach. That special marriage license would not be for her. "I long for my own clothing."

Caroline rose also, dipping a respectful curtsey. "Thank you for helping us, aunt. I hope that it may never be needed and Lucy will swiftly see sense."

"As do I, my girl." She waved them off. "Unless you care to stay for breakfast."

Her stomach rumbling, Caroline declined, afraid that her aunt might change her mind and make her stay.

She and Alex fled the bedchamber, making their way out of the Waverton house with alacrity. They hastened into Alex's carriage and he gave orders for them to drive to his townhouse.

"Alex, what possessed you?" Caroline blurted, unable to believe he'd cajoled her aunt to have her stay with him.

He glanced aside at her, a seemingly casual look, but Caroline had spent enough time with him now not to be fooled. Her comment had hurt him. "You do not have to stay with me if you do not wish to."

Caroline nibbled on her lower lip. She ought to refuse his offer and retreat behind her scaffold of respectability, but she also wanted to spend as much time as possible with him before he married Lucy. It was very, very wrong of her, but she couldn't help herself.

"I am sure I will survive," she replied, her voice nonchalant, wondering if this fooled him as little as he'd fooled her.

"Will you?" His question seemed not directed at her immediate stay, but beyond. Caroline chose not to answer it.

His townhouse stood close to her aunt's. Once again, Caroline concealed her head with a hood, letting just a sliver of her blond hair show.

From the corner of her eye, Caroline thought she saw curtains twitch. The neighbors were awake and watching—unless Radbourne's house encompassed more of the block than normal and his servants were taking a look at their new mistress.

The butler ushered them inside. Along the side of the staircase, the last of his staff fell into line. Alex's grip tightened on her elbow and he led her forward.

The housekeeper bobbed into a deep curtsey, followed in succession by the other maids. None of them, she noted, seemed to be under the age of forty, which indicated, at least, that Alex didn't care to poach sexual favors from his own staff.

"My lady," said the housekeeper. "Welcome to your new home."

Caroline shot a glance at Alex. His thinned lips warned her to silence.

"It is very kind of you, Mrs. Bell," he interposed. "We plan to stay a few days only. Is the adjoining bedchamber prepared?"

"If you will give us half an hour," the housekeeper replied. "Perhaps once you have broken your fast?"

He nodded, smiling. "Excellent." He steered Caroline toward another door, revealing a small but pretty dining room. He pulled back a chair for her and took a seat beside her.

"Alex," Caroline confirmed, "they think we are married!"

"It will serve," he returned in an equally low voice. "Servants gossip too."

Caroline didn't like it, but she saw the wisdom of his decision. She managed a strained smile as the first of the breakfast dishes arrived.

He grinned at her, a sudden lightening of his features that made her breath catch. "They will expect the marriage bed to be shared tonight." He winked. "I think we should do our best not to let them down."

Her mind reeling, Caroline sipped the freshly poured tea. "Alex, but think how they'll feel when they meet the real countess? Won't they feel duped?"

"There's no need to worry about them." Alex got out between bites of bacon. "I do not plan to return here once we retrieve Lucy. A few years away, they may well have forgotten exactly what you looked like."

"But—" At his quizzical eyebrow, Caroline let her protest go, nibbling on a slice of toast instead. Alex led her down a wild path, so very wrong and yet she felt inexorably drawn toward it. Soon, very soon, she would have to walk away and act as if nothing had happened between them. "I think I will rest. I am sure you have much to do."

"I'll order a bath drawn for you. It will be nice to remove this travel dirt."

With that, he kissed her, a soul-searing kiss that sealed her fate, and strode from the dining room.

14

With Alex busy in his study, marshaling and dispatching his troops, Caroline, bathed and dressed in only a clean shift and her stays, tried to rest.

Her mind wouldn't let her. It buzzed with all the "what ifs" of this disastrous affair. Would Lucy even speak to her again if she found out? Why did Alex refuse to let her slip out of his life even for one night?

Unsettled, she slid out of bed, pulling on a sheer peignoir over her stays and shift. She left her chamber, sparing only a glance at the door that connected her room to his via a small closet.

Not wanting to be seen, she kept to the upper floor, strolling along the hallway and observing the artwork, mostly of horses and dogs. She didn't expect any servants to approach her, let alone be spotted, but she feared dealing with the housekeeper. That was Lucy's responsibility, not hers.

Caroline started down another hallway, wondering if she ought to dare and descend a level. This part of the hall held the family portraits, or at least, Caroline guessed them as that, considering the family resemblance some of them had to Alex.

A throat cleared.

She turned. A tall, dark-haired man in plain brown livery stood toward the end of the hall. Her breath caught.

"It *is* you," he said, striding toward her and catching her hands. She allowed his familiar behavior, not usual with a servant, because when had she not?

"Luke," she breathed. "I had wondered . . ."

He grinned at her, his swarthy skin showing he now spent much of his time outside. "You are as radiant and as beautiful as always, my lady."

Caroline glanced beyond him and then back over her shoulder.

"You are right," he said, gripping her hands a little tighter. "We must not be seen." He opened a nearby door and practically dragged her into the room.

She barely had time to register the room as a small guest bedroom before Luke was upon her, catching her up in his arms and kissing her.

She squirmed free. "No, Luke. We cannot."

He frowned. "You have forgotten our friendship so fast?"

"You know I have not." Caroline tugged the neck of her peignoir closer about her, arms folding over her breasts. "But time has passed. It's different now."

"Because you're married to *him*." Luke's lip curled.

Caroline stared at him. Could she trust him enough to tell him the truth? He'd sounded angry. "Last time, it got you fired."

He grimaced ruefully. "You'll give me a good reference again."

She shook her head. "What we had is in the past. You must leave it there." She hated that her voice sounded so pleading.

His eyes narrowed. "You're in love with him."

Her lips compressed and she lifted her chin. "I'm being well satisfied," she declared archly. "I am glad to see you are well, Luke, but we cannot—"

He huffed. "I put up with your high and mighty manners to get a taste of you." Caroline gasped, hand lifting to her mouth in shock. He hadn't cared about her? "But you'll do as I say, or I'll go to that new husband of yours and tell him what a slut you are."

Caroline's lips inadvertently twitched. Alex knew that already. She foresaw trouble if Alex found out about this former, low liaison. "You must not."

Luke grabbed her shoulder, his grip pinching her. "Then you will go on your knees and beg me, bitch." His bruising grip forced her down—anything to stop the excruciating pain. With one hand, he unfastened his breeches. His cock sprang free.

Caroline gazed up at him, tears in her eyes. "You cannot make me."

"I've always wanted to do this—to make you pay for the humiliating positions you forced me to assume." He released her only to grab her blond hair, close to the roots, pulling her head back. She whimpered, fresh tears springing forth. "It's your price for my silence."

Her gaze fell on his cock right in front of her face, hard and red. He jerked her toward it. How had she ever loved him? Ever wanted this? She tried to turn her head away, but a savage jerk reined her in.

"The hell with your silence," she murmured, anger and fright at war with each other inside her. "You're fired."

He laughed, a chilling bellow that had Caroline twisting toward the door, in fear of being overheard. Luke's grip held her in place.

"Fire me after," Luke snarled. "You owe me this. I suffered for you, now it's your turn."

He shoved her head forward, her compressed lips sliding off

the head of his cock. She braced herself against his thighs, try-ing to push herself away, but trapped by the terrible grip on her hair.

"What a pretty picture," Alex drawled from behind her.

Luke's grasp loosened and Caroline pushed herself away, sprawling backwards.

"Alex," she gasped, turning to him and hoping he read the picture of her tears aright.

"Oh, don't let me interrupt." He leaned against the jamb of the door.

"It's not what you think!" Caroline protested, still back-pedaling from Luke.

Luke's dark eyes flamed. "It's exactly what you think, m'lord. Your wife is a slut and demanded she satisfy me. What red-blooded man would refuse?"

"Liar!" shrieked Caroline, struggling to her feet. "Alex, he's lying."

"And is it also a lie that we were lovers before this happy re-union?"

Caroline quivered to a standstill, struggling to breathe. "I would not say the reunion is happy," she whispered.

"Enough." Alex strode forward, interpolating himself be-tween Luke and Caroline. "You are fired. You'll get a good ref-erence so long as you keep your mouth shut. Pack your things and get out."

Luke's bravado crumbled and he left without a further word.

Caroline staggered to the narrow guest bed and sat, forehead resting against the bedpost. "Thank you," she whispered, her voice hoarse with her tears.

"Don't be so quick to thank me."

She looked up at him, to see him standing before her, arms folded. His fair face purpled with anger.

"Is it true? You were lovers? And how many other footmen have you bedded?"

"Just the one," Caroline admitted, tired beyond words, her shoulders slumping. "I thought he loved me, naïve little idiot I was. He just wanted to get a leg over the mistress." She lifted trembling fingers to her lips, staring at the open door. "Why did I not see that before?"

Alex crouched down before her. "Caro, look at me."

Reluctantly, she faced him. She didn't want to see his condemnation, his disgust. "You must despise me now."

"On the contrary . . ." His voice trailed off, a fierce look of concentration on his face. He sat beside her, close but not quite touching her. "When I first saw you on your knees before that man, I admit it, I felt betrayed and angry. When I saw you were resisting, I wanted to knock the man's block off . . ."

He took a deep breath. "I swear, Caroline, I will never ever do violence like that toward you. Never."

Startled, she blinked away the tears. "Never is a long time, Alex," she murmured.

"I know," he whispered. He leaned in and kissed her salty lips. He kissed the tip of her nose, just as she curled her arms about his neck, and fixed her with his intense blue eyes. "I mean it."

She sought out his mouth with hers, not wanting to hear more, not daring to say more herself. Problems abounded with his vow and she didn't want to think about any of them.

Alex responded to her kiss with a soft groan, enfolding her in a tight hug. His lips pressed against hers, coaxing them apart. His warmth seeped into her chilled skin. Caroline hadn't even realized how cold she'd become until he held her. She held him tight, relieved that this crisis had passed, relishing his heat.

He drew her down to lie with him on the narrow bed, his hand sweeping along her curves. "I do not think I can wait until this evening," he whispered, nuzzling her neck.

Caroline squirmed against him, hooking her leg over his thigh. "Me either."

Slowly, he drew down the filmy peignoir from her shoulder, baring the thin strap of her shift and stays. He placed long kisses against the revealed flesh, each kiss building the warmth within her.

She had not expected such tenderness. She held him loosely in her arms, her fingertips brushing over his short blond hair, content to bask in his attention.

Bending down to kiss the tops of her breasts, he stroked her through the stays, his tongue darting beneath the concealing cotton. Almost by accident, the tip of his tongue flicked over a nipple and Caroline gasped, instantly transported to another level of heat.

"Alex," she moaned. No longer content to be loved, she clutched at him, wanting him closer, the new fire demanding much more than gentle loving.

Rearing back, he removed his coat and his shirt, unfastening the buttons on his pantaloons. His cock freed, it rose straight from its nest of dark golden curls. Caroline took the opportunity to slip off her translucent peignoir and work on loosening her stays, a garment she had not worn since leaving her home. She felt Alex's gaze upon her and struggled with the stay's cord, her arms behind her back.

"That's a very fetching picture you make, Miss Caroline," Alex almost growled, idly stroking his cock. "Like a captive princess."

She grimaced at him. "These damn stays!"

He smiled, a slow, sexy smile that should have made her stays melt off her. "I second that motion, my dear. Why are you wearing them now?"

Caroline regarded him with muted horror. "I can't not wear them! Did you not notice that my dresses fit terribly?"

He brushed away her protests with a wave. "Not really. Now what are we to do about them, before I perish here?"

Her gaze dropped to his cock, the head a dark red, almost purple. She licked her lips. "My stays do not cover where your cock belongs."

She wriggled on the narrow bed, hitching her shift up over her hips, revealing her creamy white thighs and her quim, still concealed by her golden curls. Her hand dropped as if to cover herself, but she pulled her cunt lips apart, revealing the glistening flesh between.

Her middle finger traversed the length of her cunt, gathering her juices and circling her clit, a light teasing that made her catch her breath.

She heard his breath hitch also. He leaned over her, shifting to kneel between her spread knees. He captured her lips in a savage kiss that absorbed her breath. Their mouths fused, their tongues tangling, and Caroline folded her legs behind him and over his calves, drawing him even closer.

In the next breath, she was on her back, Alex's weight upon her and her head poised over the edge of the bed. She gripped the back of his neck, clinging to him, continuing their deep kiss. He supported her neck, ravishing her mouth more thoroughly.

His cock pressed against her wet quim, pushed between her hairy lips, and probed the entrance of her cunt hole. Hardly able to breathe with the anticipation, waiting for Alex to plunge inside her, Caroline bit down on his lower lip.

She released him. He kissed her hard, his tongue plunging deep into her mouth, and she tasted his blood. His cock breached her, driving all the way in with one swift thrust.

Caroline groaned her joy into his mouth. This is what she had yearned for, this is what she wanted. Him inside her, joined to her. She kicked her heels against his buttocks, wanting the feel of his balls against her.

Alex obliged, cradling her shoulders to affect deeper penetration. Caroline tilted her hips upward, her cunt clutching at him, her head falling off the side of the bed.

Hoisting her legs higher, Alex kneeled, pulling her onto his cock and fucking her with short, hard thrusts. For a long moment, Caroline watched the flex and release of his muscles, the golden planes of his muscled chest, his biceps bulging from holding her in place.

Caroline let herself go, powerful heat washing through her, draining into her cunt and into her dangling head. Her gaze swam, blurring, and she shut her eyes against the dizzying sight. She gasped for air, each thrust driving the precious air from her lungs.

Each of Alex's thrusts struck a certain part of her cunt's tunnel, sparking sharp delight. He let go of one leg to thumb her clit, driving her to an even higher plane of ecstasy. Her entire body thrummed with it, an endless ride on the crest of release. It felt like she had found release, she'd had experience enough to recognize the sensation. Yet it didn't end and promised more, so much more.

It hit her, a blow that drove the last of the air from her lungs in an astonished scream. Her entire body tensed against the sexual overload and then thrashed, her body undulating under Alex's persistent fucking.

Dimly, she heard him groan, but it faded away into darkness and sweet oblivion.

When she woke, she found herself lying along the length of the bed, cuddled in Alex's arms. She blinked up at him, still breathless. "My God," she gasped.

His face filled with relief. He traced her jaw. "You were not unconscious long."

"I—I lost consciousness?" She gaped up at him.

He claimed that open mouth with a kiss. She kissed him

back, flicking her tongue over the wound she'd inflicted on his lower lip. He drew away, a reluctant frown shadowing his face. "It was powerful for me also."

She smirked up at him. "How powerful?"

"Well, I think the servants thought we were killing each other. You missed that embarrassing moment."

Fresh heat washed over her cheeks. Her parts still throbbed and echoed with the power of her release. "Oh dear."

"It was supreme," he continued, winking at her in acknowledgment that he'd seen her blush. "You came and compressed my cock until I thought I would die, but I couldn't stop fucking you. I wanted to explode into you, but couldn't and then, oh my God, Caro, you came again with such force."

She blushed again at the wonder in his face. She traced his cheek, his chin, his lips with her fingertips, wanting to remember him like this. Open, vulnerable, and still aroused.

"I can't describe it, but I don't think I've given up so much jism in one go in my life."

Caroline raised a blond eyebrow. "Impressive."

He grinned back. "I thought so. Indeed, I fear I have nothing left to satisfy you with tonight."

She laughed at that, feeling a lightness of heart she shouldn't feel, but giving in to the delight she'd shared with him. "I am sure you will be restored by the time we retire for the evening."

"I want to retire right now," he murmured, bending forward to nibble at her ear. "Let the rest of the world go to hell."

It sounded nice and for once, Caroline was too deliriously happy to raise her objections. When his mouth closed once more over hers, she felt sure she'd done the right thing.

"What do you mean she's staying with us?" Maggie shrieked, arms folded. Lucy turned away from the altercation. They'd reached the outskirts of London and the argument ranged between leaving her at the gates and skirting the City until they reached Watling Street, or just going through the City and dropping her off at her home.

That she remained with them had somehow made matters worse. She turned back, Maggie's dire warnings of arrest and death washing over her.

"Nobody will look for me among you," Lucy said. "I am not dressed as I was and I haven't bathed. Nobody will give me a second glance."

"Except your sister knew you were traveling with us."

"We did our best to throw her off the scent," put in Jane Jones, clutching her husband's arm.

"She may still be clinging to that straw," Maggie shot back. "They may be looking for us."

"We can't travel separately." Michael looked ferocious, ready to tear Maggie into pieces for challenging his command. "If what you say is true, they'll still be looking for a sergeant and a blond woman."

Lucy pulled the shawl from her shoulders and draped it over her head, clutching it under her chin. "What blond woman?"

"We go around," Michael declared. "I will have no more talk on the matter. We stick together and we don't stop until London is behind us. Is that clear?"

Maggie grumbled something under her breath but with a nudge from her bulky husband, nodded her assent.

"Right." Somehow, Michael seemed larger, stronger. "We've wasted enough time. Let's go."

He led them away from the city gate, skirting the city that had long ago overspilled its walls. The women followed in a tight bunch, the other soldiers guarding them from all sides.

Few dared to come within the reach of the rifles, even though the bayonets remained unfixed. Not even the unruly denizens of London's underworld crept out from the shadows and tested them.

At length, they moved into the city, needing to cross the

Thames via one of the bridges. Lucy hunched her shoulders, turning to Jane to make sure not one curl of her hair, dulled by the dirt of travel, was visible.

Night had fallen by the time they passed the bulk of London. Michael called to make camp on the edge of Hampstead Heath. "It would be foolish to travel further. The heath is full of thieves. A double watch tonight."

Lucy helped the women prepare the evening meal and boiled the tea. She thought the danger Maggie had prophesied would isolate her further, but Jane's acceptance of her had softened the other women toward her. All except Maggie, that is.

At last, serving everyone else brimming tin mugs of weak tea, Lucy settled next to Michael, handing him a cup. She sipped the liquid—she'd hardly call it tea—feeling it warm her insides. She inhaled the steam appreciatively.

"You've changed," Michael remarked, his cup balanced between his hands.

She glanced aside at him, her shawl slipping back slightly. Having made camp, she didn't feel quite so vulnerable and let it slide off. "I have?"

"I remember you turning your nose up at the tea once."

She grimaced at her cup. "Believe me, you haven't had real tea, but this is hot at least."

His severe face broke into a smile, making him look boyish. "You make a good cup."

Her eyes narrowed. "You haven't touched it yet."

Michael obediently took a sip and swallowed. "It is good, Lucy. I never expected you to take to this life."

"Neither did I," Lucy replied, "but it is not so bad. I won't lie to you and say I don't miss the luxuries of my old life; I do."

"You'll be going back to that soon enough." Michael stared into the black hole of his tin mug. "But I am glad you're making the effort."

"The scandal will not allow me to my former life, unless I

am in some way fortunate. It will be a much simpler living."
She smiled. "This is a good primer for me."

His gaze softened but he didn't return her smile. "I wish I
could spare you from that and—" His gesturing arm took in
the entire camp—"this."

The smile vanished from her face. "Take me to the Peninsula
with you."

He frowned. "I've explained—"

She touched his knee. "I know. I'm sorry. I should not have
brought it up again. But it is nice to dream."

His eyes, made dark by night, narrowed. "It's dangerous to
dream."

Lucy slipped her arm into his. She didn't want to argue with
him. "No more will be said about it." She squeezed his arm and
moved away. "I must help with serving the evening meal."

Midway through helping Maggie, she noticed Michael rise
and go to sit with some other men, deep in conversation. He
took a heaped plate from her without comment, the conversation pausing until she had moved on.

Frowning, Lucy rejoined the women gathered closer to the
fire. She nudged Jane. "What are they talking about?"

Jane shrugged. "I have no idea."

"Jane wouldn't know, she's a first timer." Maggie paused to
scoop a mouthful of stew into her mouth.

The two women turned to her with querying expressions.

"There's highwaymen, not shy in harassing the King's men,
especially those who have womenfolk along. He'll also be
talkin' to them about leavin' us behind. Remindin' them what
he told them back home."

Lucy frowned. "Do you stay in Dover?"

Maggie bellowed. "No! The parish turns us out as soon as
the men are gone. We have to make our own way back home,
without the men."

Lucy sucked in her breath. Without the men's protection

and their ability to snag additional game, the women had a difficult journey home. "Why did you come then? Wouldn't it be
easier to stay at home?"

Jane sighed. "And miss a moment of living with my husband, and the chance of going with him overseas? I'd rather be
with him than be apart."

Lucy couldn't argue with that. She hugged Jane's shoulders.
"I'm sure you'll be able to go."

"You don't know anything, do you?" sneered Maggie. "Did
the sarge not tell you about the lottery?"

"He did," replied Lucy, stung. "What is wrong with hoping
Jane gets to go?"

"What about the rest of us?" Maggie demanded, hands on
hips.

Rendered speechless, Lucy released Jane and stumbled back.
"I—I didn't mean . . ."

She turned, abandoning the fire. Her warm cheeks cooled in
the night air, but she still felt too embarrassed to return. She
didn't dare go too far. Maggie's warnings of highwaymen and
thieves kept her close to the camp. So long as she was away
from that horrid Maggie.

At last, she returned to her own blanket, finding Michael
still with the other men. She'd gotten used to the days of long
walking and late nights filled with lovemaking, but without
Michael around, she rapidly tired. Rolling herself into her blanket, she fell asleep.

Sometime later, she woke from a pleasant dream involving
Michael to the touch of a fire-warmed hand on her thigh. She
froze. Had the farmers tracked them down and . . . ?

A scream fought to rise in her throat. *It couldn't be! Think
rationally!* She sucked in air . . . and inhaled a familiar scent.

Michael. She fought to hide the small smile of relief and relaxed under his touch. His lips brushed against her cheek, so
lightly she thought she might have imagined it.

His warmth no longer hovered over her. His hand lay against her thigh. Somehow he'd peeled back both her blanket and lifted her skirt to bare her legs.

She slitted her eyes, the light of the dying fire a rosy red against her eyelids. It had to be late, nobody else about the fire stirred at all. She closed her eyes again. This was their own private world.

Michael's palm slid up her thigh, up under the hem of her skirt. His thick fingers fanned out over the tops of her thighs, the tips tickling her nether curls.

Lucy held her breath at his slow inching toward her quim. She should relax, make believe she still slept and that Michael seduced her unaware body. It reminded her of their first time, but she wouldn't let him end it too soon this time.

He cupped her quim, and Lucy realized he lay alongside her. But more importantly, his finger feathered down through her curls, finding the top of her slit. He pressed down, not penetrating to reach her clit, but exerting pressure to wake her desire.

He succeeded; from that one point, fire spread along the lips of her quim, reaching her cunt hole and starting a well of moisture rising up from within.

Michael pressed harder, the blunt tip of his finger breaching her crack. He found the swelling tip of her clit, circled it, eased the pressure and circled it again.

She wanted to moan, she wanted even to sigh, but to do either would break the spell that she slept. It appealed to her, this seduction without her permission. If it had not been so gentle, she may have thought otherwise.

Giving her throbbing clit one last flick, Michael slid past that eager nub of flesh, digging deeper between her nether lips. He reached her cunt hole, circling the taut entry. Lucy whimpered, wanting his fingers inside her, but Michael froze.

She'd given herself away as being awake. She sighed again

and shifted her limbs, pretending to seek a more comfortable sleeping position. Her legs just happened to end farther apart, giving easier access to Michael.

He rewarded her by dipping his finger into her cunt, up to the first knuckle. Lucy wanted more, much more, but had to pretend indifference. No more moaning. Not even lifting her hips. She would resist the temptation to move. It made each of Michael's caresses much more precious.

While his finger plunged in deeper, Michael's thumb located her clit and stroked it into fuller life. Lucy's parts throbbed with Michael's persuasive touch. Desire flooded her senses, overwhelming her need to maintain the façade of sleep.

All her good intentions went for naught. She moaned again, her hips shifting beneath his hand. He didn't stop this time, a second finger joining the first in palpitating her smooth tunnel.

Lucy flung the blanket from her, twisting her upper body toward Michael. His mouth covered hers, his hand still covering her quim. She welcomed his kiss hungrily, giving up all pretense. She clawed at his coat, almost ripping the buttons off in her effort to reach his bare skin.

He chuckled under his breath, unfastening his coat and his overalls before she could do any further damage to his uniform. Eagerly, she slid her hands under the rough canvas material and pulled his shirt free of his loosened pants.

The first contact of her hand to his skin sent a thrill through her, no matter how many times she touched him. He was warm to the touch, despite the cold night.

The night air seemed to have no effect on her. She burned for him. His skin felt soft under her touch—that is, until she pressed down to feel the ripple of muscle beneath. She loved the apparent softness of his body compared to his rough hands and hard cock.

Michael rolled atop her. Her hands slid higher up his back. His cock nudged her thigh and then slid forward, into place.

She wanted him deep inside her. Now. She slid her hands down to his buttocks, squeezing the cheeks. His butt flexed and he swooped inside her.

She cried out, muffling it against the bulky shoulder of his coat. His cock filled her, satisfied her. Until he started to move within her, reminding her there was more than the significant bliss of having him inside her.

His thrusting enflamed her further and she locked her legs around his hips. Meeting each thrust with one of her own, Lucy urged Michael on: harder, faster, more.

He nuzzled her neck, his panting breath hot against her sensitive skin. The ground felt hard and lumpy against her back, but Lucy didn't care. Her need for him swelled over the minor complaints of her back, filling her to overflowing with her approaching release.

Despite her long straining toward it, her release hit her without warning, an ecstatic overflow sweeping against Michael, and into him. He stiffened above her, groaning low, joining her in her coming.

Lost in him, Lucy sensed him there with her, caught in the swirling explosion.

15

Some hours after their fresh understanding, Caroline and Alex had adjourned to his bedroom. Twenty-four hours later, they remained abed. Caroline ached all over in a most pleasant fashion. She had lost count of the number of times they'd had sex, pausing to either slumber, spooned together, or to nibble on food Alex's valet had discreetly left for them at various times. Caroline hadn't even noticed him come and go.

After another round of exciting sex, the room dark except for a profusion of freshly lit candles, Caroline declared herself famished.

Alex extinguished the taper in his hand and rang for his valet, who appeared almost immediately. Neither Alex nor the valet minded Alex's splendid nakedness.

"Bring a selection of cold meats, bread, and cheese up from the kitchen. Something a little more substantial than you have been bringing us." Alex paused, looking over his shoulder at Caroline. "Unless you wish to dress for dinner?"

She tugged the ends of her translucent peignoir over her otherwise naked body, blushing. "Hardly."

The lascivious grin he gave her made her heart pound faster and her cheeks turn to fire. He turned back to his valet. "We'll dine up here. Bring up a bottle or two of my best claret as well, will you?"

The valet bowed, his gaze pinned most firmly onto the carpet, not daring to look at either his master or his new mistress. "Of course, my lord. Shall I clear the tray?"

Caroline eyed the remains: grape stems and apple cores, the green tops of strawberries. Closing her eyes, she remembered Alex biting into a juicy strawberry and tracing the bruised fruit over her bare breasts and licking up the juice.

Without thought, she lifted her hands to her breasts, teasing her nipples into taut life. They were sore from all the attention and so needed little prodding.

She heard Alex say, in a rough, sexy voice, "Take it. Make sure there are more strawberries also."

Could the man read her mind? Opening her eyes, she grinned at him, giddy to see that intense look of desire on his face. He prowled back to the bed, climbing onto the mattress and crawling toward her.

From the corner of her eye, Caroline saw the valet let himself out.

She remained in her seated, curled-up position on the bed, her legs tucked under her, watching him approach. He moved like a golden lion, each movement sure of his capture.

And why not? She was his in more ways than she had ever expected. As he reached her, she unfolded, the peignoir falling to either side of her.

"Is it possible that you still want me?" she teased in a throaty murmur.

"Mmm," he purred, rearing up from all fours to kiss her. It was no polite kiss; they'd gone far beyond that. Their mouths meshed in mutual hunger, their tongues searching and sucking. Alex hauled her against him, all hard lines against her softness. She sank against him, reveling in this temporary submission, letting him hold her up.

He fell back, with her on top of him, their mouths only parting for a moment. She rubbed herself along him, her breasts already heavy with renewed desire, feeling his cock harden at the jointure of her thighs.

Groaning into her mouth, Alex rolled her over, catching her arms and drawing them above her head. She struggled against him—she'd always struggle, no matter what silent, sexual contract they'd signed.

He forced her legs apart, releasing one of her wrists to hoist her hips higher. She lifted them eagerly, wanting him and only him, and wanting him now.

She gazed up at him, and saw herself in his blue eyes, gazing down at her with such intensity that her breath caught. His eyes burned with unspoken words, words she knew he'd never say, for he'd only break her heart even more.

Feeling tears build, she blinked them away, her free hand at the base of his neck drawing his head down to her. He kissed her, hungry and hard. At the same moment, he slid into her—tongue and cock delving inside.

Caroline cried out, the sound muffled by his mouth. She felt every part of him inside her, her cunt so sensitive after their frequent lovemaking.

He slid in and out, the wet sounds of their sexes meeting sounding loud in her ears. She moaned again, every part of her afire and clamoring for release.

Alex grunted above her, pistoning in and out of her, in short, fast thrusts. Precious breath escaped her, and she clung to him, trusting in him to see her through this exquisite torture.

Groaning, Alex hauled her legs up over his shoulders, bending her in two, her thighs compressing her breasts. The new position allowed for deeper penetration than before, and he fucked her hard and fast and deep, her swollen clit squeezed by her legs.

Completely in his power, unable to even tighten her cunt about his pounding cock, Caroline cried out, an endless moan while she hovered on the very edge of coming. Her nails raked his sides. She was close, so close . . .

Someone cleared his throat.

Alex thrust deep inside her and looked toward the door and the noise. Caroline turned her head away, not wanting to see who interrupted them. She focused on his cock poised inside her: so large and thick and good.

"My lord, a messenger has come." It was his valet. "Two, in fact. The other can wait but this . . . you said you wanted to hear from him the moment he had any news."

Caroline's lips shaped the word, but she dared not give it any sound. Lucy.

Alex nodded down at her, and with a regretful expression, slid from her wet cunt. "Very well. I'll be down at once." He gazed down at Caroline, his gaze lingering upon her face and her heaving bosom.

She knew how she must look to him: lips swollen, flushed skin, utterly wanton. "Should I—should I dress?"

He gave an abrupt shake of his head. "Let me see what the news is first. I won't be a moment." He rose, pulling on a long velvet gown of darkest burgundy, stepped into some slippers laid out by his valet, and followed his man downstairs.

Caroline stared at the bed canopy, not truly seeing the pleated crimson satin. She felt bereft, empty. Was this a taste of how it would be without him? Cold and alone?

She shivered and crawled under the covers, pulling them up to her chin, waiting for his return.

She didn't have long to wait.

"They've found her," Alex said, striding into the room. He

pulled apart the cord that held his dressing gown and let the velvet garment slide off his body.

Caroline almost forgot Lucy in watching his magnificence. "She is with my aunt?"

Alex shook his head. "One of my men saw a small group of soldiers and women skirt the city. He says they've made camp on the edge of Hampstead Heath."

Caroline sat bolt upright. "The heath? That dangerous place? We should go—" She gaped at Alex, who instead of dressing, clambered onto the bed. "Alex? We should go."

"I have no desire to approach a group of nervous soldiers in the dark. If Lucy's sergeant has any sense, he's posted a watch, and my dear, I have no intention of getting you or I shot."

"You would take me?"

He settled beside her. "You would stay behind?" She shook her head. "I thought so. No, Caro, we shall either catch them on the road to Dover tomorrow, or beat them there." He leaned forward and pressed his mouth against the base of her neck.

Between his lips, his tongue swirled on her skin. Caroline moaned softly. "Are you sure she will be all right?"

"Positive." He breathed the word hot against her skin, his mouth sliding up to draw her earlobe into his mouth.

Caroline's eyelids fluttered closed. Her fingertips swept as lightly as butterflies down his back. He groaned and hauled her to him, pressing her body against his. His skin, slightly cooler, soon warmed with her contact.

He lifted the swell of her breast, his thumb flicking over her sensitive nipple. His mouth found hers in an impassioned kiss that bore her down onto the bed. Alex made short work of the sheets that lay trapped between them and soon they lay breast to breast, groin to groin, her legs loosely wrapped around his.

He peppered her skin with kisses: from chin to ear to throat and down to the vee of her breasts, seemingly in no rush to fuck her. Caroline luxuriated in his tender kisses, secure beneath his weight.

A man's throat cleared.

Alex's head shot up from where it had been buried in her bosom and mouthed to her: 'I will kill him.'

Her lips twitched, trying to conceal her amusement.

The light in his eyes danced before he looked over his shoulder at his valet, and in his chilliest tones, inquired, "Yes?"

To his credit, the valet stood firm. "My lord, you may recall that there was another message that you deemed important?"

Alex waved at him to get on with it.

The valet cleared his throat again. "Yes, well, it, ahh, it appears your mother has arrived and is demanding an audience."

Alex pulled away from Caro. "Good Lord!"

At Alex's outburst, his mother sailed into the room. For all her years, she remained a magnificent-looking woman, her white hair piled impressively upon her head and dotted with diamonds that glittered in the candlelight. Her silver diaphanous gown dropped from its high waist, concealing the fact she no longer had her girlish figure.

Caroline shrieked and scrambled to hide behind Alex using her long blond hair to conceal her face. Of course, she recognized the woman, the Dowager Countess of Radbourne. She'd been present not only at Caroline's coming out, but also at Lucy's, inspecting the newcomers to the Season with an eye for finding a bride for her son.

An eye like a hawk. The Dowager Countess never forgot the smallest error, or a face.

"Really, Alex!" his mother said. "I have waited and waited for you to present your bride to me. Indeed, I heard you visited the wretched girl's aunt the moment you arrived in London! What reason do you give for shirking your duty to me?"

"Mother." Alex's arm slid behind him, protecting Caroline with a comforting touch. "Could this not wait until tomorrow? We are abed—"

"I *see* that," his mother snapped. "I have come to see the foolish bint you have chosen to tarnish our bloodline with."

Behind him, Caroline sucked in her breath, bristling. Alex shushed her to silence. Quivering, Caroline remained still—his mother must not find out he had the sister in his bed, not his future wife.

"That is," the Dowager Countess continued before either Alex or she protested, "if she is the former Miss Lucy Waverton."

"Of course I am!" Still hidden behind Alex, Caroline pitched her voice high and breathy. "How dare you!"

He started at the unusual pitch in her voice. "I thought you'd be pleased that I'd finally got leg-shackled." Alex had chosen to let the insult slide. "Tomorrow, Mother, we shall come to you and I'll present C—Lucy to you then."

Caroline hoped she was the only one who noticed his slip.

His mother raised an eyebrow. "The girl has nothing that I don't already possess, son. Why should she not be presented to me now?"

Gasping, Caroline clutched at Alex's shoulders. "Oh no, Alex!" Caroline kept her voice high. "Please don't make me!"

He patted her thigh. "You're terrifying her with your barbaric attitude." Alex's calm voice seemed to have little effect on his mother's ire. "This isn't the 1770s any more. Allow me to present her at her best."

"She isn't at her best in your bed?" His mother croaked out a hoarse laugh and stepped closer. Caroline cowered behind him.

He heaved a sigh. "I have been so taken up with her excellence in my bed that I have forgotten my other duty to you, so consumed was I with completing the duty of getting you a grandchild. Mother, I beg your apology and ask that you give us leave to greet you properly in the morning."

Peeping over Alex's shoulder, Caroline saw the older woman's eyes narrow before her shoulders sagged almost imperceptibly. She sighed, relieved. Alex had won this particular skirmish.

"She has her coloring, at least. Very well," said his mother. "I expect you before ten o'clock." Her brows rose archly. "If you can manage to rise and ready yourself at that hour."

Alex bowed from his seated position on the bed. "As you wish, Mother. Good night."

His mother inclined her head and departed the room, the valet following behind her.

Alex sagged back against Caroline. "Damnation, that was close."

Caroline hugged him from behind. "Indeed. You were wonderful." She hugged him harder.

He patted her hands joined at his waist, twisting to look over his shoulder at her. "I think she suspects you are not my wife, but some doxy."

She flinched. "That doesn't matter." Caroline's hands drifted below his waist, smoothing out over his belly, fanning out across his thighs, and back to the center, where his limp cock waited for her rousing touch. "We shall be away in the morning, before she figures out that something is truly amiss."

He dotted a kiss on her cheek, leaning against her. "Quite right."

Caroline paused in her caressing. "Alex, you spoke of a grandchild. We have not—"

Shushing her with a kiss, Alex stroked her cheek soothingly. "If we have made a child, Caro, I will provide for it and take care of you. I have been foolish not to think—" A grin broke through. "But then, it has been impossible to think around you."

She grimaced. "Thinking hasn't exactly been our strong suit. Alex . . ." She mourned the loss of him in that one word.

"Hush," he murmured, drawing her to him. "Don't think about it. Don't think about it. Enjoy us in the here and now."

Swallowing her sadness, Caroline reclined against the headboard. She brought her hands to work upon his cock, bringing the limp muscle back to life, her fears vanishing. She thrilled at how the soft flesh grew hard and then harder by her touch alone. She explored his expanding cock, satiny soft skin over rigid muscle.

With delicate care, he drew himself out of her grasp, rising and turning. Caroline slid to lie flat on the bed, looking up at him. He lay beside her, partly on her, encompassing her in his arms, her leg between his.

He stroked the hair back from her face, regarding her with such tenderness that Caroline held her breath. "Caro, I want you to know how much I have enjoyed our time together."

His fingertip traced the outline of her cheek. Caroline remained silent, watching him, memorizing the sweet agony of his features.

Bending his head closer to hers, he whispered, "I don't want it to end."

The admission wrested one from her. "Neither do I."

He kissed her, a long, slow, sensuous kiss filled with longing. She arched up against him, wanting to be closer to him, wanting this kiss to last forever.

For a long, dreamy while, it seemed she'd get her wish, Alex content to just kiss and kiss her.

He ended the kiss, and Caroline's eyes fluttered open to find him gazing down upon her again. The expression on his face . . . She had never expected a man to look at her quite that way.

"I'm glad you don't want this to end either. It means, I hope, that you will take my proposal seriously."

Proposal? Caroline's heart thudded wildly.

"I cannot do without you, Caroline, and yet I'm honor-bound to marry your sister. Stay with us, Caro, and become my mistress."

He'd hinted at it before, so the idea didn't shock her, and indeed, most of Society would see her as his mistress already.

"I couldn't do that to Lucy," she croaked.

Alex closed his eyes, acknowledging the pain. "Do not answer now. I want you to think about it. Do not think I am unaware of how your life will be after I'm married and you have returned home. There will be gossip . . ."

Caroline sighed. "I have dealt with that before. Lucy's happiness has to come first."

"Why does it?" Alex frowned, rearing back. "You're not her mother any more, Caro. You sought pleasure on this journey with me. Why not continue it?"

She reached up and touched the side of his face. "This time has been beautiful, Alex, and I will treasure every memory of it, but—"

He covered her mouth with his fingers. "Don't say it," he rasped. "I won't believe you, if you say it. I wish I hadn't brought it up, but this may be our last night together."

Caroline's breath hitched, a band growing tight about her chest. Their parting hurt more than she had expected. "Just kiss me, Alex." Her vision blurred with tears she refused to shed.

With a soft moan, his lips covered hers. She squeezed her eyes shut, welcoming him with her body. He shifted to lie between her legs, his cock parting her nether lips.

"You will miss this," he murmured, his voice hoarse.

"With every breath," she replied, eyes open once more, arching her hips to meet his.

He slid in, slow and perfect, sinking all the way in. He rotated his groin against hers, making her gasp. He held himself inside her for an endless moment. Caroline squeezed her cunt muscles about him, wanting to imprint the memory of his cock inside her, wanting to remember exactly how it felt.

Alex drew out slowly, as if a magnet fought to join them together again, and, resisting all the way, he slid back even more deliberately.

"I won't forget you," he breathed, pausing to run his fingertips across her bosom and the hard nipples that just a moment ago had pressed against his chest. "Every time I see Lucy, I'll be reminded of you and your fire."

A sob escaped her lips, a tear streaking down and vanishing into her hair. He'd accepted her answer already, had recognized his impossible dream wounded her heart.

He was letting her go.

"Please—" She raised a hand and covered his mouth with her fingers. "Don't speak of her again tonight." Her voice hitched. "I want to remember us, just us."

It was selfish of her, selfish of them both to have even started down this path, but it might be their last night together. Just being in London made Caroline realize their affair drew to an end.

Alex kissed her fingers, gently pulling her hand away. He bent down and covered her mouth with his. He stroked her hair, the lazy thrust of his hips a slow counterpoint to the palpitations of her heart.

Even though he moved as in a dream, the golden tension started to build, a rising wave on which she floated in iridescent bliss. Even the air she breathed in transformed into gold, tasting of a warm summer's day.

Sweat sheened their bodies, her hands slipped over his perspiring skin, skimming over his shoulders and back and down to his narrow waist. Beneath her touch, his muscles flexed and released in an endless motion of thrusting in and out of her.

The golden wave cosseted and comforted her. Here, safe

from all harm, she lay in his arms and in the beauty he wrought with the tender fucking of his cock.

In a strange way, they flowed together, moving back and forth in time with the other, like the tide against the pier. Only the other existed, his breath in her mouth, his cock in her cunt, their bodies meshed together. Nothing else mattered but this endless connection, merging.

Caroline didn't think she'd be able to explain it to another soul, but when Alex broke the kiss and reared back, driving his cock into her with greater force, she knew there was one who understood.

His faster thrusts plunged her beneath the golden wave, her highly sensitized body falling out of the dream, overwhelmed by the intense sensations rocketing through it.

She burst free, her limbs wrapped around his body, soaring on a release that had no end. She came and came again, harder, when Alex gushed his jism into her.

They remained locked together for a long time. Caroline's nerve endings thrummed with the aftershocks of the intensity, the slightest move from Alex making her gasp.

He slid from her and, rolling to his side, gathered her into his arms, their legs still tangled. He said nothing, breathing heavily, as did she, waiting for the last of the sweet release to subside and sink away from their bodies.

Caroline had no regrets, save one: that this couldn't continue and she had to let him go.

The travelers got a late start, moving out across the heath and away from the road. "Last time I came through," Michael explained, "we took Watling Street straight down to Dover. It was just us soldiers so they left us alone, but when I arrived in Dover, I heard of attacks on the womenfolk. We don't need the cart anymore. Everyone carries something."

He fastened a makeshift pack onto Lucy's back. She clung to the straps and staggered forward with the others. The men drew the almost empty cart off into some bushes, covering it with branches and letting the animal graze nearby, hobbled but still able to seek nearby water. The women would collect them on their return north.

Grateful that Michael kept close by, Lucy grew accustomed to the additional weight on her back. She let go of the straps, and reached out for his hand.

He accepted it, gathering her soft hand into his large, callused one and giving it a squeeze. A surge of comfort washed through her when he didn't let go, content to hold her hand and keep the connection between them alive.

They stopped to rest throughout the day but as evening approached, Lucy sensed Michael's nervousness through his touch, his fingers flexing.

"What is it?" Lucy murmured, breathing in the cleansing salty air of the nearing coast.

He glanced over at her, his brows lowered. "It feels like we're being watched. We're not going to make it to Dover tonight and whoever is out there knows it."

Lucy tried not to let her fear show, squeezing his hand to show she understood.

He shot her a smile. "That's my brave girl." He sighed. "I want you to sleep close to the Joneses tonight. Don't go anywhere alone, promise me. I plan to take at least two watches—too many of us are green."

We're running out of nights! she wanted to protest, but she kept silent.

If it weren't for his sense of duty, he'd never have rescued her from her terrifying flight from Radbourne.

Who may still be looking for her even now. She shivered. Keeping off the roads, even with a cart, had been a godsend.

She glanced across at Michael, her heart aching. *I don't want to lose you any sooner than I must.*

That night, she missed the warmth of his body snuggled up against hers, even though, in the past, he had slipped away to take a turn on watch, returning when his turn was done.

Not tonight.

Jane shook her awake, the heavy morning mist blanketing the sun. Shivering, she joined Jane in a short trek to nearby bushes to relieve themselves in some privacy.

Soon after, Lucy rose, stepping forward and straightening her skirts with an impatient twitch. She wanted to find Michael before she even started to help with breakfast. With Jane following, she moved through the bushes back to the encampment.

The heavy thuds of hooves froze her in place. Jane joined her, clutching her arm, the fingers twisting tight into Lucy's flesh.

Glancing down at Jane's white face, Lucy held her breath. Had Radbourne found her?

Jane tugged on her arm, pulling her forward. "Run!"

Lucy glanced over her shoulder, fear surging. Four men on galloping horses, black cloaks streaming out behind them. One of them spotted her and Jane and changed direction.

Jane gave up and let go, running for the camp and screaming. No longer absorbed in morning ablutions and making breakfast, the soldiers scrambled.

The men grabbed their rifles, starting to load them. Their movements were clumsy and jerky, the powder spilling over their fingers gripped around the barrels.

She saw Michael run into view, bellowing orders, his gaze sweeping the scene. He flung his rifle butt into the ground and loaded, taking a fraction of the time of the others.

Running forward, he spotted her, and waved his free arm for her to move. His face twisted with anger and concern. Then, he turned from her, shouting at his men, ordering the women to gather.

He spared her another despairing look and ordered his men into line.

The ground shuddered beneath her feet. Lucy took one uncertain step, then another, and soon she ran, heading not for the women, but for Michael. Michael would keep her safe.

A large bay horse, muscles rippling, appeared alongside. She caught sight of a man's leg, the breeches stretched tight over his thighs, and a brown muddy boot.

The horse passed her, wheeling in front of her, kicking up dirt into her face. The animal charged her, its rider leaning out to one side, arm extended.

She turned to run the other way. He snatched her up, flinging her face down over the saddle, knocking the breath from her.

The ground rose up to meet her, hillocks of green between the chalky brown of mud. She clung on to the saddle, some leathery part on the side. Her vision blurred, each hoof-fall knocking the breath out of her anew.

Shots rang out, a ragged coughing from the line of soldiers behind them.

Cursing, her captor wheeled the horse about again, gouging its sides. He hauled Lucy up before him, using her as a shield for his body, one hand gripping the reins. Upright again, and able to breathe, Lucy had to admire his skill in handling both the horse and her.

She sought out Michael, seeing him race forward, bayonet fixed to his rife, a silent snarl masking his features. He ran not for her, but the nearest horseman, whose pistol smoked from recent firing.

Michael bayonetted the rider in the shoulder, hauling him

off his mount in the next breath. Mounting it, he wheeled the horse around. His legs flapping at its flanks, he made directly for Lucy and her captor.

Michael shifted the grip on his rifle, holding it like a lance, the sharp end glinting with blood in the sudden sunlight.

Her captor changed his hold on her and raised a firearm of his own. Lucy reached for it . . . the gun discharged by her ear, blinding her with the discharges of smoke and powder.

Eyes watering, she tried to blink her tears away and see if he'd shot Michael.

16

A fierce shove took the breath out of her, and Lucy tumbled off the horse and onto the ground. She rolled, hoping to escape the horse's hooves.

She ended up on her behind, her skirts tangled about her. She looked up. Her captor had toppled off the horse also, and now clutched at his shoulder. Michael's rifle protruded from it, still shaking from the force of Michael's throw.

He had to have thrown it. He'd been too far away to skewer her captor with it.

The man and his horse blocked her view of the rest of the skirmish and, most importantly, of Michael. She struggled to her feet, tugging her skirts aright, still looking for him.

The riderless bay trotted away. Lucy's heart leapt into her mouth, seeing Michael upright. He staggered over to her captor, his uneven gait and smeared coat suggesting he'd been hurt.

Before she could take a step toward him, Michael reached the wounded man. He savagely hauled his bayonet out of the man's shoulder and plunged it down again into his chest.

Squeaking, Lucy hid behind her hands, turning from the bloody sight.

The next moment, hands clasped her upper arms. She struggled, dragging her hands away from her face.

"It's me, Lucy lass. It's me." Michael's voice, rough and hard, yet filled with concern, brought her back to herself.

She blinked into his face. He drew her into a hard hug, grunting when Lucy returned the fierce embrace with one of her own.

He pulled away, wincing and reaching for his shoulder. The sleeve had torn and blood welled up through it.

"You're hurt! Let me—"

He brushed off her ministering hands. "Still work to do, Lucy love." He darted in for a quick kiss and loped across the grass to where the skirmish petered out.

Lucy followed, more slowly, not looking at the dead man as she passed. By the time she got there, it was all over, the other attackers either dead or driven off.

"Leave the dead," Michael ordered, suffering to let Lucy tend to his wound. "Let them bury their own."

The victory had not come without a cost. Two of Michael's men lay dead from the attackers' pistol shots, and another wounded but mobile. The women milled around, consoling the two new widows.

Lucy watched them from the corner of her eye, not wanting to leave Michael and offer her own condolences. She sat on a crumbling log next to him. One dirt-and-blood-encrusted hand held up his head, his dark locks feathering through his fingers. He stared at the dirt at his feet, his distraught company ignored.

"Michael." Lucy secured the bandage on his arm. "Michael, you did everything you could have done."

He grimaced, not moving. "I lost two good men."

"I saw how fast you moved, getting everyone into line and

ready to fire." Lucy paused, lowering her voice. "And you didn't hesitate the moment you saw I'd been captured." She stroked his arm. "If I came with you to the Peninsula, at least you wouldn't have to worry about not being able to act at the sight of me in danger anymore."

Michael remained silent, staring sightlessly, his hands twitching as if he replayed the entire skirmish in his mind. Lucy rested her arm around his shoulders. If only she could relieve him of all his pain.

At last, he squeezed her hand, which rested on her lap. "We need to bury our dead," he muttered, his voice gruff. "We'll make arrangements for a proper burial when we get to Dover."

She rose with him, moving away to join the women, while he walked off in the other direction, muttering about a burial detail. She took one look at the sobbing women and murmured, "I'll make some tea."

Jane helped her. "They'll have to go back home now," she whispered, giving the tea a stir. "It will be hard for them."

Lucy nodded, murmuring assent under her breath. "Is Joe unhurt?"

"Yes, thanks be," Jane replied, pouring the tea into the mugs Lucy held out and carefully placed on the ground next to the fire. Together they made a number of trips to the women until everyone was in possession of a soothing cup.

After the funeral service and a halfhearted breakfast, the two widows bid them farewell. "We'll take the cart back to the edge of Hampstead Heath and wait for you there," one of them said between sniffles.

This provoked further tears from the other women, for those who returned would be the ones who lost the lottery to travel overseas with their spouses.

Lucy hugged her knees to herself. She had not even that expectation. She'd farewell Michael in Dover and little could be done about it.

At length, the two women departed and the remainder of the troop walked to Dover in the last remaining hours. They reached the outskirts of Dover in the dark, finding a temporary encampment filled with soldiers and camp followers.

"Stay here and don't wander off," Michael ordered them.

Lucy stepped forward, a beseeching expression on her face. "Take me with you?"

Michael wanted to. He wanted to squire her about the encampment and show every man how lucky he was in finding this treasure, even if she was only his for a very brief while longer.

"I'm going to the commander," he told her, unable to resist caressing her shoulder and arm. "If you are recognized . . ."

She bowed her head, accepting the implied threat of her being forcibly parted from him. "Do not be long."

Michael strode quickly through the encampment. Nobody hailed him, which meant his regiment camped somewhere else. He reached the only building in the immediate area, a two-room cottage the army had requisitioned for its use.

He saluted his way in and found his commanding officer at dinner with a number of other officers. Michael saluted smartly. "Sir, myself and ten others reporting for duty, sir."

His colonel looked up at him, his peppery gray beard smeared with a streak of gravy. His bright blue eyes peered up at Michael over rosy cheeks. "Ah. It's you, sergeant. You're late. What misadventures have you gotten yourself into now?"

Michael shrugged, keeping his face blank. "Bit of a skirmish on the heath with robbers. They got two of ours, we got four of theirs."

"Hope you do better in Portugal, lad!" The colonel slammed his hand down onto the formerly white tablecloth, now spattered with grease, gravy, and wine droplets. "That all?"

"Yes sir."

"Find any pretty blond women on your way?"

Michael cocked his head to one side, realizing that news of Lucy had preceded him. A chill settled in his stomach. "Sir?"

"Girl was taken near Durham. Folks seem to want to lay the blame on our door." He looked up at Michael through his bushy white eyebrows. "Even you're not that stupid."

"Yes sir." He essayed a cautious remark. "We did hear some lass had been stolen by a gent. Gossip's all over the country. That the one?"

The colonel nodded. "See her?"

Michael avoided the question. "So why aren't they lookin' for the gent then?"

"Seems she did a runner." The other officers chortled in amusement. "Didn't want to marry him after all. He's determined to do the right thing by her and marry her anyway. Which is more than I would have credited the man once. Nice to see he's got a bit of backbone and honor to him after all."

"Marry her or rape her, sir?" Michael bit the inside of his cheek. He'd let a little too much anger creep into his voice.

The colonel's eyes narrowed. "You know something?"

"Lots of gossip about it." Michael tried to keep his breathing even. He wouldn't lose Lucy to that reprobate rake yet.

"The chit's sister, charming young woman, came along with him to make sure he honors his promise. I imagine she's got plans to sue him for breach of promise if he backs out. Not that Radbourne can't afford the expense."

Michael released the breath he didn't even realize he'd been holding. "All's well that ends well then, sir?"

"Shakespeare, Hall?" The colonel shrugged. "If the girl can be found. See any other troops while you were traveling?"

"No sir." His answer didn't necessarily mean there weren't any, only that he hadn't seen them. He didn't know of any other troops supposed to head south, but the colonel had been on a recruiting drive in his district and beyond.

"Very well." The colonel waved him away. "Our regiment is

camped by the city limits. Go join them and you will all be briefed on the morrow. The tides are currently in our favor and we may ship out sooner than expected."

Michael saluted again, crisp and sharp. "Yes sir. Thank you, sir."

Lucy rushed to meet Michael on his return, her heart full. He bundled her up into a fierce embrace, lifting her off her feet. Something haunted his lively features. "We need to talk later," he whispered in her ear, putting her down. He turned to the rest of them and gave orders.

Before they moved off, he took Lucy's shawl and lifted it from her shoulders, draping it over her head. "You are being looked for here," he whispered.

Eyes wide, Lucy tightened her grip on the shawl. "I will go walk with Jane," she murmured.

Later, after everyone settled amongst their new regiment and found spaces to sleep, still clustered in their small group, Michael led Lucy away from the fires into the dark downs.

He hauled her close to him. Welcoming his warmth and concern, she laid her palms against his chest, trying not to clench them into fearful fists.

"What are we going to do?" Lucy began the dreaded conversation. She searched his worried expression, the dread rising, threatening to choke her with its bile.

"Nothing," Michael decided. "I won't let them take you, Lucy, to become that man's playmate. I promise you that." He paused, a frown marring his forehead. "The colonel said Radbourne has your sister with him."

Lucy clutched the straps on his red coat. "She's here?"

Michael nodded. "To make sure Radbourne marries you."

"What?" Lucy sucked in her breath. "Could it be a trick?"

Michael's frown deepened. "The colonel has no reason to lie. Not when he's fishing for information. I will go into the town tomorrow, find your sister, and discover the truth."

The dread rose higher. What if he discovered the truth, that she'd been a willing participant in Radbourne's seduction? "I should go," she breathed. "Why would my sister tell a stranger the truth?"

His grip tightened on her shoulder. "Lucy, I think there's nowhere else for you to run. Throw yourself on your sister's mercy, perhaps she'll spare you the marriage." His gaze dropped. "It's too much to think she'll allow you to be with me, a common soldier, or even wait for my return from the wars."

"Hush." Lucy covered his lips with her cold fingertips. "Michael, you are anything but common . . ."

He drew her hand away from his mouth and kissed her. "Thanks, but Lucy, you know—"

"No, I don't want to hear it."

"The colonel suspects me. Chances are tonight is our last night together. I'm willing to wager that the colonel will make a surprise inspection—"

"Then I will not be here. I won't allow you to get in trouble because of me. You could be demoted—"

"—and flogged," Michael added. He kissed her brow, stilling her shudder. "Thanks, lass, for thinking of me, but it will be worth the extra time with you."

"I'd rather end this with grace, not disgrace," Lucy said, stroking his stubbled cheek. "We have this one night. In the morning, I will go, and with luck, my sister will let me return, but if not . . ."

"Don't say it," Michael's voice grew hoarse. "If there were a way to rescue you from this . . ."

Lucy smiled, her lips twisted, longing rising inside. "You could marry me. I would be safe with you then."

He gazed at her for a long time, his body taut. At last, he let out a long sigh. "Who would marry us? The whole of Dover must be buzzing about his pursuit of you. Not one priest would marry us and risk Radbourne's fury."

"Perhaps he won't want me when he sees me."

"The colonel says the man has honor. He'll do the right thing by you—"

"—and make me miserable." Lucy swallowed the dread. "Let us speak no more of this. If this is our last night, let's make it one to remember."

She pressed against him, hooking her leg over his. Lucy sought out his mouth, sliding over his stubbled chin and finding his lips, so thick and sensuous it was sinful to find them on a man.

She took his mouth without reserve, her teeth skimming over his flesh and plunging her tongue deep into his welcoming mouth. He responded, his tongue jangling with hers, answering her each thrust, delving into her mouth. His cock jabbed her belly with fresh hardness despite being trapped in his overalls. She rubbed her groin against its ridges, wanting the barriers of overalls and skirts to be gone.

"Slow down," he gasped, "or we will be finished before the night is half done."

She paused, propping herself up by an elbow and looking down at him. "Will we?" she teased in a husky voice. "I want you now, Michael Hall, and I want you inside me."

Catching the flash of his teeth grinning in the dark, Lucy found the buttons on his overalls and unfastened them, peeling back the flap.

She took his stiff cock in both hands, running hands up his shaft one after the other in a circular motion. Her fingers encountered a stickiness and she bent to taste the head of his cock. He'd tasted her parts; it only seemed fair to return the favor again.

Her tongue flicked out across the head. She smiled at his soft groans. She tasted him, a hint of musk, laving her tongue all over his swollen flesh.

His fingers entwined in her tangled hair, a light pressure

against her scalp, but no more than that. She kissed the leaking tip of his cock and let her mouth slide down it, slowly engulfing him.

Michael groaned again. His hand slid up her calf and reached her thigh. Kneeling, she parted her legs, allowing him access to her private parts. His fingers fumbled along her wet slit and Lucy closed her eyes in sweet anticipation.

The tip of her tongue stroked under the ridge on his cock, and she almost wriggled in pleasure at the sound of his sharp intake of breath. His cock felt huge inside her mouth, hot and throbbing like the place between her legs.

She took in more of him until his cock pushed at the back of her throat. She backed off, pumping the visible remainder of his shaft with her hand.

Fucking him with her mouth, her head bobbed, never going deep, but sucking on the tender tip to prevent it from escaping her lips. His hips jerked beneath her, and a thrill of power rushed through her.

She did this to him. She aroused him and made him come. Give this up? She wanted to never do so. A soft moan escaped her, her lips tight about his cock.

His fingers worked their magic, teasing her folds apart, his thumb strumming her clit while another finger plunged into her wet hole, fucking her at the same tempo as her mouth on his cock.

The rising tension of approaching release washed through her and blinded her to all else but him. Soon, she'd find release and she guessed from the furtive jerking of his hips that he wasn't far off either.

His cock slipped from her mouth with a wet, popping sound. "Michael, I want you inside me. Not in my mouth, in my cunt."

"Then do it, sweet, before I explode."

Raising her skirts, she slipped free of his hand and straddled him. She wasted no time: his cock fitted against her cunt and she bore down on him, feeling him inch inside until his balls brushed her bottom.

She leaned over him, watching amazed as he licked his fingers, fingers that had been inside her.

He drew her down for a kiss, even though it meant he slid out of her a little. Lucy's heart pounded in her ears, tasting his jism, tasting hers, inhaling the musky male scent of him.

She'd give anything to remain impaled upon his cock, just him and her, in a sea of everlasting sexual bliss. The tug of her heart caused tears to rise, reminding her she actually possessed feelings for Michael. She didn't want to lose him. Not now, not ever.

Banishing the thought, Lucy broke the kiss, driving her groin down upon him, burying him deep. She arched her back, her hips grinding against him, grabbing him with her cunt muscles while she pivoted on his cock.

Their soft panting filled the night air, puffs of white breath rising above their writhing bodies, the campfires glittering gold and red in the distance.

Lucy paid no heed to that, setting the pace, a slow grind around and against his cock.

"Lass, lass," he begged in a low groan.

Her head tilted back and a despairing cry issued from her throat. She bent her head, braced herself against the cold earth, and quickened the pace, rising and falling on his stiff cock until ecstasy swept over her, drowning her in fire.

Michael gripped her hips, holding her in place, while he pumped into her, until at last he came, his hot jism shooting inside her. Even lost in her release, she felt it, and secondary shudders raced through her.

His grasp loosened and Lucy fell forward, seeking his mouth. They kissed, a breathless twining of tongues. She wanted to tell him how she felt, but didn't dare say the words, showing him with her mouth how deep her love ran for him.

Eventually, they snuggled together, Lucy still more on Michael than off. The buttons of his coat dug into her, but she didn't care. He held her tight, a voiceless promise to hold her in his heart, or so Lucy imagined.

She gazed up at the night sky, at the stars that twinkled, and wished there wasn't a tomorrow.

Dawn barely touched the horizon when Lucy woke, shivering. Michael slumbered next to her. She sat up, looking down at him. Enough light existed for her to see the long dark eyelashes at rest, the proud line of his nose, his stubborn chin, and his sensuous lips, ripe for kissing even when asleep.

Lucy decided against one last kiss, creeping away from him. With the growing light, she made out the direction for the town of Dover and headed for it, not looking back.

17

Caroline looked up from the book she'd been trying to read, without success. She'd started it to take her mind off Alex's absence and the thoughts of losing him to Lucy.

Alex doffed his hat, tossing it onto a small table by the door to her room. He stayed elsewhere, having been at pains to gain them separate rooms in different buildings in case Caroline's aunt turned up.

Her cozy room, let out by a local merchant and his wife, had not given any peace to Caroline's thoughts. The plain ivory walls turned golden by the fire, reflected their fading affair, the heart of which still beat strong within her.

Caroline closed her book. "Alex."

"I didn't find her." He slouched into a chair opposite. "Clarke says he knows the colonel of the soldier's regiment and will introduce me on the morrow." He sighed, rubbing his face. "This is such a mess."

Caroline agreed, rising to perch on the arm of the chair. She rested her hand on his shoulder, enjoying his touch on her hip and thigh. A gentle, almost reverent touch, one made casually. "She may not have arrived yet."

Alex grunted, his hand dropping away from her. "Should have by now." He leaned back, tilting his head to look up at her. "You look remarkably pretty."

She raised a blond eyebrow. "I'll accept that as a compliment."

His lazy smile made her melt inside. "It was meant as one." He found her hand in her lap and drew it to him, lacing his fingers in hers. "You are a remarkable woman."

She smiled at that. "I am a scandalous woman, you mean."

He let out a dramatic sigh. "There is just no letting me flatter you, is there?"

"With Lucy possibly camped out there? Knowing I may see her tomorrow?" Caroline shook her head. "I have to prepare myself, I—"

Rising from the chair, Alex turned, leaning over her and shushing her with a gentle press of fingers against her lips. "We have one night left, Caro love. There will be time enough on the morrow to prepare yourself." He took a breath. Longing for her suffused his features. "Or no need to at all, if you'll consent to be my mistress."

She kissed his fingers and then turned away, unable to meet his intent gaze. "I cannot give you that answer until I have seen Lucy." Already, misery welled up within her.

His forehead rested against the top of her head for a moment, his fingers tracing the outline of her cheek. He understood. "I will not ask again tonight."

He touched her chin and tilted her head up to look at him. Caroline blinked away the tears before he saw them. He must not see how distraught she had become. Essaying a watery smile, she reached up and caressed his cheek.

More than anything, she wanted to tell him her feelings for

him, how much she wanted him, how much she loved him. She looked away again, afraid her emotions showed on her face.

"Caro?"

She slipped off the arm of the chair, putting some distance between them, although she wanted nothing more than to be held by him.

He came up behind her, wrapping his arms around her. He pulled her against him, lips nuzzling her neck. She leaned against him, eyes closing, and enjoyed the warmth of his body against hers.

Almost without her noticing, he loosened the ties of her peignoir, parting the silky fabric to explore what lay beneath. She wore nothing but her shift, a soft linen that Alex caressed, swooping over the mounds of her bosom, exploring familiar territory with the lightest touch.

Caroline caught the back of his hand, pressing it against her body. She wanted to be held, to be loved, not worshipped like a tender virgin.

He slipped his hand beneath the loose yoke of her shift, reaching to cup first one breast and then the other in his large hand. He thumbed over her nipple, lightly at first, all the while kissing her neck.

Caroline reached behind her, smoothing her palms up his muscled thighs and to his butt, pushing him against her. Her back arched, presenting her bosom to him for more attention. He tugged on one nipple and then the other, his groin grinding against her buttocks.

Through his pantaloons, the hard line of his cock strained to reach her, rubbing against her soft bottom. It set her afire, consuming her sorrows with the promised joy of ecstasy.

She fumbled for the buttons of his pantaloons. Her skill didn't extend to undoing buttons behind her back and she sighed in frustration.

With a chuckle, Alex let go of her waist for the brief time it took for him to free his cock from its confines. Caro took the opportunity to shed her peignoir, the fine silk puddling at her feet.

She started to turn, but he stopped her pivot, hauling her against him again. His cock jutted against her buttocks, rocking against her crack.

With both his hands, he hitched up her shift, hustling her forward until they reached the ivory plastered wall and her shift bunched about her waist.

Caroline gasped, pushing back off the wall but being held in place. "Alex, it's bad enough you are here, unchaperoned. If somebody notices, if somebody hears us . . ."

Alex gave a soft chuckle. "Then you'll have to be quiet, won't you?"

"Alex . . ." Caroline groaned. Silent while he wrought delight upon her? Impossible! But if her reputation was to be spared at all . . . She gritted her teeth, not wanting to be denied this last encounter.

Pressed up against the wall, Alex rubbed against her. She had not thought of her back as an erogenous zone, but his wandering hands, the pressure of his body, his thrusting cock against her bared buttocks soon changed that impression.

She parted her legs, pushing her behind against his eager, slick cock, wanting him inside her.

His hand curled around her hip and down to her blond nest of curls, parting her nether lips and probing deeper for the well of wetness that indicated her readiness.

Her sex fluids drowned his exploratory fingers. He spread the moisture from her cunt, slicking her clit in the evidence of her desire. He swirled about her swelling bud, coaxing forth a fresh swell of her sex fluids.

Caroline bit back a moan. She was ready. She was more than

ready. She wanted to push back against him, bend her body so that he fit against her, inside her. She wanted to grind her groin against the wall, trapping his hand against her cunt, to keep him toying with her tender clit.

His finger slipped deeper, despite being caught between her and the wall, finding her cunt hole and circling it before dipping inside.

It had the effect of drawing her hips forward. Caroline was more than willing to hump the wall to gain her satisfaction. Anything. When would he give himself to her?

He stepped back, his hand slipping from her wet cunt, and she wriggled back, almost turning to see where he went. He grasped her hip with one hand, and at the probe of his cock between her buttocks, Caroline faced the wall again, arching her back and presenting him with her eager, wet slit.

She braced herself against the wall, feeling his cock draw nearer to her eager cunt and jam against her opening. He grabbed her hips and, with one deep thrust, he entered her.

He circled his groin against her buttocks, letting her feel every part of his thick cock. He withdrew and started fucking her in short, fast thrusts, making her breasts bobble.

Caroline hung on, loving every moment of it, soaring on wave after wave of heat. Her breath came fast, and she bit back her moans, the sound muffled deep in her throat.

Alex fucked her in a relentless rhythm, the sucking sounds of their joined sexes sounding loud in the small room. The wet sounds increased Caroline's state of arousal. She pushed back, meeting each thrust, wanting more of him.

The crest of her release rose within, along with pride that she hadn't yet cried out. Her lower lip swelled from biting back her cries.

His hand snaked around her hip and down again to her blond curls, wet with both their sex fluids. He found her swollen clit poking out and flicked it.

Caroline didn't know how she stopped herself from screaming, a high-pitched sigh racing from her mouth.

He teased her clit, rubbing and flicking it, all the time pummeling her cunt with his cock. She tensed and trembled, biting down hard on her lower lip. She tasted blood and the surge of release swept her away. She bucked wildly against him, her cunt massaging every iota of his cock.

Alex groaned, his hand slipping away from her clit and digging into her hips. He fucked her hard, slow, and deep, finally subsiding.

Face down, Caroline panted. "Glorious," she gasped out.

He bent over her and placed a kiss on her back. "Indeed, and you didn't scream once."

"I didn't?" Surely the entire town had heard her whimper. Her senses still resonated with the power of her release.

"And now to bed," Alex murmured, his cock slipping out of her. He gathered her in his arms and carried her to the narrow bed. "I want to make love to you face to face."

Caroline's eyes widened as her head bounced off the soft pillow. *Make love? Did he mean that?*

When Caroline woke the next morning, Alex had gone. They'd shared her narrow bed, the bed of a spinster, not a couple, after a second, tender lovemaking session that brought tears to her eyes, and to his.

The indent on the pillow where he'd lain had lost all trace of his warmth. She sighed, getting up and washing herself in the basin provided. The cold water freshened her and she dressed. She knew, without him having to tell her, that Alex had gone to see this colonel.

She'd nibbled at the items on the breakfast tray brought to her room, when a knock sounded at the door. Caroline frowned. Her hosts' servants either didn't know their place or somebody else demanded entrance. "Come in."

A woman dashed in, quickly shutting the door behind her. She wore a drab gray highwaisted gown, her head covered with a dark woolen shawl. She looked at Caroline, a trifle breathless.

Caroline gaped. "Lucy?" She leaped from her chair and ran to her, arms spread. "Oh Lucy, it *is* you!"

Her sister hugged her back. "It is. I am sorry if I worried you."

Pulling back, Caroline regarded her. Lucy's skin was gray with grime. Her sister seemed on the verge of tears. "From the moment I heard that Al—Radbourne had taken you."

"Is it true? That he's with you? I saw him leave . . ."

Caroline started in surprise. "He didn't see you?"

"I didn't look like this the last time he saw me." Lucy grimaced.

"He wants to marry you." Caroline's tongue flicked over her sore lower lip. She hoped it didn't look like Alex had smacked her.

Lucy shook her head, withdrawing from Caroline's loose embrace. "I cannot. Caro, I *won't*."

"Because of your sergeant?"

Lucy started. "You know of him?"

"We managed to stay in the same inn. You'd taken a tumble in the river and they'd given you a room. The innkeeper's wife was most informative." She caught her breath. She wanted to ask if Alex had raped her, but couldn't bring herself to do it, just yet. "She suggested you were lovers."

Lucy nodded. "Yes. It's true. We became lovers not long after I ran away from Radbourne." Her head tilted to one side, a tear escaping. "Do you truly mean to marry me to Radbourne?"

"His decision didn't change once we'd learned of your—your sergeant."

"His name is Michael," Lucy supplied. "So I have no choice?"

Caroline sighed, tired. "None of us do, Lucy. Radbourne is doing the honorable thing."

"After what he did?" Lucy's breathless exclamation gave Caroline the opening she needed.

"What did he do, precisely?"

Lucy opened her mouth to reply.

"Be honest with me, Lucy," Caroline warned.

"He abducted me."

"Was there a gambling debt?"

Lucy hung her head. "Yes. He said something later about teaching me a lesson. But he was drunk, Caro. I don't think he really knew who I was initially, and so he carried me off. When he'd sobered, he convinced me that the only recourse was to marry him."

Caroline frowned. "So you agreed? But—No, come and sit. Have something to eat." Caroline didn't know how she managed to sit so still and quiet while Lucy wolfed down her food: toast, eggs, and a couple of slices of ham. She left very little for Caroline, but she didn't begrudge a single bite. "So you agreed? But why did you run away?"

"I agreed." Lucy took a deep breath. "I cannot deny he is a handsome, attractive man, but then I discovered something else very unattractive about him."

"Aside from his indulgence in drink?" Caroline didn't know how she got the question out so casually. She wanted to lean over the small table and shake her sister and demand to know whether or not Alex had raped her.

"He—he called out another woman's name." Lucy's cheeks, beneath all that grime, stained a deep red. "Oh, Caro, I am so ashamed!"

"He—he bedded you?"

"But I shouldn't be speaking of such things to you! You're unmarried and—"

Caroline cut her off. "We've already established you've taken a lover, Lucy. It's a little late for protestations. You were willing?" She softened her voice. "Come, Lucy, you can tell me. I will understand. I haven't been angry at you about your Michael, have I?"

Lucy paused. "Will you be?"

"Angry about Michael?" Caroline shook her head. "You were alone and frightened. If he has taken advantage of you, then I will be angry at him, not at you."

"I—I seduced him." Lucy sank back against her chair, seeming to breathe easy for the first time.

"Radbourne?" Caroline frowned into her tea.

"No, Michael. It was the only thing I could think of to make him protect me."

"Surely, it was his duty . . ."

"He wanted to leave me at the nearest village. If Radbourne had found me, I don't know what I would have done. I was desperate."

"Do you love this Michael?"

"Yes," Lucy whispered.

"And Radbourne? What made you so afraid of him?"

"I wasn't afraid. I was ashamed. Ashamed to have been seduced by him—"

Caroline cut her off. "He didn't rape you?"

Tears spilled down Lucy's cheeks. "I know I have said so, and I can see by your face you have heard the same, but he didn't. I said it only to protect myself, otherwise Michael and the rest would never have believed me, never have taken me with them." She sobbed. "I was willing. I was willing!" She buried her head in her hands, crying gut-wrenching tears.

Going to her at once, Caroline knelt by Lucy's chair. "Lucy . . . Little sister . . . He was going to marry you. What was there to be ashamed about?"

Looking up, Lucy hiccuped. "He—he didn't love me. When he . . . when we . . . well, that's when he called out this other woman's name. I was furious with him, furious with myself." She turned her beseeching gaze to Caroline. "If I'd married him, he would have found someone else for his bed. I couldn't stand that!"

Caroline winced, ducking her head and withdrawing to her seat. Exactly what Alex had proposed to her. "And would that be so bad?" she asked, almost under her breath.

"It's a ridiculous, romantic notion, but I want a husband who loves only me! I don't want to share him with anyone."

That gave Caroline her answer. "In time, perhaps a love bond would form . . ." Oh, she hated saying those words.

Lucy shook her head, vehement. "I love Michael. I plan to go to the Peninsula to be with him."

Caroline gasped, pressing her hand over her heart. "To war? But Lucy! You could be killed!"

"That's what Michael said. He says it's impossible for me to go. Only a few wives from the regiment get to travel with them, and I'm not even married to him. And he won't marry me. He won't leave an obligation, a responsibility behind. That's the kind of man he is."

"He doesn't want you in danger. I like him already." Caroline managed to smile. She didn't know how she'd sort out this mess, but she'd try. "When do I get to meet him?"

Lucy stared. "Why would you want to do that?"

"I want to see what kind of man it is that has you following him all over the world, whether he'll have you or no."

At her gentle smile, Lucy sniffed away the last of her tears and a giggle escaped. "He's gorgeous. I came to you, Caroline, because I was hoping . . . hoping that you wouldn't make me marry Radbourne."

Caroline took a deep breath and released it. Did she answer her own needs if she let Lucy go? Was it best for Lucy?

"I've learned a lot about living on the road," Lucy supplied. "I wouldn't be a hindrance."

"Well, I am sure there are plenty of rivers you can fish people out of," Caroline remarked dryly, buying some time. She sighed. "What will Father say?"

"Will Father care? It's one less dowry he has to pay."

"But I can't let you go out into the world with no money. How on earth would you survive? How would you get to Portugal without funds?"

"You can draw on the Waverton money. Father would be satisfied with the explanation that you got rid of a family scandal by sending me over the Channel."

"Lucy . . ." Caroline begged. "It absolutely must be Michael?"

"Absolutely. He's the best man I've ever known."

Caroline flung up her hands. "I believe there is a small bank in town." She eyed her sister. "You certainly need better fitting clothes."

Lucy shrieked, leaping up and hugging her sister, almost knocking over the breakfast table in the process. "I need sensible clothing for living in the open." Her hug tightened. "Thank you, oh thank you!"

Pulling Lucy off her, Caroline blinked away her own tears. "You must write, and write often, and if you get into any trouble, just send for me and I'll come."

"All that way on your own?" Lucy teased.

Caroline grinned, and no thought would smother it. She loved her sister dearly and to see her alive and in good spirits made every sacrifice worthwhile. "I managed to come this far."

"With Radbourne." Sitting down again, Lucy shuddered. "How could you stand to be with him?"

"I like him very well." Caroline smoothed her features.

"Your eyes are dancing," mused Lucy, her eyes narrowing with suspicion. "Did you—Oh! Were you going to give him up for me?"

Lucy's anguished voice almost put Caroline into tears again. She took a sobering breath. "You had first claim on him, sister dear."

Before Lucy quizzed her further, Caroline rose, smoothing out her skirts. Back to being the respectable sister. Let Lucy think her elder sister pined for the earl in vain. She wouldn't disabuse her of the notion. Not, at least, until she replied to Lucy's first letter from overseas.

"Now, we should go," Caroline said, extending her hand, glad to have dressed before breakfast. She reached for her pelisse and wiggled into the tight sleeves. "I don't know when Al—Radbourne will be back. He's gone to the encampment to look for you."

Lucy threaded her arm through Caroline's. "What will you tell him?"

Caroline smiled. "I will think of something, don't you worry about it."

Walking alongside Colonel Chase, Alex scanned the milling activity around him. Tents appeared to be erected in a haphazard fashion. More soldiers had slept out in the open, their blankets rolled up and stashed out of the way.

Soldiers marched in formation. Others cleaned their guns and their kit, mended uniforms, kept fires stoked. Still others jogged throughout the camp, running messages.

"Here we are," the colonel said. "This is the group that arrived last night."

Alex saw a dark-haired sergeant straighten up from his crouch by the fire. A handsome-looking devil, his sour expression soon buried under a carefully blank one as they approached. Alex guessed this must be Lucy's lover.

If the colonel were indeed right. Perhaps the sergeant didn't like interruptions from the officers.

"Good morning, sir." The sergeant saluted.

"Where is she?" the colonel demanded without preamble.

The sergeant blinked at him, giving every attitude of wanting to be helpful. "Where is who, sir?"

"The girl. The one you stole from this gentleman." The colonel indicated Radbourne. "A Miss Lucy Waverton."

Alex saw the sergeant's glance flick to him, eyes narrowing before returning a more innocent expression to his colonel. "I am sorry, sir, but I don't take young ladies against their will. This is the same girl you mentioned last night?"

The colonel's bushy white brows beetled. "I'll have none of your insolence. You'll be flogged, man, if you continue to defy me."

The sergeant looked penitent but in Alex's eyes, something didn't seem quite right. "She is not here." He stepped aside, gesturing to the small camp. "Ask around. Perhaps somebody saw something I didn't. I don't dare speak for all the men I brought with me to serve you."

The colonel grunted and stomped past, leaving Alex to follow him in his wake.

Alex paused, giving the sergeant a long look up and down. He'd hoped that this simple act of superiority would make the man crack, but he was cannier than that, enduring his gaze and staring straight ahead.

Striding quickly to catch up with the colonel, Alex withstood the unfriendly expressions sent his way by each of the questioned persons, both men and women. Only one, a buxom redhead, gave him a leering once-over.

They made the circuit and returned to the sergeant, who'd waited for them. The colonel grimaced at Alex. "I'm sorry we didn't find her. May have given this lout too much of a warning." He glared at the sergeant. "Sergeant Hall, I expect my company to be loyal to me, not their sergeant."

Hall saluted. "Yes sir."

Alex left with the colonel without a backward look at the insolent army man. Had the colonel been mistaken and offered up the first group that had arrived from the north? Practically everywhere in England was north of this windy town. But no, that sergeant knew something.

He left the colonel with the barest of courtesies, asking the man to contact him if he heard anything more. He doubted he'd hear from the colonel again.

Striding along the rutted tracks into the town of Dover, Alex tried to avoid getting much mud on his boots. He expected Caroline's disappointment, but he also hoped at least a part of her would be happy to have him to herself for one more night.

A redcoat stood on the side of the road ahead of him, at a point midway between the town and the encampment. Alex kept his face in a featureless mask, not slowing his step at all.

He should have taken the carriage out, but he'd needed the fresh air to clear his head from thoughts of Caroline. He thought of walking right past the sergeant, but the man stepped onto the road in front of him.

"First, I was just gonna shoot you in the back, but that'd mean the noose for me."

18

"Wise man." Alex stood in a relaxed position, one leg slightly akimbo from the other. "Why on earth would you want to do that, pray tell?"

"Because you raped Miss Lucy Waverton," the sergeant growled, his tanned face darkening with anger.

Alex raised a calm eyebrow. "I did no such thing."

"You didn't fuck her?" Hall lowered his rifle and pointed the affixed bayonet at him.

"Oh, I fucked her," Alex replied with a breezy calm he didn't feel. "With her permission," he added in the next breath. "I don't force women to have sex with me." He preened his blond locks. "Generally have to fight them off."

Sergeant Hall snorted. "Then why'd she run from you?"

"That's what I've been trying to figure out. She was in the throes of passion. I've never seen a virgin display such wantonness—and you can be sure that I plucked her cherry. She up and left while I snoozed afterward. From a moving carriage, no less."

"Prove it."

Alex's eyebrow went skyward again, and his lips flared into a sneer. "My good man, how on earth do you expect me to prove it?" His gaze narrowed, his charm vanishing beneath the steel. "It's clear you know her, that you are, in fact, her lover. Where is she?"

"I don't know," he answered. "She left this morning while I still slept."

"I see she's kept the habit of leaving her man without bothering with good-byes, or explanations."

"She had to go," Hall continued with a stubborn frown. "We knew the colonel'd show up today. Played his hand too openly last night." He jabbed his bayonet at Alex, stopping just an inch from his coat button. "You say you didn't, she says you did. I'm inclined to believe her."

Alex huffed an impatient breath. "Listen, my fellow, if I were as bad an egg as you think I am, I'd not bother with marrying the chit. I made a mistake—"

The bayonet pressed against his coat button with a soft ping. "The rape?"

"Carrying her off. Was in my cups. Didn't touch her until our second day on the road. Know that for a fact. Offered her marriage, promised her a good and happy life. She accepted. I kissed her, one thing led to another, and before I knew it, she gave me the ride of my life." Alex's eyes narrowed. "Sergeant Hall, she was on top. Hardly the position for a rape."

The sergeant sucked in his breath, actually considering his words.

"Is she well?" essayed Alex. The sergeant nodded. "If she swells with your child, I will raise it as my own. With us so fair and you so dark, I'm sure we'll be able to tell. Even send word to you, if you like."

"You think she'll come back to you?" the sergeant sneered.

"Of course," Alex replied, seeing doubt flare in the man's

eyes. "I can offer her the world: the life of luxury to which she's been bred, anything her heart desires."

The sergeant stepped back, raising his rifle. The bayonet's blade swished by Alex's nose. Hall stepped onto the raised mound on one side of the tracks. "Go, then. Keep her safe."

Without another word, the redcoat turned on his heel and marched across the moor.

The man's capitulation fair took Alex's breath away. Would he so easily give up a lover to another like that? Like . . . Caroline? Sobered, he headed toward town.

The main street of Dover sloped down toward the sea. Rising up from the docks, the shops and stalls had been set up with their wares: fresh produce from the surrounding country-side, pretty ribbons fluttering in the breeze, and other delights.

He spotted Caroline, dressed in a new highwaisted gown of simple gray silk, a gown he hadn't seen her wear before. She stood at a vegetable stall, haggling over the price.

He hadn't thought of her doing such domestic duties, but he supposed she did, perhaps with the housekeeper or going her-self. Seeing her enjoy such simple pleasures warmed him from head to toe.

She turned. Shock blasted through his system, dispelling any notion of domestic bliss.

Lucy.

He leaped forward, seeing her spot him at the same moment, and grabbed her arm, weighed down by a heavy basket. "Lucy!" Words failed him, he didn't know what to say, what to demand of her first.

"Why did you run?"

Lucy turned up her little retroussé nose. "That is none of your business, sir. Unhand me."

"You are aware that I've been trying to recover you for the

last week? Stop this nonsense and come back with me at once. Your sister has been most anxious about you."

"And you haven't?" Without waiting for an answer, Lucy continued, "I have already seen and spoken with her. You may release my arm."

"You have? With Caroline?" Alex stared at her. This self-possessed young woman wasn't the flirty flibbertigibbet he'd kidnapped barely over a week ago.

"Yes," Lucy's calm voice filled him with uneasiness. "I will not marry you, my lord. Not in a thousand years. My heart lies in the army now."

"Caroline's letting you go back to that sergeant?" This meeting seemed to run beyond his control. "That's nonsense!"

"Speak to her if you do not believe me."

"Why should I believe you? You have been blackening my name up and down the country." He cocked his head to one side, regarding her. "Rape, Lucy? Really?"

She flushed at this, breaking eye contact at last. "I had no choice," she muttered. "You wouldn't understand."

"Fortunately, our marriage will end such speculation."

Her head shot up again. "I will *not* marry you." She backed off a step. "I will not!"

She turned and ran, the heavy basket banging against her thigh. Alex let her go. He should pursue her, drag her to Caroline, and confirm her story, but he knew where she fled: to Sergeant Hall.

"Michael! Michael!" Lucy's cry carried across the encampment. She didn't care if others gaped. She'd kept her displays of emotion to their blankets, but excitement and fear drove her to shout.

Michael looked up from cleaning his rifle, making no move to rise. She saw him take in her new attire, the laden basket.

She dumped the basket at Jane Jones' feet, her eyes only for her Michael. "Michael, you will never guess!"

He looked back at his work, blacking smeared across both the rag and his hands. "You saw your fiancé." His voice sounded flat and deadly.

"Well, yes," Lucy acknowledged, "but he let me go. As did my sister! She's allowing me to be with you!" She put her hands on her hips and glared down on him. "Will you stop that for a moment? Why aren't you excited?"

He didn't shift in the slightest, picking up a piece of the gun (Lucy didn't know which piece, it looked like a stick) and sighting down it before putting it back in its place. "Because you shouldn't be here."

Forgetting her new gown, Lucy plunked herself on the ground beside him. "They won't come looking for me again."

"Don't be so sure. The earl sounded quite smitten with you. Odd behavior for a rapist." This time, he slanted a look at her, under his dark brows.

Lucy's hands twisted in her lap. If she were to spend the rest of her life with him, he needed to know the truth. "I—I may have exaggerated a little. I told you I didn't know what it was."

He glowered at her, his black brows converging. "Exaggerated? Tell me, what position were you in when he raped you?"

"Ahh . . ." Even now, Lucy had the urge to lie, to protect herself. "On top."

"Bloody difficult to rape a woman when she's on top of him," Michael growled. "Get out of here. I won't wed a liar."

"You cannot push me away," Lucy snapped. "Not now. I made a mistake in lying to you, and I made a mistake in hoping I would never have to tell you the truth."

"What is the truth?" The words dragged from his lips in icy denial of everything they'd shared. Shared based on a lie.

The truth came spilling out. "Radbourne convinced me that

marriage was our only course, after his error of abducting me. He seduced me, to seal the deal, I suppose. I was too lost by that point to think rationally. Then he called me by another's name, and at the first opportunity I ran. I lied to you so you would keep me from him. I could not think of any other way to do it."

His rifle lay untouched in his lap, but he didn't respond. At last, he asked, "When would you have told me about this lie?"

"You gave me opportunity enough. I couldn't bear the thought of your disappointment, or losing you. And I won't lose you," she continued, daring to grab him and shake his arm. "I won't. I've been an idiot, I admit it, but I love you, Michael."

"You will be better off with Radbourne, Lucy." She caught her breath at the sight of his pained expression. "He said he would take care of you and any child we've created."

Unthinking, her hand went to her belly. A child? The thought hadn't crossed her mind. "I don't want him," she replied simply. "I want you."

He shot her a dark, tortured look, his voice dropping to a low burr. "It's too dangerous."

Lucy tried another tack, sensing he verged on forgiving her. "I have my sister's blessing to be with you."

"It won't make a difference when I sail without you," Michael bit off. "Go back to Radbourne."

She paused. She wanted to tell him she had money but feared he might find it an insult to his masculinity. "I will follow you, Michael. Somehow, I will follow."

"The life is rough—"

"I know, I've lived it." She grasped his large hand in both her small ones. "Please, Michael, please. Give me another chance."

His lips parted, thin and hard. In that moment, Lucy thought he'd deny her. Instead, his head lowered, drawing her into a long, soulful kiss.

Thrilled that she had somehow convinced him, Lucy wrapped her arms around his neck and pulled him down on top of her.

The door opened and Caroline paused in her pacing. "Alex, I have news," she blurted.

"So she *was* here then. I didn't quite believe her." Alex sat on a chair by the door and pulled off his still-muddy boots. "Why did you let her go? Why does she think she isn't going to marry me?"

"You saw her?" At his nod, Caroline continued, approaching him, making it as far as the end of the bed. She grabbed the bedpost to steady herself. "Alex, she's well and truly ruined. She and the sergeant have been lovers and she wants nobody else."

"So, the colonel was right in his hunch. That sergeant has had her. He came to challenge me on the road."

Caroline dashed to him. "Are you hurt?"

"No. The sergeant backed off when I told him I'd take far better care of Lucy than he ever would."

"Oh. Oh, dear." Caroline settled on the arm of his chair, gazing down at him.

"It gets worse. I disabused him of the notion that I'd raped her. Lucy may get a surprise when she returns to the army camp."

"She told me the truth," Caroline whispered, stroking his blond hair.

His smile up at her was twisted, raw. "So you believe me now?"

Caroline sucked in her breath. "The last lingering doubts are gone." Lucy's honesty inspired her to do likewise. "I hope Lucy and Michael work it out."

"That's Sergeant Hall?"

She nodded. "She's had the roughest time on the road, Alex,

and yet she's managed to fall in love. She's a changed woman, more . . . resilient."

"I noticed that too."

"She has money to book passage to Portugal, as well as for supplies to last her a while. They will work things out."

"Men don't like to be lied to."

"They will work it out." Caroline believed her words. Lucy's lifelong stubbornness combined with her newfound skills would ensure it. "And if they don't . . ." She took a deep breath. "Alex, nobody would blame you if you didn't marry Lucy now. She's gone far beyond the pale."

"I told that sergeant I would take good care of her, and I will."

"My sister has always come first. I will not see her abandoned, and I have not done so with my decision. I thought hard about it, believe me. You do not have to marry her."

"I do believe you." Alex gazed across the room, his forefinger rubbing at his lower lip. Caroline held her breath. She dared not to speak, not wanting to push him any more than she already had done. Had she made a mistake in letting Lucy go?

At last, he looked up at her, his expression warm. "You are right, Caro, I do not have to marry her."

Her heart started to beat in triple time.

"But I will if that sergeant deserts her."

Caroline pressed her hand to her chest, trying to stop the pain blossoming outward. She bent over him, resting her head on his, their fingers tangling together in a bittersweet embrace.

They sat like that for a long time. Caroline didn't want to move, didn't want to release him to the world and to her sister. Not yet, not yet. Alex appeared to be in no hurry either, his thumb stroking her palm.

A sharp rap on the door startled them out of their dreamy communion. Not wanting to leave him, even for decorum's sake, even if it were Lucy outside, Caroline raised her head and bid the person enter.

A soldier stood there, a common private. His arm shot out, a crumpled note in it. "For Miss Waverton."

Caroline ignored his widening eyes at the sight of their intimate position and accepted the note. "Do I need to reply?"

The private shook his head. "No, ma'am." He bolted out the door, leaving them.

Caroline unfolded the crumpled paper. "It's from Lucy." She looked up from the note and met Alex's troubled gaze. "He's forgiven her." She handed him the note to read.

He read it. "She is lost to us then."

"She promised me she will write and get in contact if she's ever in difficulties." Caroline brushed the hair off his forehead. "We know where she is. We can drag her back here, if you prefer."

Alex grimaced. "The one time I want to do the right thing, and it is taken from me by some common lout." Caroline started at that. "Oh, he's decent enough, I admit."

She relaxed against him, kissing the top of his head. He pulled her down onto his lap, claiming her mouth for an impassioned kiss. Relief and hope swept through her.

He broke off the kiss, framing her face in his hands. "There is one more thing I need to put right, and it has tortured me that I would have had to let it go—to let you go." His gaze swept over her face. "You have haunted my every waking and sleeping moment, made me curse that my responsibilities meant I couldn't have you forever. Marry me, Caro."

Her fingertips skimmed down his nose and across his cheek, wonderingly. "You want me forever?"

"You've made me feel more than any other woman." His intense gaze fastened upon her, hungry for her answer. "What's it to be, Caro?"

Her smile started small but soon widened. "I will marry you, Alex."

She had no chance to say any more for he hugged her tight, his mouth finding hers in a kiss so passionate that it struck her soul.

Morning came with news. "The regiment ships out on the first high tide," Michael announced, having let the runner go on his way to the next regiment. "Pack at once and be down at the docks. Ladies, the lottery will be held in the customs house near there. Go when you are ready and secure your lottery ticket."

Lucy bundled up her things, having shared the contents of her basket the previous night. She slung it over her arm, the basket now filled with a blanket and other sundry items. She made to follow the stream of women heading for the town.

"Lucy! Where are you going?" Michael called her back.

She smiled at him. "To offer my support."

Michael frowned at her.

"Michael, they only give wives a ticket. You said yourself that not all of us will be able to go. If I can be a comfort to them . . ."

He grinned at her, full of warmth, although his eyes were still wary. "Thank you, lass."

She turned and hurried after them.

At the customs house, she jostled with the regiment's wives pushing Jane ahead of her so she'd receive a ticket. Jane got one, turning to smile hopefully at Lucy. To her surprise, the beleaguered clerk thrust a ticket at her and she accepted it.

Maggie glared at her, but said nothing, collecting a ticket of her own. The women of Michael's troop stood clustered together, clutching their tickets close to their chests, afraid to have them snatched by another.

The room was stifling and the stench overpowering from the unwashed masses. Waving her hand in front of her face, in the hopes of getting fresher air, Lucy saw that some soldiers had joined them, all sergeants. Michael stood among them.

He acknowledged her presence with a short nod and a smile before the severe expression returned. With a gasp, she realized that he'd come to keep the peace. Only a small handful of women would win their way into the regiment's rosters.

A burly man up front called for silence. The high-pitched nervous chatter dropped away, all eyes upon the low dais and the men upon it who held the women's fate in their hands.

"Twenty-seven. Two seven."

All gazes fell to the piece of paper in their hands. A woman shrieked, waving her ticket in the air. The women around her grabbed at it, but she shoved it into her bodice and forced her way to the front.

"Forty-nine. Four nine."

"Thirteen. One three."

Jane squealed, jumping up and down. Lucy and Maggie got her between them and pushed their way to the front. Lucy grinned as Jane gave the name and rank of her husband.

Two more numbers were called. Lucy looked over and saw Maggie's face grow grimmer and grimmer, her skin turning as red as her hair.

"Six. The last number is six."

Nobody shrilled their excitement. Looking down, Lucy unfolded her palm and saw the number written clearly on her ticket.

Jane saw too. "You won! You won!" She hugged Lucy, who looked around in a slight panic. She saw Michael's surprise and his beaming smile at her.

Almost blindly, she shoved the ticket at Maggie. "Here. Take it."

Jane and Maggie stared at her, their jaws dropping.

"Just take it, will you?" Lucy persisted. "Before someone else does."

In a daze, Maggie snatched the ticket and marched forward.

"Why did you do that?" Jane called out over the rising wails of the unsuccessful women. "I thought you loved him."

"I do," said Lucy, saying no more until Maggie returned clutching her proof of passage.

"Why did you do that?" Maggie demanded.

Michael pushed through to them, hearing the question. "Why, Lucy?" His tanned face had gone ivory in shock.

"I didn't plan on getting a ticket," Lucy explained. "We're not married. Besides," she added, "I have bought passage already. I will not be far behind you."

"You bought passage?" Jane's shriek almost drowned out Michael's low interrogation.

Lucy turned, hugging Jane and then finding herself engulfed in a hug by Maggie. "Go!" she said. "Go board before they change their minds!"

Laughing, they departed, Maggie protecting the smaller Jane from the buffeting crowd.

Lucy turned her attention back to Michael, who should have been doing something to break up the riot that threatened to brew around them.

"I bought passage," she said. "I've funds enough to last the campaign, I hope, and if not my sister will send more, or we'll do without. This isn't just my riches, Michael," she said. "It's the regiment's."

"Your sister will do this?" He stared at her, eyes round and disbelieving.

"Yes." She grinned at him. "From what Private Jones told me, she's in love with Radbourne herself. I'm not surprised now she didn't put up much of a fight. She didn't surrender until she was sure of my happiness."

Michael shook his head, still disbelieving. "Why didn't you tell me this sooner?"

Her grin widened. "I wanted it to be a surprise. Do you think the regiment's chaplain will marry us now, or will we have to wait until we are together again in Portugal?"

He whooped, wrapping his arms around her waist and hoisting her up, swinging her around. Her boots clipped the legs of women around them, but Lucy didn't care. She had her man and would keep him forever.

Michael set her down again, claiming her mouth in a hot kiss. She twined her arms around his neck, holding him tight, her tongue tangling with his. Hunger flamed between them, sexual desire that hadn't been assuaged last night and she feared would never be again.

He pawed at her gown, groaned when she thrust her hips against him, kissing and kissing her as if that alone would seal their destinies together forever.

Pulling back, he panted, surveying her flushed face. "I have to go. I need to get the men on board, and Maggie and Jane. I will see you in Portugal?"

"You will," Lucy breathed, and reluctantly released him. "I must find the other women of our troop. They'll need provisions to get back home. There's not enough in the cart."

Michael glanced around. The customs house had almost emptied, the women streaming out after the lucky wives and officers. He knew the docks would be bedlam, but in the absence of the army, the customs house resumed its normal business.

He drew her outside and pressed her against a column, letting her know with the harder length of his body how much he wanted her.

He brought his lips down upon hers, kissing her hard. Her soft curves molded to his body, striving against him.

Pulling away, he cupped her face in his hands, memorizing her. "I don't want us to part."

Lucy smiled, her eyes shining with unshed tears. "Nor do I. I will meet you in Lisbon, I swear it."

Their mouths joined. In a frenzy, Michael delved into her bodice, bringing his rough palm against her soft breast, grinding his hard cock against her groin.

He wanted to haul up her skirts and bury himself inside her—this vision of genteel nobility, this woman, rich in passion, who wanted only him.

"I am not worthy of you," he whispered against her ear, his tongue teasing the tip.

"You are," she breathed, arching her body into his. "Oh, you are."

Don't miss the sexy sneak peek at
MIDNIGHT CONFESSIONS by Bonnie Edwards.
Coming soon from Aphrodisia . . .

Faye took a breath, smoothed her palm across her thigh to hike her dress and crossed the threshold into the darkly lit hotel bar.

Alone.

On a mission she'd been planning for two weeks, and wanting for longer. Sex with a stranger. An I-don't-want-to-know-your-name kind of stranger.

Desperation was a harsh mistress and demanded sacrifice. And Faye was desperate. Propelled into the bar by a heat under her skin she could no longer deny, her craving seemed to explode outward, from her skin, her hair, the ends of her fingertips. She was on fire and it amazed her that no one in the hotel lobby had called 9-1-1.

She paused just inside the entrance to glance around for a likely candidate. At first she was disappointed. The sparse crowd was sprinkled around the edges of the room. Light came from table top candles and subdued ceiling bulbs made to look like the night sky. For a bar called the Stargazer, it made sense.

Faye noted couples having a quiet drink, men on cell phones

with laptops open, a woman with shopping bags sporting expensive logos at her feet while she sipped a martini. Her mouth was set grimly and she downed the drink fast, nodding for the next before the glass was set back on the table. An obviously bad day.

The only men of interest were a group of rowdy suits at a table left of the door. Four men in their early thirties, happy, celebrating. Her inner heat cranked up unbearably at the sight of all those delicious-looking men to choose from. She kept her gaze forward, to hide her interest, but had to ease out a breath. She half expected to see fire blaze from her mouth she was so hot.

Need. She'd never felt such need.

Forcing her legs to take her past the men and toward the bar kept her focused.

A silence hit the table as she strolled by. She wanted to turn her head to look, but if she did, she knew she'd stop and one last shred of pride wouldn't let her. She would not stand there to be ogled openly.

Moisture pooled at the image in her mind of four men touching her with their eyes, skimming her arms, her breasts, her legs, taking inventory of all her secret places and wanting to be there, inside her hot, hot skin. She took a hard breath, suddenly awash in heat.

If she wasn't careful, she'd end up with all of them at once! One could kiss her mouth, two could suckle her breasts and one could pleasure her lower. Melting in the heat of her own fantasy, she finally made it to a bar stool.

Her nipples peaked so hard the lace of her bra felt like burlap and scratched against the raised buds. She shivered with the yummy feel and imagined one of the men soothing the roughened nubs with an expert tongue. She imagined a wet mouth suckling at her and restrained herself from tilting her head back to offer more. She shivered.

One of those men at the table would surely read the signs of her arousal. One of them would want to tap into it, exploit it. One of them would want it bad.

And bad was what she needed.

This craving had built for months. At first it manifested as an unsettled feeling when her Great Aunt Mae Grantham had passed away. She'd put down her need for sex to wanting to reaffirm life.

That had seemed a natural response, but then the unsettled feeling grew into an itch she couldn't scratch. She'd had more sex, but she'd become even less satisfied than usual. All the while the craving tore and clawed at her, bringing sexual frustration to a pinnacle.

Everything she'd done, everything she'd tried, had brought her to this moment, to these men. These strangers.

She kept her back to them so they could sort it out amongst themselves. In a few minutes, when they saw she was alone, one of them would stroll over, maybe lean against her forearm where it rested on the bar. He'd burn with the fire on her skin. He'd order a drink, see if she shifted away.

When she stayed put, he'd look at her and smile. She'd cross her arms under her breasts and, without flinching, give him an eyeful. She'd chosen this bra for maximum uplift. The top of her areolas peeked over the edges of the cups, the rosy flesh obvious from above.

The dress she wore had practically chosen *her* instead of the other way around. She'd found it in her back room inventory, in a stack of men's fedoras, folded like a scarf. She never would have looked for a dress there. She'd checked the tag and found it had been worn by a B actress in a 1957 sex kitten flick. Not possessing much cachet in the vintage clothing business, but a whole lot of 'hot' in the seduce-a-stranger realm.

She smiled and felt her sexual aura shimmer again as she hiked up the tight silk hem to mid thigh and slid onto the bar stool.

She tilted her hips just so toward the men and placed her beaded clutch on the bar top. She smiled at the bartender and leaned toward him, her nipples grazing the round leather rolled edge of the bar top. Enjoying the pressure, she swished her nipples back and forth to ease herself.

Big mistake. At the faint abrasion, moisture pooled and slid down her channel to wet her g-string. She crossed and uncrossed her legs to appease her inner ache.

The bartender had been wiping up a spill a few feet over but let the cloth he used dangle as she settled herself. Her focus had turned inward when she'd felt the moisture between her legs. Now, she turned her gaze to him, sure he could see sparks from her eyes.

She tilted her head and he woke from wherever his thoughts had taken him and came over to her. Young, handsome, and randy, he leaned across the bar, a good look at her cleavage.

She shifted to make the flesh move. "Aren't you breaking some bartender's code by staring at my breasts?" But she squeezed them together again just to ensure his interest.

He grinned and looked into her eyes. "What can I give you tonight?"

"I don't know. What do you have that's juicy and wet? I'm a thirsty girl."

His eyes flared and he folded his arms on the bar. Strong forearms, with a sprinkling of hair showing out of the sleeves of his brilliant white shirt.

"You must work out. Your upper arms bulge with muscles. You look very strong."

One of the suits moved in beside her before the bartender could answer. "I'll have a whisky and soda, and for the lady?"

He followed the script and with a look that scorched peered down her scoop-necked bodice. She gave him a slow, welcoming smile and crossed her legs again. He caught the movement and traced a fingertip from the pink-painted nail of her index finger, across her knuckle and along the vein in her hand to her wrist.

When he stopped the delicate caress she thought she'd beg for more. She bit her lower lip, wetting it, plumping it, preparing it. He watched her mouth with deep focus. Their bodies turned toward each other, their heads dipping even closer.

A strong jaw, even teeth, and intelligent eyes made up her first impression. His control of the situation was apparent when he looked at the younger man and cocked an eyebrow. Quick as that, the bartender bowed out of the equation.

Faye had found her man.

He smelled of success and money and she blinked up at him as if surprised he'd be so bold. His forearm burned along the length of hers on the bar, right on cue.

She swivelled her ass toward the other three men the man had left behind. An appreciative hiss came from one of them.

She imagined the man beside her skimming his hand down her back to cup a cheek and squeeze. She had to blink to dislodge the image.

His eyes were hazel and hot, his hair neatly trimmed, his hands the hands of a businessman. Clean, neat nails. She'd already learned his gentle strength when he'd traced her finger and hand.

His lips were hard, though, just the way she liked them. She saw them bearing down on her own, demanding she yield her mouth to his. The strength of the fantasies she was having unnerved her. They were so powerful she wondered if she projected them onto her forehead for all the world to see.

She'd never been so imaginative. Never so hot, never so needy, never so alive.

"I haven't decided what I want yet," she said, finally remembering to reply to the stranger's question. "I can be very picky."

She cleared her fantasies away with great effort and took stock of him. What she saw fit her requirements. Healthy looking, interested, no wedding band and keen intelligence. Yes, he'd do.

"I'm Faye Grantham," she said, tossing away her anonymous sex fantasy. Giving her real name came naturally and she wasn't an easy liar.

"As in 'grant'im his wish?'" One side of his hard mouth quirked up.

"If you'd like."

"I'd like."

"Miss, can I get you something?" The bartender interjected, all business now.

"Like I said, I'd like something wet, something juicy." She arched her neck, trailed her fingertips down her throat. "Maybe an icy drink, I like the way they cool me when I'm hot." Her fingers drew down farther along the line of her cleavage.

There was a long moment of silence from the two men as they watched her fingers trail between her breasts. Her nipples stood out prouder, the areolas hard.

"Do you have something that will cool me off? Something juicy and wet?" She emphasized the *t* sound, drawing it out only to clip it off at the end.

The gulp the young bartender gave was audible. "A bellini. You'll like it, I promise."

The man at her side, older, more experienced, narrowed his gaze. Then he slid his hand to her back, just above the low material of her dress.

His fingertip drew slow hypnotic circles on her naked flesh. Her spine straightened in response, lifting her breasts higher. She looked into his eyes and saw the promise of a sure thing.

He was hers for as long as she wanted to play.

"I don't need that drink after all," she said. "I think I see what I need right here."

She slid off the stool, making certain to brush the length of his body. Her pebbled breasts skimmed his chest, her knee bent as it caressed the side of his leg. Moisture gathered inside at the thought of sex with this man with the hot eyes and hard mouth. She licked her lower lip in anticipation.

"You have a room?" she asked him on a husky note, surprised at the deep timbre.

He nodded and turned his head to the bartender. She liked the sharp angles of his profile, took a complete inventory and burned again. "Champagne. Suite twenty fourteen," he ordered from the gaping young man on the other side of the bar.

She slid her eyes to the younger man. "Make it the best you've got."

She turned, took her clutch from the bar top and headed toward the exit that would take them through the lobby and up to his suite. Her hips swayed seductively, her shoulders straightened and she could feel the heat of his stare through the silk of her dress.

"My card," he offered. He took her elbow in a firm grip to guide her through the tables. She took the card, glanced at his name in spite of not wanting to know it. Mark McLeod.

It was a good name. She didn't recognize the company logo, but it didn't matter; they'd never be in touch again. She slid the card into the outside pocket of her clutch next to the very convenient letter from Watson, Watson and Sloane.

She looked up at his profile once more. Strong chin, bold nose, hard lips and great shoulders. She warmed through and through at the idea of skimming his collarbone with her mouth, her teeth leaving small marks of possession along the path.

He did not look back at the table of companions he'd left behind. No, his focus was on Faye and on Faye alone.

She knew he'd keep it there. How refreshing.

They strode across the lobby together, his fingers firm on her arm. Her breath quickened with each step; her breasts bounced, each movement a secret abrasion on her sensitized nipples. Her knees quaked at the knowledge of what she was about to do. Sex with a stranger in an airport hotel room.

Cool-headed logic flushed through her body, washing away the rapacious desire that had brought her here.

The inherent danger in her plan finally rattled her. Faye glanced at Mark out of the corner of her eye as they walked together. He looked like a decent man, a kind man. A normal man. A hot and ready man she'd deliberately enticed. She couldn't go back on her offer now.

Her body wouldn't let her, she realized as the warmth in her loins spread upward again. She tried to tamp it back, but it was useless. This was a battle she'd lost many times in the last three months. Her body wanted what it wanted in spite of her attempts to hold herself in check.

She wanted to scream her need out loud, but she didn't have to. Mark had picked up on her sexual craving, had responded and answered the call of woman to man. He knew what she wanted and he would give it to her.

Once alone in the suite with Mark, anything could happen. Any sexually deviant behavior he favored could occur and she'd be trapped in it with him. But wasn't that part of the whole thing? The fantasy of being unable to put a stop to things, of being swept up into something forbidden, exciting and wild. Excitement mixed with a healthy dose of fear twitched and grew and made her pant.

Mark slid a finger over the elevator keypad and grinned into her eyes. "Okay?"

"I'm fine." Fear mixed with anticipation was a heady blend, arousing and spicy.

"You're more than fine, Faye. You're a dream come true." He let go of her arm and ran his hand down her back to cup her ass just the way she'd envisioned earlier. Thrill trails followed his movements. "You're perfect."

"Really?" She bit her lip. She shouldn't sound so ingenuous, so stupidly inexperienced. He'd be surprised enough by her behavior once they were alone.

The elevator doors opened and they stepped inside the smoke-mirrored quiet. They turned as one to face the doors, bodies thrumming, heat rising, minds racing with images of what was to happen when the door closed, hiding them from public view. Mark frowned at a harried-looking bellman with a luggage cart.

The bellman nodded and stepped back. The last chance to change her mind disappeared as the doors slid shut, closing Faye in with this stranger. This Mark McLeod.